A SERIOUS WIDOW

A Serious Widow

CONSTANCE BERESFORD-HOWE

First published by Macmillan of Canada 1991
First McClelland & Stewart trade paperback edition 1993
This trade paperback edition 2001

National Library of Canada Cataloguing in Publication Data

Beresford-Howe, Constance, 1922–
A serious widow
ISBN 0-7710-1105-9

I. Title.

PS8503.E76S47 2001 C813'.54 C2001-901146-6
PR9199.3.B47S47 2001

We acknowledge the financial support of the Government of Canada
through the Book Publishing Industry Development Program
for our publishing activities. We further acknowledge the support
of the Canada Council for the Arts and the Ontario Arts Council
for our publishing program.

Typeset in Minion by M&S, Toronto
Printed and bound in Canada

McClelland & Stewart Ltd.
The Canadian Publishers
481 University Avenue
Toronto, Ontario
M5G 2E9
www.mcclelland.com

1 2 3 4 5   05 04 03 02 01

This book is for
Tom Lockwood, Q.C.,
and his family,
with affection and thanks.

A SERIOUS WIDOW

Birth and Death Notices

HILL, Edwin J. – Suddenly in Toronto on September 30, 1988, in his sixty-eighth year. He is survived by his wife, Rowena, and daughter, Marion. Funeral service at St. Michael's Anglican Church on Monday, October 3 at 3:00 p.m., followed by interment at Pinewood Cemetery.

Toronto *Globe and Mail*
October 3, 1988

"I'm Nobody! Who are you?
Are you – Nobody – too?"

Emily Dickinson

"Who are *you*?" said the Caterpillar.

. . . Alice replied rather shyly, "I – I hardly know, sir, just at present – at least I know who I was when I got up this morning . . ."

Lewis Carroll, *Alice in Wonderland*

PROLOGUE

I held my tongue and spake nothing

Of course I didn't argue when poor weeping Marion insisted that I wear this silly hat. It doesn't fit – daughters' heads for some reason are always bigger than their mothers' – and the wind keeps shoving it to one side, so I feel like the stooge of some knockabout comedian. As for the black veil (also her idea), it embarrasses me more than words could ever tell. The glum web of it falls between me and the ceremony, the tiny clump of mourners, the prose of Latimer and Cranmer, all of which I expected would make this whole thing seem real. Instead I see everything through silk chiffon, darkly. And all the others can see is Survived By His Widow, concealed by her grief, clad in almost royal dignity by her new status as Relict. Well, it's an identity, of sorts.

Teach us to number our days

Teach us to numb them, as far as possible, from now on, if you don't mind. The days that stretch ahead of me are so full of various kinds of anxiety they don't bear thinking of. Simply because it's gone, the past defines itself as satisfactory – well, anyhow, safe, and not without its comforts. Now it's been cut off with such finality and no warning, I stand on the brink of nothing but questions without answers. Do widows have to pay income tax? How do you make out a cheque? And what do you do with a dead man's under-wear and socks?

The wind creaks the almost leafless boughs of the oak over our heads. It's a dark afternoon, with a cold smell of decay and damp about. I will be all right, though, as long as it doesn't rain. Why this should matter so much I have no idea, except that among all the other fears, it's only common sense to choose a small one: if it rains, Marion's hat will be spoiled, and she will be annoyed. Pretend that's the worst rain could do. But if it falls today to blur the distinction between grey sky and grey earth, or between life and death, it might well tumble me weightless as a space traveller and obliterate me as totally as Edwin. Yes, better stick with lesser fears; for example, no will in the house – we've looked everywhere else and found nothing . . . All very well for Cuthbert to say that's no real problem . . . Where on earth could Edwin have . . .

Thou knowest, Lord, the secrets of our hearts

Yes, but for God's sake don't tell anybody mine. Among others, that while his death was totally unexpected (though not from time to time unwished for), it's brought me nothing that could be remotely described as grief. There, there, they say, by way of comfort. At least he didn't suffer. No, he just dropped dead in his Adidas outside a dry-cleaner's shop, with the Walkman plugs still in his ears. You've got to cry, Marion says sternly, it will do you good. Don't keep it all inside. And why not? If she only knew, inside is the best place for it. Shock, they murmur knowingly. Try surprise. Try relief.

Who shall change our vile body

Yes, indeed, changed at last. That finicking little click in his throat. The brief, pre-sleep tattoo of farts. The square of plaster always dropping off his cracked heel. Why would he keep jogging, at his age? If he'd been a couch potato like everyone else, none of us would be here now, in his case dead, the rest of us cold, scared, bored and depressed, secretly needing a wee and looking forward to the sherry and sandwiches to come. God must be a bit of a knockabout comedian himself, because it was health, of all things, that in the end did for Edwin's vile body – numbered his days and then finished him off.

We give thee hearty thanks

Well, that may be going a bit far.

It hath pleased thee to deliver this our brother

Speak for yourself, Canon Foster. He was not my brother. Two – generally three – acts of incest every week, in that case. Multiply by thirty years and you get a pretty grim total. That's not counting menstrual time off, of course, or his regular week in Ottawa.

And our secret sins in the light of thy countenance

Not that he had any, secret or otherwise. Model citizen. A clean record, if ever there was one. Never, ever, in the wrong about anything. Law-abiding, thrifty, church-going, scrupulous, decent, monogamous, sober . . . the Seven Deadly Virtues.

Our perfect consummation and bliss, both in body and soul

Well, spiritually the closest I ever got to that state was after his regular audit of the household accounts, on those rare occasions when I managed to fiddle things out to balance debit and credit. Bodily, now, is another thing altogether. Must be about the same for everyone's body, I guess, or why all these big promises about bliss in the world to come? My nose is itching fiercely . . . that's a sign of some kind. Guilt, probably, for these subversive thoughts. I rub my nose through the veil. Frowning, Marion thrusts a hand-kerchief into my gloved hand. She is all smeared and bleared with crying. Surprising, really, this abandon in a woman whose strongest passion always seemed to be teaching First Aid. The other mourn-ers control themselves much better. They shuffle and cough in the rising wind.

Receive the kingdom prepared for thee

One of the straps meant to lower the coffin discreetly into the hole is mishandled, and slips. The youngest of the undertaker's grave-side aides mutters something that sounds very much like "Shit." The coffin lurches. Marion grips my hand. She is afraid I will make an unseemly commotion by crying out or fainting. Canon Foster at my elbow tactfully tries to turn me away from the open trench, but I can't move. Behind the folds of my veil a rictus halfway between tears and a mad grin stiffens my face.

From the beginning of the world

Because just at that inappropriate moment, across the open grave, I have discovered Edwin standing, his bald head bared to the wind. His dark overcoat is buttoned close over the bulge of his little paunch. His left foot toes in slightly, just as it always did. Our eyes meet and hold. Marion now sees him, too. Her arm slackens under mine; then she gives a long sigh and sinks to her knees. The stout Canon briskly slings his prayer book under one arm and ducks down to retrieve her. Years of genuflection have kept him in good shape for occasions like this. Like someone in a dream, Edwin clarifies and grows larger. He clears his throat with an audible small click.

"My name is John Edwin Hill," he says to me. "I am his son."

One or two curious faces turn to look at him, pale discs in the darkening air. The others are busy jostling each other to brush down Marion's coat and retrieve her handbag. I stand numbly looking at John Edwin Hill as if we were alone – as, in a sense, we are. There is a surflike sound of water in my ears that makes me think fleetingly of Vancouver and the novels of Ethel Wilson. Vaguely I put up a hand to straighten Marion's hat. Then, with a jerk, I pull it off, veil and all.

"How do you do," I hear my colourless voice tell him. "Of course you must come back to the house." A gust of wind scoops up a handful of dry leaves, spraying them high in the air, and it begins to rain.

CHAPTER ONE

❧

"**H**is son!" says Marion sharply, as the limousine door closes us in. "That's ridiculous. As if Dad could have a son without ever mentioning it to us!"

"He was married before, you know. And you've only got to look at the man."

"Well, yes, but that's not proof, Mother. Nothing of the kind. Lots of people – resemblances can – he couldn't possibly be – Are you listening?"

I am, but not very closely. The suburbs of Toronto glide past us serenely, as if the world were a rational place. Thickening rain blots the tinted limo window. Marion leans towards me, her eyes flashing in the home-bound headlights of rush-hour traffic. Her colour is high. Our graveside encounter with incalculable chance has shaken her, first out of, and then back into herself.

"Mother, you surely realize that this man, whoever he is – maybe some distant relative, at most – has simply come here to

6

claim – he's some kind of trickster trying to con you out of Dad's estate, or part of it. Now I want you to leave this to me. Don't you worry about it. Dear old Canon Tom will cope with the guests – I've had a word with him – and Cuthbert and I will take this fellow aside. We'll soon sort him out."

"Will you?"

"Of course. It won't take long." She pats my cold hand briefly.

"I wonder where the corkscrew is for the sherry."

"Are you all *right*, Mother? We're nearly there. Here, do take my comb and do something about your hair."

Marion has been addressing me in exactly this tone of voice, one that combines scorn with pity, ever since she was two. I have grown so used to it I even find it vaguely reassuring. Totally incompetent women may be snubbed a lot, but people do look after them.

"Now remember," she says, "just leave everything to me." The car glides to a stop outside our modest Don Mills semi. I wonder what the driver, who looks like a retired African emperor, makes of our tiny patch of front lawn on which lolls the garbage can I've forgotten to take in. We clamber out of the low-slung, upholstered depths, and rain flicks small, cold kisses over my forehead and cheeks as I fumble with my hat and gloves. Marion is already waiting impatiently for me at the door. The second limousine full of mourners is purring to a stop at the curb.

In a corner of the living-room, while Tom copes with the other guests, Marion confronts the stranger. "And this is our lawyer, Cuthbert Wesley," she tells him, offering the information together with a glass of sweet sherry. (She evidently doesn't trust the paler decanter of dry, in case it might be stronger. Nor does she add that Cuthbert, while he played chess with Edwin regularly for the past thirty-odd years, has only once given us any legal advice, and that was when we mortgaged this house, a generation ago.)

"Hem, my name is John Hill."

"Pleased to meet you, Mr. – Hill."

This is a manifest lie. Cuthbert's round face, now he is close enough to focus his thick-lensed glasses on the interloper, looks much more alarmed than pleased. But then, I remind myself, he is, like me, very easily alarmed. Tom, on the other hand, playing host with casual expertise in the background, seems entirely unperturbed. He has linked the other guests into a small, chatty group and is now refreshing himself with a generous swig of sherry. With real or assumed calm he examines a nearby framed sepia photo of my grandmother, born in 1910 and wistfully named Hope. She returns his tolerant glance with the look of mild, sweet apprehension I remember so well, and in fact see in my own mirror every day. Yet she never heard the words *terrorist* or *nuked* in her life, and was consequently quite a lot less afraid of everything than I have always been.

I stand a little behind Marion, stealing frequent glances at John Edwin Hill with the detached curiosity of shock. He looks, in fact, less like Edwin than I first thought. Someone else's input – presumably his mother's – has given him a short, straight nose and fine-pored white skin. He is, in fact, altogether better looking than Edwin, a discovery in which I take little or no comfort. My eyes keep wandering around the room, where everything looks subtly different today. All my books, for one thing, have been hastily huddled out of sight, like the bottles of a secret drinker. The house even smells different, filled as it is with newly delivered pot plants, sent by Edwin's business acquaintances as a substitute for attending the funeral. The clay pots are shrouded in wrinkled foil in various unattractive colours, and the plants themselves are ugly yellow or maroon chrysanthemums smelling of pepper. Only one, a hibiscus with gay, frilled trumpets of blossom, has charm; but it looks altogether too frivolous for a funeral.

"The food, Mother," Marion mutters to me. Belatedly I remember the sandwiches and whip off their protective plastic. Tom takes the platter from me with a flourish to offer it round with a bowl of olives.

"Nothing for me, thanks," says John Hill. "I'm afraid my turning up at the cemetery came as rather a shock to you ladies –" and here he makes a little bow to be divided between Marion and me "– but my home is in Ottawa, and I only saw the obituary notice yesterday in the *Globe*. When I tried to phone, I found this number was unlisted. Then my plane was delayed, so the service was nearly over by the time I . . ."

"Yes, well, Mr. Hill, we won't want to keep you here unnecessarily," Marion says crisply. "Perhaps you'd care to identify just who –" She is the kind of person who likes to get straight to the point, indifferent to the possibility it might be more civilized to go around a longer way. I'm never sure whether this makes her admirable or just crass.

There is a brief interruption while Tom escorts up to me various sidesmen and the People's Warden to murmur sympathy and say goodbye. I thank them. They disappear. Tom reappears at my elbow protectively just as Hill, having set down his glass, draws two rather foxed and dingy documents from his breast pocket. "My parents' marriage certificate," he says, unfolding the first. "And," producing the second, with the air of a polite bridge player taking a trick, "my own birth certificate dated, as you see, one year later."

Tom's face suddenly crimsons under his thatch of white hair. He presided over my marriage to Edwin in 1957, after all. "May I?" he asks, appropriating one of the Hill documents, which, I now see, looks dreadfully authentic with its yellowed silk tassel and border of lilies. Then he blows out a long breath, as if relieved. "Ah, I see. This certificate is dated 1944. Edwin, of course – this first marriage – he gave me the clear impression that by the time I knew him he was a widower. And childless. Of course I saw no reason to doubt his word then or now – with respect."

"My mother and I are both, hem, alive and well, Canon."

"But then – but surely then – there must have been a divorce," says Cuthbert. He looks agitated. This may land in his lap after all – a legal rather than a moral problem. He takes a large gulp of sherry, which makes him blink and produces an outbreak of fine perspiration on his bald forehead.

"There was not and never has been any divorce," says Hill firmly. His rhetorical style so intrigues me I have some difficulty grasping what he actually means.

"No, that's ridiculous," says Marion in a thin voice. "My parents were married at St. Michael's. If it comes to certificates, Mother has hers, too."

Something like a grim little smile flickers on Hill's thinnish lips. "Your mother and mine have both, I'm afraid, been kept in the dark all this time. Business, hem, or so he claimed, kept my father down here for three weeks in every month; but for the past twenty years or more he's always returned to his home in Ottawa and to us. I'm sorry – this can't be any more pleasant for you than it is for me. In fact, finding out he had a second family here has been a considerable shock to me. In any case, like you, I'm an only child. I'm here to carry out my responsibility to my mother, as I'm sure you understand."

"But if this is true, how amazing of Edwin," I say, more to myself than to anyone in particular. However, no one appears to hear me. Tom gently urges me into a chair and gives my shoulder a comforting pat. Cuthbert is peering at the birth certificate, his mouth dubiously pursed, as if fearing to find no loophole there. Marion stares fiercely at her half-brother, her eyes bright with tears of outrage. This, at least, is easy to understand. The very last thing the poor girl ever expected to find herself is a bastard.

And as for me, I think, what do I find myself? A kept woman? That's what I've been content to be, after all, for the past thirty years. Why does the phrase have such an ugly ring now?

"Well, I'm afraid this may complicate matters a little for Mrs. Hill," murmurs Cuthbert, refolding Hill's papers. A masterpiece of understatement, we all feel. He fumbles to find space for his empty glass beside a yellow chrysanthemum. "It opens the possibility that – well, the fact is, we've not yet been able to find a will, though Edwin always gave me to understand . . . He certainly used to say very firmly that no responsible family man ought to be without . . . But for some reason Mrs. Hill – er, Rowena and I haven't been able so far to locate . . . and we've searched his office downtown, of course, as well as this house quite thoroughly . . . it's all very –"

"Well, I've also brought along," remarks J. E. Hill, calmly producing another elderly-looking document, "a holograph will my father made about ten years after my birth. That is, when it appeared I was to be an only child." He shows this paper to Cuthbert, who looks at it, frowning. "As far as I know, there is no later will. And now if you'll allow me to call a taxi, I must get back to my mother. She has a heart condition and naturally all this has been a great shock to her. As for this will, Mr. Wesley, you'll find it quite in order. Our lawyer will be in touch with you shortly."

He folds and puts away his bit of paper with care. The others look at each other with varying expressions of shock, dismay and chagrin. As for me, I sit there dumb and motionless, like the survivor of an explosion, while through the house plaster dust and rags of paper still drift down.

Once Hill's taxi has taken him off, I hope with something close to desperation that Marion, Tom and Cuthbert will all go away, too. More than anything in the world at this point, I need to be alone.

The true nature and identity of Edwin Hill are now apparent; but who, then, and what, is Mrs. Edwin Hill the Second? Only in solitude can I ever hope to find the answer – if there is an answer.

Not one of them, however, shows the least disposition to go home. Marion disappears into the kitchen to make coffee. The men sit down with a heavy air of permanence. My new and awkward status causes them to avoid looking at me, I suppose out of delicacy. Instead they stretch out their legs and stare at the toecaps of their polished funeral shoes.

"Turned much colder," remarks Tom, glancing towards the window where sleet is now scrabbling against the black glass.

"Yes, hasn't it," agrees Cuthbert. "Much colder."

They clear their throats. "Early for frost," adds Tom.

"Very early," says Cuthbert.

Marion comes in with a tray and dispenses coffee efficiently. She glances at me warily and says in a bright voice, "Barometer's right down. What a change from this morning."

"Yes, indeed," says Tom. He expertly hitches up his cassock to permit the crossing of one stout leg over the other.

"Time of year," murmurs Cuthbert, who never drinks coffee, furtively hiding his cup behind a plant.

"It's appropriate for funerals," I say rather loudly. "Especially this one. Because it seems I'm more widowed than most."

They all look at me apprehensively now, as they might eye an unexploded grenade. Marion's face puckers. For once in her life she is not sure how to deal with me. Cuthbert's glance, a flash behind the thick glasses, exposes brief morbid curiosity. Tom's eyes rest on me with a queer, speculative gleam of quite a different kind. I get out a handkerchief and blow my nose, to stifle a hysterical impulse to giggle.

"Well, I suppose we really ought –" begins Cuthbert, bracing his short legs to rise.

"Yes, you'll want an early night, my dear. So if you're sure there's nothing more for the moment we can do –" says Tom.

To encourage them, I am already on my feet. "No, no; you've been so kind, both of you –"

"Of course I'll stay here with you tonight, Mother."

"Oh, please, dear, there's no need for that."

"The apartment won't fly away without me for one more night, Mother."

"Of course she'll stay," puts in Tom with authority. He approaches me to place a kiss in the middle of my forehead. "Be at peace, my dear, and believe that God will provide."

Provide what? I want to ask him. Comfort, or some more practical form of aid? All of you are too polite to mention it, but you know as well as I do this is going to leave me destitute – I suppose you realize that? But Cuthbert is now squeezing my hand between his two small, warm ones. "I'll talk to you tomorrow, Rowena," he says. "There just has to be a more recent will around here somewhere. I know we'll find it, sooner or later." He pats his breast pocket where he has carefully stowed away the card of John Hill's lawyer. "And in the unlikely event we can't," he goes on, "there are steps we can take, you know, to protect you from – I mean, after all, we have the Family Law Act now that provides appeal procedures for common-law – er, cases like this." He juts up his chin, in the centre of which a dimple nests, in quite a spirited and aggressive manner, and gives my hand a final, reassuring squeeze.

The wet night then, at last, swallows them up, to my heartfelt relief.

"Now, Mother," says Marion, with a nurse's severity, "it's bed and two Aspirins for you. I'll clear up down here."

"It's only eight-thirty." And I look with incredulity at the mantel clock. Is it possible that so much has happened in the space of so few hours, after all those stagnant years? How ironic, to say the least of it, that I should have spent the greater part of my adult life trying to prevent (so far as possible) anything happening – and now here I am in the centre of this débâcle. Wreckage litters the room in the shape of dreg-stained coffee cups, a sticky-lipped empty decanter, drained glasses and (on Tom's plate) one small, dry survivor of the sandwiches.

Marion whisks into and out of the room, tidying up in her deft fashion. She retrieves the last cup from behind a mantel photo of herself looking magisterial even at a fat six months.

"Go to bed, Mother," she tells me, not unkindly.

"Yes, I'm going."

"Off with you, then. No use trying to discuss anything tonight."

She vanishes into the kitchen. But I stand there numbly as if looking for answers in the air, which is still thinly spiced with John Hill's cigarette. The clock ticks ponderously on. In the mantel mirror my own face slowly comes to meet me. I stare at it curiously. Astonishing that no change at all can be seen in those familiar, mildly enquiring eyes with the anxious pucker between the brows. The confused-looking greyish-brown hair, the indecisive mouth, are just as they were sixty hours ago, when Edwin failed to come back from his life's last jog; or when, two hours ago, his son rose from the dead. To find myself so totally unchanged after all that is so bizarre it sets my heart to hammering.

"Take this," orders Marion, thrusting a mug of steaming Ovaltine into my hand. "And these." She folds my other hand around two Aspirin. I turn towards the stairs, only too pleased to obey. "That's right, up you go. I'll just do these dishes and then tuck in, too. It's been quite a day. Now you go right off to sleep. I won't disturb you tomorrow – got an early meeting. I'll be gone before you wake. Good night."

It is obvious that Marion has as urgent a need to be alone with herself as I have, so I say, "Good night, dear," and plod upstairs with my Ovaltine.

Once in my own room, the door closed, relief sweeps over me in a wave so enervating it is all I can do to pull off my clothes before creeping into bed. There I try to calm the various frantic little pulses that for hours have been tapping at my head and neck. But the newly exposed enigma of Edwin, instead of retreating, only expands itself hugely. The questions no one – including me – dared to confront over the funeral baked meats now present themselves without compromise. How could Edwin, of all people, possibly have conducted a double life so long and so successfully?

That riddle threatens so many of the other certainties I once thought I had that a spasm of shivering overtakes me, making my teeth chitter together. Think about something else, I tell myself desperately. Think about Nana. Remember that time you were in bed with measles, and the bliss of being allowed to stay home from school. It was February, and she bought you a cutout book of valentines; and forever after, that bright, clear red, the white snow falling past the window, the warm bed and her protective love, all produced a joy that still lives. This train of thought briefly calms me. But as I gulp down the Aspirin with a sour mouthful of Ovaltine, I think, in all those years, then, I never really knew Edwin. None of us did, least of all me. How astonishing to think about the perfect order of his bureau drawers, his treed shoes, his unvarying daily routine – bath, shave, dress, office, evening paper, after-supper cup of tea – all his fussy, abstemious, predictable ways – yet all the while . . .

I turn out my bedside lamp as I hear Marion's step cautiously ascend the stairs. She pauses, then, satisfied I am asleep, goes into her old small room across from mine. Before closing the door she thriftily clicks off the hall light. And I find myself suddenly grinning in the dark. Well, some things at least are now clearer than they once were. No wonder he was such a penny-pincher all our married lives. The civil service pay of a purchasing officer is not lavish enough to support two households – not without considerable strain. So now I know the reason for all that coupon-cutting and bargain-hunting that made every shopping trip as complex, but much less fun, than a tour abroad. That was why repairs were mostly done badly and at home, the thermostat kept at sixty-seven degrees, the hot water hoarded. To be fair that was also why his best suit was shiny with age and why, years ago, he gave up his six-cigarettes-a-day habit. Yes, a lot of things are clearer now. Like that time he didn't speak to me for three days because I bought oranges at eighty-nine cents a pound instead of sixty-nine cents. Not more acceptable. Just clearer.

But these minor insights are not, after all, much real help. The central question – or one of them – remains: who was the private man inside? What about that weekly, faithful attendance at St. Michael's? So all that was just a part of the cover? And what a convenient, respectable façade it gave him! All those vestry meetings, and passing the brass collection plate on Sundays with such po-faced dignity – and all the while he was commuting between the beds of two Mrs. Hills. Disgusting old hypocrite! For a moment physical nausea creeps through me.

As it ebbs, I think half-reluctantly, on the other hand, you almost have to admire the cool duplicity it took. The logistics alone must have taken endless ingenuity. "The old cousin I stay with has a thing about telephones – won't have one in the house. If you really need to reach me in Ottawa, you can leave a short message on the office machine . . . No, dear, you would not like to come along. It's an amazingly dull town, unless you happen to be on the embassy circuit. You're much better off at home. Besides, hotels cost money." The time and inventiveness that must have gone into such manoeuvres in both cities!

And how neatly he did it. To slide with such agility from one base to the other, never rousing the faintest suspicion – in me, at any rate. I will doubtless never know about the other Mrs. H. She may well have been more alert than me. Or less unwilling to suspect. It's even possible she guessed the truth long ago and simply accepted it. There are women tough enough for that. But I'm not one of them, as he probably well knew.

But why, I wonder, did he find it worthwhile to go to so much trouble? Which of us wives was he so unwilling to lose? Not me, surely? But to think of the strain of leading that double life – the daily risk of discovery and scandal – what on earth made him choose that? Like an actor who can never leave the stage, wipe off the makeup and go home. Yet such a life must have had some fascination of its own for him, even though he was a man who never gambled in all his days.

On the other hand, if it comes to role-playing, isn't it true that I've lived a secret life, too, for as long as I care to remember? Acted (not very well) the part of mother and housewife, while in the privacy of my own head, I've lived another existence entirely, with Mrs. Wilson and Prince Charles. A hidden, dotty, and very real life, concealed successfully from everyone, even my own child. Of course I've never done anything remotely as bold as Edwin's disappearing act. Just the same, I've practised my own brand of subversion. That nondescript face of mine in the mirror has been a convenient mask – an image that satisfied everyone around me. A protection against everything, chiefly the use of power. Because, offered the enticing apple in Eden, I would certainly have refused it for fear that it might give me indigestion. And this means that, of the two Mrs. Hills, I am surely the one more to be pitied.

This backhanded tribute to myself makes my eyes fill with easy tears. But from the moment of Edwin's resurrection in the cemetery, I made a firm resolve to give up crying for good. Weeping, in circumstances like mine, is both pointless and bathetic. Laughing might in fact be a lot more appropriate. Fleetingly I think of that decanter of dry sherry, still full, downstairs on the buffet, and am tempted to creep down and have some of it. I even wonder vaguely whether this might not be a good night to get drunk. If only I were the kind of widow who could empty the bottle, kick off her shoes and dance to one of Scott Joplin's rags. Instead I'm the kind who, after half a glass of anything alcoholic, feels dizzy and considers throwing up. I think unfriendly thoughts about the Ovaltine and push it aside. Then, with a long sigh, I turn on my side and close my eyes.

The quiet room, the bed occupied only by myself, the city's mutter and semi-darkness, gradually relax me. But after a minute or two, I grope for the mug and drink off the now-cold remainder of the Ovaltine. There, Nana. There, Marion. I've been a good girl. For what that's worth. Soon after that I drift towards sleep. My last coherent thought is to wish tomorrow could be indefinitely postponed, because I am in no way ready to face it.

CHAPTER TWO

"**I** cannot imagine what got *into* you," Edwin says, accusingly shaking a bill at me. "Have you any idea at all what funerals *cost*?"

My eyes jerk open. A long knife of sun parts the faded chintz bedroom curtains. Thanks perhaps to the Aspirin, I have slept deeply and long, and for a minute or two I lie blinking at the light, drowsy and relaxed, my memory blank. Then Edwin's tattered old bathrobe on the back of the door brings everything back in a flood. The weight of all there is to do, and decide, and cope with now – all for what? for whom? – seems to pin me flat to the bed, as it did the day after Marion's birth when, confronted with parenthood, I thought simply, I can't do this.

The phone in the kitchen shrills. (Edwin always vetoed an upstairs extension: too expensive.) I would have liked to pull the blankets over my head and ignore the call; but as he once said of me (without smiling), I am the kind of woman who always scurries to answer phones, because the slightest delay might offend the caller. He added, "She also hates turning off the TV in case it might hurt the actors' feelings," at which everyone smiled but me. The phone trills once more. Marion has evidently gone to work. Barefoot, I stumble downstairs and pick up the receiver.

"Rowena? Cuthbert here. Good morning."

"Yes. Hello."

"You had a decent night's sleep, I hope. Good. Good. Well, now, I've been rummaging round doing a bit of research about your – er – position. Because, as you know, my work is mainly in real-estate transactions, that sort of thing; so this is outside my usual . . . Anyhow, if you want me to act for you, of course I'll be more than willing."

"Oh, yes, please."

"Well, then, this is the procedure. Pending any discovery of a will, I find the thing to do is file an application for Dependants' Relief. You're eligible for this since you and Edwin lived together for more than three years, and had Marion. I've been looking into the Family Law Act, and I also made a call to Hill's lawyer –"

His voice fades in and out of my ear. The window frames a square of sky as bright as fresh blue enamel. The backyard tree, a boring sort of maple generally, today has a Japanese charm, with a chalk line of hoar frost traced on every bough and twig. Guiltily I jerk my attention away from it.

"Meanwhile, Rowena, it would help if you had another really thorough look around the house – people often tuck wills away in peculiar places, you know – in books, or in boxes of old papers or whatever, so if you'd just –"

The front doorbell gives a ring so loud it makes me jump. "Sorry, Cuthbert – someone's at the door. Can you hang on a minute?"

"That's all right – I'll call you later."

"Thanks."

Clutching my old robe close, I unlock the door and inch it open, keeping as much of myself concealed as possible. A tall woman with a fur coat slung untidily round her stands there with something in her hands. I peer at her inquiringly. The sun on a glaze of melting ice makes such a dazzle it half blinds me. Leashed to her wrist is a turbulent spaniel, which at once tries to leap into the house.

"Stop that, Arthur," she says, hauling it back. "Pam Wright from next door," she adds, kindly helping me out. "I just thought you might find this casserole useful. So much to do, and so many bloody people no doubt dropping in, you won't want to bother cooking. It's steak-and-kidney pud, with just the most tactful *hint* of garlic."

"Oh, thank you so much." After an awkward pause I take the dish from her. It is still warm.

"Do let us know, won't you, if there's anything we can do," she goes on. "John would be so glad to run any errands or whatever in the car."

Her high voice is familiar to me after three years of a shared house wall. So is her personality and a surprising amount of her private life, both of which drift freely to me on summer evenings over the partition dividing our back porches. In spite of this, till now I had only a vague general impression of what she looked like. "It is always a mistake to get chummy with the neighbours," Edwin told me in our earliest married days. "Believe me, dear, it never fails to lead to trouble." Of course I believed he knew best about this, as about everything. Even years later, when I knew better, I made no protest. The Wrights having newly arrived from England, he dismissed them from the first as snobs, though they were obviously nothing of the kind. For the sake of peace, I refused their first friendly invitations to drinks, and since then our connection has extended only to "good morning" over the back fence, or "lovely day" when we meet on the street. Today I realize for the first time she is deaf; the button of a hearing aid is exposed when she turns to discourage Arthur from lifting his leg against the doorpost.

"This is very kind of you," I say. "And thanks, too, for the lovely plant you sent. Very kind."

Arthur is now straining to lick my bare feet. She jerks him back. "Sorry. He's a fool of a dog, rather." (Edwin would have agreed whole-heartedly. He disliked all animals, particularly this one, which is an indiscriminate barker. But I rather like his bright eyes and boundless enthusiasm.)

"You must get in, Mrs. Hill – it's cold. Be sure to let me know if there's anything we can do . . . call any time. Ta ra." And off she whisks, the fur coat and the spaniel's ears flying.

Which plant was theirs? I wonder as I put the casserole in the fridge. Oh, yes – the hibiscus. My feet are icy, so I pad swiftly upstairs to dress. A large quantity of air sharp with frost has pushed its way into the house like a trespasser, but I don't mind. It seems to freshen the place up. On my way past the thermostat I nudge it up a notch to compensate. After all, no one is here to object.

Now, I tell myself, it's time to get practical. By way of a start, I zip up my skirt and make the bed. What should I tackle now? The thank-you notes for the cards and flowers? But what, given my present state of mind, could I say? And what name could I sign to them? Furthermore, it's a chore that brings to mind one hot night last August on the porch when I overheard Pamela telling her husband what happened when she forced their eight-year-old to write his grandmother a thank-you letter. "Well, as a sort of bribe I let him use the new typewriter. After a bit I went along to see how he was coping. And my dear, the letter read, 'Dear Gran, the weather here is fine, I hope you are fine. Thank you very much for the fuck shit damn.'"

I was half shocked at the time, and relieved that Edwin was indoors. Now my mouth twitches in a smile. No, my thank-you notes will definitely have to wait. Let's see, now, what was it Cuthbert told me . . . Wills turn up in old boxes or books – well, I can make a start on that, perhaps, before Marion gets home.

On the top shelf of our clothes cupboard there is a shoebox full of old photos and letters . . . the sort of thing one doesn't really want to keep but for some reason hesitates to throw away. After some groping I find the box, and when I pull it down, as in an archaeological dig, an old hairpin, two coins and a lot of dust come with it. After sorting out the old snapshots and some laboriously printed birthday greetings from Marion at the Brownie age, I come upon a yellowing packet of letters in Edwin's neat hand. They are postmarked more than thirty years back. I look bemused at my old name on the envelopes. There is nothing else in the box.

I find myself reluctant even to handle, much less reread, these letters. Nostalgia plays no part here; they were never, in the usual sense, love letters at all, and I wonder now why I ever kept them. Circumspect, decent and discreet, like their author, they began soon after my grandfather Clive first brought him home for dinner. Edwin, he told us, was a new customer; he'd just recently moved here from Ottawa; he was living in a bed-and-breakfast place and could use a decent home-cooked meal. I slipped away dutifully to lay another place, glad of the excuse to disappear. Edwin looked very old to me; even then, just approaching forty, he was balding, a little paunchy. I was seventeen, just out of high school, with a summer job filing invoices for a big construction company. I loathed the long, dead, boring days, and also the tittering, bold-eyed girls in the office, endlessly chattering about their sex lives, or speculating about other people's. "In this day and age, every girl should be able to earn her own living," said Clive stoutly, because he had recently noticed that it was the twentieth century, poor darling. And Nana, who hoped this dictum wasn't true, neverthe-less added gently, "That's right, dear. We won't be here to look after you forever." But the thought of a long, long future filing invoices depressed me more than I could ever tell them.

Of course it wasn't that first evening, but perhaps a month afterwards, that Edwin (now a regular visitor) began to fix on me a peculiarly sad, intense gaze. It combined reluctance with an almost fixated absorption, and at first it puzzled me. Anything he said to me was always scrupulously correct; he certainly never touched me; yet I knew there was a clear connection between that gaze and the wise tittering of the office girls. I was not at all pretty, but my teenage acne had disappeared, and I was agreeably enough rounded here and there. Anyhow, for these or other reasons his eyes fastened on me as if helplessly fascinated, and of course that in turn soon began to fascinate me.

Gradually my acute shyness with him (as with all strangers) wore off. The first time he asked me to go for a walk with him in the park one bright June Sunday, I accepted with only a mild qualm of alarm. As time went on, we fell into the habit of these Sunday walks, whatever the weather. Considering the sequel, this prim and innocent courtship echoes now in my mind with a sour kind of irony.

Once in a while – though not often – he took me to a movie. But we were both much more at ease outdoors, walking in the sun, sitting on benches eating warm chestnuts from a vendor, and talking. He did most of the latter. He had a good deal to say about things like politics and the economy, and I listened with respect, though privately I preferred to hear the tales about his various landladies. One was a Seventh-day Adventist with thirteen cats. Another had an episode of DTs while serving breakfast. Never once did he so much as hold my hand. I found this reassuring and chatted away to him freely about the stenography course I was taking, to prepare for a higher destiny than that of filing clerk. I confided to him that shorthand made my head ache. I admitted to him that I much preferred the English literature course my grand-parents were letting me take at night. "They don't really see the point of Chaucer and Lawrence, you know; but it's like . . . writers like that . . . they let you walk into a whole different world, and that makes you different, too, do you know what I mean? I know it sounds silly, but –"

He smiled tolerantly. "My main concern is your being out alone on the streets at that hour," he said. I saw nothing unusual in this attitude. My grandparents were, I knew, a little overprotective sometimes, but I only loved them more for it. I was glad to be able to tell him that Clive drove me downtown weekly to these classes, and picked me up after them. And the following winter when Clive's cancer was diagnosed and he had to sell the car and close down his little printing business, I dropped English Lit. without too much regret. After all, I had the reading lists; I could and did go on by myself, becoming in the end a sort of addict. Not long after that Clive died, and Nana had a heart attack that left her paper-pale and all but weightless.

It was then that fear began to haunt me. An unimaginable future orphaned of her as well as Clive presented itself, not just as a threat but a reality. I was eighteen by then, but I'd never been on my own, economically or any other way, nor had I the slightest wish to be so.

Then, one Sunday, after the doctor had called and pursed his lips over Nana in a dissatisfied way, Edwin suggested our usual walk, though it was a cold, drizzling day without charm. Under a shared black umbrella we strolled in silence along the paths plastered with wet leaves. Then he said abruptly, as if the words had forced their way out, "I wish to God, Rowena, I could take care of you."

"Do you? Do you really?"

He stopped short and looked into my face. His own wore an almost tormented expression I could not easily account for. "It's what I want more than – more than you can – but it wouldn't be fair . . . I mean it's out of the question, of course."

"Do you mean you want to marry me?" I asked.

A peculiar look of shame crossed his face. There was a long, tight silence while the thickening rain tapped the umbrella over our heads. Then he said with a jerk, "Yes. That's what – in spite of everything, it's what –"

"Then I'll marry you," I said eagerly. It actually seemed romantic that I could feel his arm trembling. At that moment I sincerely believed I loved him. Even then, though, I was honest enough to know I also loved the prospect of never having to use that hated shorthand. I was so absurdly incomplete as a person – indeed, I still am – I actually thought relief was the chief component of happiness. Now Nana's approaching death would not leave me totally alone. And when we got home, her joy at the news corroborated mine. As for Edwin, though he looked by turns sombre and sheepish, it was clear that he found deep satisfaction in his new role not just as lover but as rescuer.

"It's true he's older," Nana said to me later that night, "but a man's no worse for being mature. As for his being married before – what of it? Experience is no bad thing, either." It did not occur to me then that there was anything defensive in these remarks. She looked at me a little sharply over the word *experience*, but as far as I could tell, this only confirmed what I'd just discovered: that Edwin knew how to kiss pleasantly. True, my standards of comparison even here were very scanty. There was the boy in grade twelve who after a school dance clamped his wet mouth over mine and sucked, like someone drinking out of a bottle. And there was the mail boy from last summer's job who pawed me through an endless double bill at the movies. When he called to ask me out again, I cried and made Nana say no to him on the phone. It was not what anyone, even in the fifties, could call a sophisticated sexual record. Edwin's first marriage, neatly curtailed (I thought) by death, was to my mind all to the good. He would naturally know whatever it was, exactly, that married people did, and how to do it. Nana's gentle hints about seeds and eggs were so far from explicit I went to the altar with the vague impression that the male fertilized the female with all the delicacy of a dandelion puffball seeding the breeze.

Somewhat sharply I replace the lid on the box of letters. No, it would be painfully embarrassing to read them again. All those decorous, misleading sentiments, expressed and evoked quite sincerely at the time – they are now far past their Best-Before date. Furthermore, of course, they are no longer relevant to anything or anybody, least of all me. Downstairs Marion's key can be heard in the lock, then her voice calling, "Mother?"

"Here, dear. Just coming." On my way down, I drop the box into a wastepaper basket. Another interment.

Marion waits for me at the foot of the stairs in the neat, semi-military Guide uniform she seems to have been born to wear. It suits her trim, upright figure; even that stiff and rather dreadful hat with its badge is becoming in its austere way. The lace-up oxfords, though, at the end of her handsome legs, can only be deplored. Altogether, Marion is quite a good-looking woman, but this does not seem to interest her at all; nor does she appear to want it to interest anyone else. She wears her abundant dark hair scraped back tightly from her face and coiled in a braid at the back; and she never uses makeup of any kind. This austerity makes me, with my unsuccessful home permanent and timid dab of lipstick, feel obscurely guilty – but of course she can't be blamed for that.

"Well, Mother," she says briskly, "what have you accomplished? Any sign of that will?"

"Nothing much, I'm afraid. And there's no sign of any will. So far, that is."

How typical this exchange is, both of us and our relationship – dryly pragmatic on her side; ineffectual and defensive on mine. Often I wonder wistfully whether somewhere outside the pages of books there are mothers and daughters who embrace each other – laugh together – even confide in each other. Years ago I used to speculate whether something I ate or didn't eat during my pregnancy could account for the bloodless distance between us two. Whatever the reason, she is always crisper and more efficient with me than with anyone else, while with her I become even more than usually neutral. In Marion's company, my normally colourless speech sinks to a level of platitudes and clichés that dismays me even as I utter them, as now when I bleat, "Have a good meeting?" Quite rightly, she does not bother answering. We go into the sitting-room where she sits down like a visiting social worker, feet neatly crossed at the ankles. "Have you had lunch?" she asks me.

"No, not yet."

"It's nearly half-past one. You'll have to watch this, you know. Women alone never eat properly."

"The next-door neighbour brought over a casserole," I say vaguely. Nothing Marion has said during these last days is actually offensive, but implicit somehow in all her remarks is the message that my present predicament is largely the result of my own weak character. The worst thing about this, of course, is that it's true. For years she has nagged me about my complete dependence on Edwin. Unfortunately, as it's turned out, I was more afraid of him than of her, and therefore took no steps to protect myself. Now, to evade her critical eye, I begin to pull dead leaves off one of the funeral plants, which looks even uglier today in the bright sunlight than it did yesterday.

"We'll have that, then. I'll heat it up." And Marion strides out to the kitchen forthwith. On her way back she pauses to glance at the thermostat. Muttering something, she pushes it down a notch.

"Now, Mother, we need to have a talk. Sit down, do – never mind those plants. It's beginning to look as if Dad made no will to provide for you. According to Cuthbert, that may mean those people in Ottawa can claim everything. And that, of course, includes this house. Perhaps you hadn't realized that," she adds more kindly when I turn appalled eyes on her.

"Because of course this property is in Dad's name, right?" she goes on. "As far as I can see, then, that small insurance policy naming you as beneficiary may be all you'll get. And once the funeral's paid for, that will leave you with maybe two thousand dollars. You can't live for long on that."

I nod, feeling rather sick, like the victim of a robbery. The air in this small room is heavy and stagnant. A fine dust hangs in the light that slots in through the venetian blind. Some ancient tombs are like this, I've read somewhere: claustrophobic little furnished cells aping the abodes of the living.

"The question is, Mother, how are you going to manage?"

"Yes, I'm afraid that's the question, all right."

"Well, the obvious solution is for you to come and live with me – at least until you can get some kind of job. My sofa makes into a bed – we could manage. Later on, if you win this case in court, we might get a bigger place. Actually it would be quite convenient for me to have someone to run the vac. around, get the evening meal and so on. I mean there's no need for you to feel –"

"It's good of you to offer, dear, but –" I cannot finish this sentence. She has been (for her) tactful and generous. How can I confront her with the truth: you would hate living with me. And that is nothing to my dismay at the thought of living with you. The frightening question is, if no alternative can be found, and she insists, what can I do? Because my one and only skill is knowing how to acquiesce, agree and be guided. And at my age it's surely too late to change. There's a negative kind of comfort in that, I suppose.

After a pause I add feebly, "I'm afraid – well – I'm sure something will turn up." (And *must* you, I ask myself, keep on saying, "I'm afraid"?) Marion is looking at me sternly, and I try to pull myself together.

"Such as?" she inquires dryly.

"Well, I don't know . . . Don't they train people to sell things in department stores?"

"Mother, you've never touched a cash register in your life."

I hardly need to be reminded that my only equipment to face the commercial world is half a secretarial course a generation old. It's not fair of me to resent her for pointing out the simple truth. Nevertheless, I do resent her, quite keenly.

"Well, then, maybe I could take in a lodger."

"You may not have this house at all," she reminds me.

"Yes, I suppose that's so." Incredible that I should, even momentarily, forget this significant detail. She is quite right to treat me like a moron.

"Well, in a few days Cuthbert ought to have a better idea just what your position is; but meanwhile we should be ready with some kind of practical plan."

There follows a frustrated silence. Marion has already revealed her practical plan, and presumably has no other. I for my part have none at all, practical or otherwise. The silence stretches itself out like a stifled yawn. Next door a shriek of laughter rises and Arthur breaks into a fit of barking. Finally I say recklessly, "Well, maybe I could be somebody's cook. Or possibly set myself up in the oldest profession. They say it pays well." I might have added with some bitterness that it was about the only job I was qualified for, but she cuts in sharply, "Oh, try not to be ridiculous, Mother."

To my surprise, she is blushing darkly, either with embarrassment or shame. In spite of all her efficiency and her calendar age of twenty-nine years, there are times when I realize that Marion is not in fact fully adult. It may also be true, I think with something of a pang, that the situation we find ourselves in may be even more painful and dismaying for her than it is for me. After all, she admired Edwin as well as loved him. A sharp mental picture comes to me, the bystander in their long-ago breakfast game – her four-year-old hands pressed over his eyes while she cried gaily, "Guess who?" Which one of us was most truly hidden then?

The timer rings in the kitchen and, released, she gets up and twitches her skirt straight. Her colour is quite normal again. "Come along," she says briskly. "Time to eat." Meekly I follow her out to the table where with a few efficient motions she sets two places and serves us each a portion of Pam's steak-and-kidney pudding. I taste it without enthusiasm, but it proves to be delicious. Suddenly I feel hungry and begin to eat almost with greed.

"Nice of Pam Wright to do this," I say between mouthfuls.

"It reeks of garlic." She pushes away her plate fretfully. "I don't know why some people have to mess around with decent food, making it trendy. Dad always used to say those people next door were like educated gypsies."

"So he did." Approving as he did of almost nobody, perhaps including himself, Edwin was able to function comfortably with few acquaintances and even fewer friends. I accepted this for so long that it's a surprise to hear myself add, "Your father used to make a lot of remarks that might be better left unquoted, don't you think?"

She glances at me, clearly surprised and offended. She opens her mouth to take exception; then closes it again. That new look of patient forbearance already so familiar to me settles over her face.

"You're not quite yourself today, Mother. I suppose that's only to be expected."

How do you know what myself is, I think rebelliously. How can you, when even I don't know any more? Just the same, it seems to me that Marion, with no resource but intelligence, is possibly even less qualified than I am to face my problems.

"Will you be all right here tonight?" she asks, getting up from the table. "The men are coming first thing tomorrow to sand the apartment floors, and I should be there to –"

"Of course, dear. I'll be fine."

"Right, then. I'll call tonight to make sure."

"Fine."

We have nothing more to say to each other. Perhaps she suddenly feels as defeated as I do, for as soon as the dishes are done she buttons on her tailored navy coat and goes away with no further discussion. The moment the door closes behind her, I rummage under the sofa cushions for my library copy of Mrs. Wilson's *Love and Salt Water*. Before sinking onto the sofa to read, I push the thermostat back up a notch.

The bright day has faded to silver by the time I next look up from my book. Some sound or other, outdoors or inside, is tugging vaguely at my attention. After a moment it comes again – a fumbling rap at the front-door knocker. With a sigh I get up to answer it, first carefully setting my open book face down on the hall table. With any luck I can probably get back to it at once. The caller is in all likelihood just someone collecting for cancer or selling real estate. But when I open the door Canon Thomas Foster stands there balancing his hat in one hand and a square cardboard box in the other.

"Why, Tom. Do come in. Let me take that while you . . ."

Once he has shrugged himself out of a bulky sheepskin coat, Tom stands revealed in an outfit that sorts oddly with his dog collar: a baby-blue cardigan with wooden buttons and a pair of baggy green tweed trousers. These indicate that his visit is social rather than professional, though Tom likes the swing of his priest's robe so much that he sometimes wears it even for an evening of bridge. With his foursquare male build, he has no qualms about wearing skirts; in fact, they are a statement of confidence, in a way.

"I just thought I'd drop by," he says, presenting the box to me with a courtly little flourish. "Thought you might be just a little – a bit of company might help. Black Forest cake in there. I know your sweet tooth, Rowena." He smiles ingratiatingly, exposing square, yellowish teeth. And I know yours, I think, smiling in return.

"How nice of you. What's the time, anyway? – it's never five! Well, we'll have some tea. Make yourself comfortable in there while I put the kettle on – won't be a minute."

But instead of heading as usual for his favourite upholstered chair, Tom follows me out to the kitchen and plumps himself jauntily astride a kitchen chair. There he looks around him at banal objects like the stove and fridge with something like a child's lively interest. Most of Tom's life has been spent dining in the officers' mess, or in parish halls swarming with useful ladies. At home, first an adoring mother and then his wife, Marjory, had seen to it that kitchens need not concern him in the least, except as a distant source of frequent, comfortable meals.

"Getting on all right, then, are you, my dear," he says, without inflecting it as a question.

"Oh, yes. Pretty well, considering."

"Ah. Of course. The whole situation requires . . . a consider-able emotional adjustment, no doubt. To forgive and forget, you know . . . we must be prepared for it all to take time."

"I'm not sure there'll ever be enough time for that, Tom."

The edge in my voice makes his pale blue eyes widen more in curiosity than surprise. "Now, my dear, that doesn't sound like you."

I fill the teapot with a gush of boiling water. "Doesn't it? Well, I wonder how you'd feel in my shoes. Forgive may be possible – but forget? No, I think even Mother Teresa would find that a bit much. Right now, if you want the truth, I feel outraged, Tom. Worse, I feel humiliated – I've been conned." Warming to my topic, I go on. "As for Edwin, I'm sure he died in a rage, you know. To be snatched away like that with nothing organized – nothing decently arranged – and everything exposed . . ." I think of those silent rages of his that occasionally for days on end would freeze the whole house. "I don't imagine he'll *speak* to God for weeks yet."

Tom smiles tolerantly. No doubt he has heard many worse things from the recently bereaved. The setting sun, flashing in and out of some transient clouds, splashes a dazzle of light at the window. Somewhere in the distance a siren whoops. A branch of the back-yard maple jerks under the weight of two black squirrels chasing each other with love or death in mind. They disappear and a little shower of snow rains down brilliantly. Life in the act of going on.

"Edwin was a true believer, my dear. He's reconciled, you must believe that. As you will be, in time."

"I'd like to think so."

"You can be sure of it," he says serenely.

In the act of slicing the cake, I pause to glance across the table at him with some curiosity. I've often wondered how much of

Tom's faith is simple professional habit and how much social expediency. One major ingredient of it, I know, is his love of high-church pomp and ritual. When Tom kisses his embroidered stole on feast days, or recites in his rich voice the drama of the Last Supper, he makes such an effective performance of it that the sceptic in me is tempted to wink. But unlike ministers of the more emotional sects, who at moments like this would certainly pray all over me, Tom only murmurs with dignity, "God bless you, my dear. And sanctify this food to our use. Amen." He then draws towards him the plate with the larger slice of cake and plunges his fork into it.

I sip my strong tea with greed. What drugs or alcohol do for other people, a powerful cup of tea does for me. It not only cheers, it very nearly inebriates. As soon as half my cup is gone I top it up. A peaceful silence settles between us while Tom gives his full atten-tion to the cake. When his slice is gone, he spreads out his square, reddish hands on the table with a sigh of satisfaction. Then he gulps the last of his tea and after patting chocolate crumbs from his grey-white mustache, clears his throat. My heart sinks. Now he is evidently, like Marion, going to try to organize me.

"More tea?" I ask.

"Yes, please." He leans a little forward, fixing me with a benign blue gaze. "I suppose, Rowena, you've considered the possibility that you may have to become self-supporting. Of course you have. You're an eminently sensible woman."

I smile faintly. "The problem is I have no skills to market, Tom. You can't count home dressmaking or baking muffins." His blue eyes are still fixed on me with a sort of attention I find vaguely disquieting.

"Well, now, you may not consider this at all appropriate or acceptable – but what would you think of a sort of part-time housekeeping job? My parishioner Miriam Whittaker has a

grandson – they live here in Don Mills – he and his wife are
setting up a small video store in the shopping mall, and they're
looking for a sort of mother's help person. They have – er – four
children between about three and ten, I believe. Perhaps this
wouldn't be suitable at all for you, but I thought – well, failing
anything better – I've been racking my old brains, but truly I
can't seem to come up with –"

"You're very kind," I say out of a dry throat. "You understand,
though, that just right now . . . But I do appreciate the thought.
Give me a week or so and then maybe I'll . . ."

My voice trails away as I try to imagine myself coping with four
children aged ten to three, part-time or any time. Mentally and
every other way I shrink from thinking about this or about anything. It depresses me to calculate that at least fifteen years must
elapse before the old age pension with income supplement can
rescue me from my dilemma.

"Will you have a bit more cake, Tom?"

"Well, maybe just a little. Quite good, isn't it?"

I lift the teapot invitingly and he passes over his cup. "Think of it
this way," he says comfortingly. "It's fortunate for you that so many
people need help in the home these days to care for the young and
the very old. Not that it isn't to be deplored, in a way. The Lord in
His wisdom gave us no children, but my dear Marjory devoted her
full time to me and our home, and that made us both perfectly
happy, though it seems such an old-fashioned arrangement nowadays. Women who stay at home have gone right out of style – with
exceptions like yourself, of course – and I for one regret it."

I murmur something affirmative. Of course I support in principle everything the feminists stand for; it's just that knowing my
own limitations has always been more than enough to prevent me
wanting personal liberation from home life. The world outside
my own four walls is so tough, rough and competitive as to be

overwhelmingly threatening. This is no doubt my fault, not the world's. Nevertheless, remembering Tom's wife brings a sort of comfort with it. While I rarely leave the neighbourhood, I do at least go shopping and to the library; but she lived entirely indoors. In the time left over from the care and feeding of her many ailments, she looked after Tom and watered their aspidistras. At the end she was a putty-coloured woman who weighed well over two hundred pounds. Her poor health had been such a long and absorbing charade that everyone, including probably Marjory herself, was astonished when a few years ago she actually died.

"Well, my dear, I must away to a confirmation class. Many thanks for the refreshments. It's always a pleasure to spend time with you."

"Thanks for dropping in, Tom. And for everything."

I go out to the hall to hold his coat and find his hat with the butler-like efficiency we both expect of me. With a heave he shrugs heavy shoulders into the sheepskin coat.

"I'll be in touch, Rowena. Keep your heart up, now. I hope, by the way, that you're careful these days about opening the door to just anyone. A woman alone here like this – there are some evil people about – you must be on your guard."

While delivering this advice he takes me by the shoulders and draws me near. Contact with the bulk and warmth of his solid form registers itself on me as he obviously intends it to do. Then he gives me a kiss, masterfully if briefly parting my lips in a way no one could call ecclesiastical. With a complacent smile and a flourish of the hat he then takes himself off, leaving me alone with my surprise.

A few hours later I begin to feel the onset of a queer kind of delayed reaction to everything. The sensation is so peculiar that

for a while I can't identify it at all. After Tom's departure, I calmly
tidied up the kitchen; I even went down to the basement and ran
accumulated laundry through the machine. After that I sat down
with Mrs. Wilson for a comfortable read. But within minutes my
attention begins to slide off the page in a most persistent and
provoking way. Even more annoying is the onset of a sort of irritable restlessness in the legs and arms that makes sitting still
almost impossible.

It occurs to me these may be twinges of conscience, so I go to
the desk to tackle the notes of condolence. But after looking
awhile at my carefully written words, "Thank you for your sympathy," I find myself unable to write another syllable, and click the
ballpoint off. After that, I go energetically upstairs ("Well, Mother,
what have you accomplished?") and begin to pack Edwin's clothes
into cartons for the Salvation Army. Rapidly I fold away jackets,
suits, the old dressing gown, sweaters, shirts . . . They seem as
much mine as his, passing through my hands as they did for years,
to be mended, laundered or thriftily sponged clean at home with
vinegar and hot water. But as I empty his bureau drawers, these
clothes begin to feel almost eerily inhabited. I morbidly imagine
they are heavy, and warm with body heat. Certainly his personal
dry, celeryish smell hangs about them yet. Soon I am reluctant to
handle them. Then, all at once, I cannot go on with it at all.
Grimacing like a scared child trying not to cry, I push the half-
filled cartons into the cupboard and close the door on them.

Downstairs the clock chimes ten. I have forgotten to give myself
any supper, but the thought has no appeal whatever. To prevent
Marion calling me, I call her and say I am perfectly fine. Then I
wander to the window for a look at the weather; perhaps a brisk
walk would settle my nerves. But outside under a bullying wind the
tree branches toss about in a distraught sort of way. Thick cloud
obscures most of the stars. Briefly a full moon emerges, high, blue

and cold as a bullet. The thought of a walk through windy city streets under that hostile sky does not recommend itself. I jerk the curtains shut and turn down the bed. A good night's sleep is probably all I need. To promote relaxation I take a warm bath. Then I switch off the light and stretch out under the blankets.

At once a confused crowd of images, ideas and memories swarms into my head. The coffin lurches on its way down by train to Ottawa. Nana's silver thimble winks as she guides my needle along a row of hem-stitching – trousseau pillowcases, those were, made of linen so fine we are still using them. Through my mind jig the lines, "With the other masquerades/That time resumes." Marion's childish voice cries, "Guess who?" Tom's bristly moustache tickles my lips. From next door come distant voices and a faint burst of music – the Wrights are entertaining. "He who was living is now dead," intones John Hill. "We who are living are now dying/With a little patience." The pillow on the other side of the bed still has Edwin's faint, sharp smell. "He is survived by his widows, the two Mrs. Hills." Downstairs the clock ticks so heavily it seems to climb the steps with beats as neat and precise as feet. Edwin coming to bed at exactly ten forty-five, pausing on the landing to turn out the hall light, entering the bathroom to brush his teeth. The toilet flushes. His shoes are neatly placed by the door. (Somewhere in a neighbouring back yard the barbaric serenade of cats rises.) He yawns. The bed on his side creaks. He puts his hand on me.

The first night or the nine hundredth, or the last – nothing really distinguished one from the other. Except that the first had an element of surprise, perhaps better described as shock. My wedding nightgown was white, of course, and embroidered by my own hands with a chain of daisies and buttercups around its modest neckline. Nothing could have been more emblematic not so much of innocence as crass ignorance.

Years later, Pam Wright on the other side of the porch told someone between hoots of laughter, "She was married five years before she found out that all intercourse isn't anal." But I did not smile at the predicament of this unfortunate lady. Ignorance is only funny to the well-informed. Nana's pretty image of dandelion seeds floating on the breeze vanished in a stab of pain. I resisted, whimpering. The shock that followed came not so much from his use of force, but from the gradual realization, many times later verified, that it was my reluctance that excited him most. How long was it before I understood that, and all that it implied about both of us? A long time, because it was not a lesson I was willing to learn. Eventually, though, I learned it. And resorted to cunning. It was all over much more quickly if I feigned ready consent.

A transatlantic plane drones high over the city. When the noise fades, minuscule creaks and sighs steal through the house. I lie there in the dark and contemplate that ugly little strategy of mine, craftily practised all those years in bed with Edwin.

There was no one I could talk to about this or anything personal, in fact, except the Prince of Wales and Mrs. Wilson, and while they've been a consolation to me, they never had any advice to offer. I've had no way of verifying my assumption that most women, like me, find the foreplay (if any) agreeable enough, but are grateful if what follows involves little or no discomfort.

I turn over, flouncing the bedclothes. My heart for some reason is racing. No, Tom's tickling little kiss – if he had any remote thought of following it up – has no hope whatever of success. Celibacy is the ideal condition, as far as I'm concerned. Death has at least liberated me from the routine carnal procedure required of wives. As for orgasm, that is nothing but a word. True, words have been my friends – my only real companions – for too many years to count. But that particular word surely has no equivalent reality. For all my reading, I don't believe anybody actually experiences such a thing. Like falling in love at first sight, it's just another of those romantic illusions; a catch-phrase to express the fantasies of housewives. My marriage, if it did little else, has left me too mature to believe in such nonsense. At least I have that much experience after the physical side of life with Edwin. Sex is the ultimate in trivial pursuits, of that I'm sure. Curious that so many poets and novelists (even Mrs. Wilson) should so often hint it is pretty well the pivot of everything.

A faint gust of laughter comes from next door. Wind rattles the window glass. My heart hammers. "Nothing of him doth remain." Oh no? The clock paces indifferently on. My own breath is loud in the dark.

Suddenly in a kind of panic I scramble out of bed and grope to turn on the light. Blinking, shivering a little, I stand there in the middle of the room, the night and my life. I know now the name of my malaise. It is anger. But what use is that kind of knowledge?

CHAPTER THREE

꽃

"Now, Sir, dear," I say to Prince Charles, "do please be reasonable. You must have known I couldn't get here sooner. I had to go to his funeral, after all."

"Then it isn't just because of my ears?" he asks, looking at me gravely before climbing into his red helicopter. But suddenly Cuthbert steps between us, his short arms extended dramatically. He wears nothing but his thick spectacles. Below the chin his naked form is plump and dimpled, its little pink appendage as innocent as a cherub's. Yet the moment he speaks, the Prince vanishes like a puff of smoke and in a voice of resonant authority Cuthbert says to me, "Fear no more." In the distance a bell rings and my eyes jerk open. The telephone. It is broad daylight. With difficulty I extricate myself from the tangled bedclothes and the dream voices.

Still thick and slow with sleep, I pick up the phone on the kitchen counter. Cuthbert's voice quacks at the other end of the line.

"I don't want to trouble you, Rowena, but I have several things here for you to sign . . . No will's come to light, I suppose. Ah, well. That wouldn't matter, you see – under the Succession Law Reform Act, you'd be automatically entitled to seventy per cent of the estate, if only that earlier will didn't exist." He sighs. "Well, I can explain it all when I see you. Would it be convenient if I drop in this morning some time? Then we can go over . . ."

"Yes, of course, I'll be here."

"See you in about an hour, then."

As I dress, I try to reconstitute that morning dream. Some detail of it seemed significant at the time, but which? Not the Prince himself, for all he stars in so many of my daytime fantasies. Our relationship, for a number of good reasons, is Platonic, but it has quite powerful sexual and emotional overtones none the less, and has provided much satisfaction over the years. The two of us have in common an over-active conscience, loneliness and a deep-rooted mistrust of our own capabilities. The novelist Ethel Wilson is another regular partner in imaginary conversations and encounters that make hours at the ironing board, for example, lively instead of tedious. She shares with me a maverick imagination, often suppressed, but more often subversively active. She is in fact the kind of writer I would be, if I were a writer. Charles inhabits the practical world; while dead but living Ethel W., with her offhand eccentricity and understated wisdom, occupies the larger realm of ideas.

Luckily no one guesses how often I am in silent communication with these two unlikely comrades. If Marion ever suspected it she would be seriously alarmed. And perhaps rightly so. But it doesn't trouble me to know, as I have for a long time, that I am a little crazy. As long as it doesn't show, I tell myself, it's nobody's business but mine. Meanwhile, Cuthbert will be here any minute; like most worriers, he is always prompt.

I hurry downstairs and put on the kettle. For obscure health reasons, he never touches caffeine, so I set out the milk to make hot chocolate for him. I've never seen any point in telling him that cocoa contains caffeine, too. A glance out at the weather suggests that he may, after all, be a little late. In sporadic gusts, freezing rain is sputtering down from a leaden sky. The Wrights' black cat, Wittgenstein, ears flattened, picks his way across the icy grass of our yard with an air of disgust.

A rattle at the front door proves to be not Cuthbert but the day's mail. Most of it consists of bills, and there are two envelopes embossed Hallmark. I add them all, unopened, to the little stack of condolences on the desk. Some time or other I will have to deal with it all; but not now. The kettle breaks into its shrill whistle, and though I long for my tea, I turn it off to wait for Cuthbert. Several times I go to the front window to part the slats of the venetian blind, but there is no sign yet of his big Buick – an assertive sort of car, I've often thought, for such a mild little man. The road shines with a menacing glaze of ice; quite possibly he will not drive at all in these conditions. Though he is only fifty-five, Cuthbert has all the prudent, precautionary ways of a celibate of eighty. Born an only child of elderly parents, he was buffeted by every possible childhood illness and has emerged small, frail, bespectacled, a sort of undeveloped man. He lives alone in an immaculate condo, his only companion a canary called Basil. In spite of all this, it seems Cuthbert is quite an effective lawyer, perhaps because he is so nearly comic to look at that people underestimate him. We have insignificance in common, at any rate. I like Cuthbert.

At last comes a rap at the door and in he steps, first scrupulously wiping his feet on the mat. He puts down his briefcase; then, one after the other, removes his old-fashioned galoshes.

"What a nasty day. I thought you might not make it at all."

"Well, I nearly didn't." Plucking off his thick glasses, he wipes them dry on a clean handkerchief, then, for good measure, mops his face. "Somebody rear-ended me at a light. Great big bison of a fellow . . . He gets out of his car waving his arms and bellowing as if it's all *my* fault. 'I beg your pardon, sir,' I said, 'I distinctly saw you in my rear-view mirror doing twenty-five miles an hour after the light turned red.'" Slowly he unwinds his scarf and folds it into a neat square. Then he tucks his gloves into a coat pocket. "My, my, some people. Anyhow, I just walked over to the corner where a couple of girls were waiting to cross – they'd seen the whole thing – and I asked if they'd be witnesses in court if necessary, and they said they would. One of them was very pretty, too – a redhead – I quite looked forward to getting her name and address! But Mr. Bison folded right up at that point . . . handed over his insurance info as meek as a lamb, and we parted on quite civilized terms after all. Just the same, my poor bumper looks pretty sad."

I make sympathetic noises and lead him into the kitchen where the kettle is just beginning to rumble again. "As long as you weren't hurt at all, Cuthbert. Cocoa all right for you? Sometimes you can get whiplash trouble from a collision like that."

He feels his neck experimentally. "No, everything seems to be all right, thanks." While I make our drinks he sits neatly at the table, elbows close to his sides and small hands folded together. "Marion quite well?" he asks.

"Fine, thanks. And how is your mother?"

These polite questions are not unrelated. I've never met Cuthbert's mother, but his references to her suggest a severely upright personality with uncomfortably high standards in everything.

"Now about these papers, Rowena – all right if I use this table here so we can . . . ? And while I think of it, I'm going to need your marriage and birth certificates, plus Marion's, and the deeds to this house, to document our case. I suppose Edwin kept all that kind of thing in his safety deposit box; but you're entitled to access as long as you make a list for the bank of everything you take out of it. All you have to do is tell them who you are, and . . . Anyhow, you'll go and get them soon, won't you, because it may be smart to be ready before the – er – the others there in Ottawa get themselves organized. And of course you must keep on searching everywhere for that will. I'm absolutely sure he left some kind of statement somewhere . . . Look through every book in the house, for instance –"

I warm both hands around the cup of tea before taking the first voluptuous sip of it. As he draws papers out of his case and sets them out neatly between us, the memory of Cuthbert's cupid-like nudity in my dream intrudes. I bury my nose hastily in my cup.

"Now this one," he says, peering at one of the documents through his thick lenses, "this one is the application for dependants' relief –" Here he breaks off, frowning, one hand flying to the side of his neck. "Dear me. That was a bit of a twinge."

"Perhaps you got whiplash after all, Cuthbert. Or it might be just a twist in a muscle. Would you like me to give it a rub? Edwin sometimes got a stiff neck and I could generally loosen it up for him. If you'll just open your collar –"

"It's nice of you, Rowena." Blinking shyly, he tugs loose the knot of his sober tie and unbuttons the collar of his shirt. He bends his head forward, exposing a white nape with a soft little drake's tail of brown hair growing down it.

"Ah," he says. "Ouch. Ah. Oh, that does feel good. Much better. How clever of you. And how kind." His arms close around my waist in a childish hug. But then, while my hand is still on his neck, he suddenly gets to his feet, roughly disordering all the papers on the table. What he has in mind is probably a friendly peck on the cheek; but, distracted by the papers drifting to the floor, I turn my head aside and his kiss lands instead on the side of my neck. Somehow he must make contact with a nerve centre of some kind there, for the touch of his warm mouth sets off a surprising reaction in quite distant parts of my body. Burning with shock, embarrassment and dismay, I extricate myself and turn away, hoping that none of these responses are visible.

"That does feel better, thanks, Rowena," he says fumbling to button his collar. "Very good of you."

"Glad it helped."

We both stoop busily to retrieve the spilled papers.

"Sorry – clumsy of me," and, "That's all right – they're all here," we say simultaneously.

With decorum we sit down, once more facing each other. "Now, as I was saying, about this application –" he begins.

Well, Charles – well, Mrs. W. – I ask silently, what do you think of that? Combine your expertise. What on earth was that all about?

"Probably," the Prince says after a thoughtful pause, "absolutely nothing." Mrs. W. preserves an enigmatic silence, though her smile is mischievous.

And now, looking at Cuthbert tapping papers together primly and pushing the glasses up on his short nose, I realize not without regret how right they both are. Leaning forward, I pin my attention firmly to the affidavit he is patiently explaining to me will have to be filed as part of my application for relief.

The Wrights' casserole dish is a very handsome one of Brittany ceramic, so it will have to be promptly returned. Later in the afternoon, with Cuthbert gone and lunch cleared away, I decide that, if only as an alternative to more important chores, I will get this little task over with. I intend simply to hand it in, thank them and come away at once. With luck perhaps their young son will answer the door, so I need not socialize much, if at all.

Before my courage can ebb away I pull on my coat and step carefully down our narrow front steps and up theirs. The sky has cleared now to a milky blue, and the temperature has risen again. Trees, parked cars, rooftops and bushes all drip and stream with melting ice. As I wait for an answer to my knock, the street lamps glow to life in a row of luminous green discs.

"Ah, Mrs. Hill!" cries Pamela, flinging the door wide. "How nice to see you. Come right along in." And before I can protest I am swept inside, dish and all. Arthur scrabbles wildly at my knees, simultaneously barking and wagging his stump. Dismayed, I find myself stripped down to my old grey cardigan and skirt and herded into the sitting-room. There I am introduced to two tall men – her husband, John, and their good-looking older son Maxwell, a Queen's student. My coat, the dish and the dog (still barking) all vanish while I say how do you do helplessly and sit down. The boy politely turns off the TV football game, but not without a wistful final glance. A somewhat heavy silence follows. John is a stoutish, amused-looking Englishman who, when he speaks at all, sounds like a telegram. This verbal habit I am soon to understand perfectly.

"How do," he says. "Foul weather."

"Foul, it's perfectly obscene," says Pamela as she whisks back into the room. "Do give us all a drink, John. I once thought nothing could be worse than English weather, but it's a marvel to me with the climate here frightful as it is, that every living soul in this country isn't a hopeless alcoholic, after all think of Russia where they actually drink brake fluid or maybe that's just propaganda, what do you think, Mrs. Hill – or may I call you by your first name?"

"Please do. It's Rowena."

"Drink," says John, advancing on a silver tray crowded with bottles. "Gin? Sherry? Rye?"

"Oh, thank you, but I hardly ever –"

"Seize the hour," he says cheerfully. "Last few days a bit rough for you. Nip of Scotch? Call it medicinal."

"Well, just a very small one, thanks."

Pamela has flopped into an overstuffed chintz chair, her trousered legs spread wide. She clutches her thick hair off her face like someone trying to control a runaway horse.

"Is your name from *Ivanhoe* then, horrible school reading, what a lot that man Scott has to answer for, the thousands he has bored to tears, and such awful sticks of women in that book, I can't think why Victorian writers were all so terrified of sexy women – look at Dickens, and all the time he had that swarm of children and a little popsie on the side, as well – I do wonder why to a man they portray women without any legs who keep on fainting all over the place, ridiculous I call it. Ah, lovely gin, thank you, darling."

I sip my drink cautiously. In the distance a phone rings, a child's voice calls, "For you, Max," and the young man darts out of the room with an apologetic smile.

"Dishy, isn't he," says his mother proudly. "A bit tense, these days, though, don't you find, John? It's that girl, of course, at twenty years old what else? – but it's hard luck, really, because in this case she's the only child of a pair of fanatic Mennonites. They're living together in Kingston – the kids, I mean – but her parents have a farm nearby and they keep on dropping in to her apartment, and Max can hardly pretend to be there just to study with her all the time, can he, so he's fixed himself up a cupboard with a chair and a lightbulb, and he darts in there and reads till they go; but you can see, can't you, that it would *not* make for relaxed nerves. How glad I am not to be that young any more."

Another modest sip of Scotch sends a wave of warmth to the ends of my toes. Somewhat to my surprise, I rather like the sensation.

"Yes, it's the start and the finish of life that are so bothersome, don't you think," Pam goes on comfortably. "I clearly remember how awful it was being a child and my parents made sure it was even worse by packing me off to an English boarding school. No, being young is frightful, it's middle age I'm finding so enjoyable. So many fewer things to bother or terrify, like pregnancy or failing exams. Not nearly so many bugbears."

"Do you really think so?" Something about her dotty conversation is so relaxing that I almost forget to be shy. "I haven't noticed much falling off, myself. I suppose it's a matter of temperament."

"How bloody right you are. Take my father, now. He was always a bit inflammable, but now he's over eighty, absolutely everything annoys him to the point of apoplexy . . . AIDS, inflation, pollution, terrorism, pornography, additives in food, the greenhouse effect (which I adore), it's hardly safe to mention anything. I don't know. His daily comes and gets his meals, and I go over as often as I can to keep an eye on things, but after ten minutes with him I can feel my eczema simply *popping* out all over me like a wallpaper pattern. Even the daily can barely stand him, and she hardly understands any English. I don't suppose you happen to know anybody, do you, preferably deaf and dumb for her own sake, who could baby-sit him evenings, just to make sure he doesn't get lost on the way to the toilet or fall downstairs? Not that it wouldn't be a blessing of sorts if he did, then a hospital would have to cope."

"Well, just possibly I might be able to think of somebody," I say warily.

The black cat Wittgenstein now comes into the room and sits with dignity on the centre medallion of the rug. His yellow eyes consider me so intently I lose momentum after this tentative opening, and fall silent again.

"Well, if ever you hear of anybody . . . Do top us up, John. Now tell me, what are your plans? I'd be off like a shot to the Bahamas or San Diego, in your shoes."

"Not for me, thanks," I say as John reaches for my glass. "No, I have no plans, really." This remark is, I think, even for me, a superbly bland summary of my present state of mind. The cat approaches and jumps into my lap with an air of nonchalance that suggests he doesn't really care for laps, but might find mine tolerable.

"Oh, good; then you have time to consider all the delicious possibilities. For instance a friend of ours – and Louise is *centuries* older than you – she went to Florida for the first time in her life right after the funeral, and within weeks, Rowena – weeks – she not only had a glorious tan and a cup for bridge, but a new boyfriend. Well, when I say *new* and *boy*, Maurice is seventy-eight; but the thing is they are living together to this day in blissful sin in Orlando, though how they manage it I don't really know, because she has gout in her knees, and he's only got one leg, though perhaps one provides enough –"

Here she catches my eye and breaks into a loud guffaw. I sputter wildly into my glass. Grinning, John claps me on the back. Young Maxwell, who has slipped into the room to get himself a beer, gives us a resigned look that intimates he hopes we will all one day grow up and cease embarrassing him. We are all just as pleased when he disappears again.

"Well, you see, the fact is I will probably be very poor," I find myself telling them.

"But, my dear, you don't mean soup-and-blankets poor."

"Something pretty close. My husband seems to have left everything to his first wife." With some incredulity I hear myself sharing this information with strangers. For one thing, it seems disloyal. But, remembering how much more there is to tell, I think defiantly, Why not?

"Well, I must say I call that rather unsporting of him," says Pam, leaning forward. She fastens on me the full beam of an attentive gaze, and it interests me to note how intelligent her eyes are, despite her random and frivolous chat. This makes me wonder whether silliness might not be as good a smokescreen as any other; or whether, on the other hand, frivolity might not after all be a form of wisdom. For a second or two she contemplates me thoughtfully. In any other circumstances I would do my best to become totally invisible, but under this scrutiny, perhaps in belated reaction to recent stress, I feel strangely, recklessly relaxed.

"Anyhow, I'll be job hunting soon," I add calmly. "Not that I can do anything at all anyone would pay for, except maybe cook. I'm not bad with boiling chickens and tough cuts of beef."

"How fascinating; John dear, we'll simply have to rack our brains and come up with something delightful Rowena can do that will pay well and doesn't need any real ability. The world is full of jobs like that, look at the government. I'm sure we can hit on the very thing, remember that woman we used to know, darling, the one with the wart on her chin – she had some absurd name like Ermentrude – anyhow, she used to pay someone to come in and play with her cat. Or there's Mike, isn't there, love, who's always looking for people to lacquer things – he refinishes furniture."

At this point a vague, floating sensation in my head warns me it is time to go. I edge my drink out of sight behind a philodendron in a pink pot and adjust my feet to deal with the challenge of getting up without falling down. The cat gives me a cold glance and hops off my lap.

"Oh, do you really have to go? – well, you must come again as soon as possible. John will find your coat. Then there's Steve, another friend of ours – he studied for years and years to be an opera singer, and then decided he didn't want to be that after all, and began to sell chicken pies that he cooked in his mother's kitchen. It nearly drove Emma mad, of course, for several different reasons, but he's actually making quite good money at it now, in a take-away shop of his own. Perhaps he could use somebody to cut up veg. As a matter of fact, we're having a little evening do here next week for Steve – he's getting married – do come round and join us – you never know where contacts may lead – I'll call you soon."

Once safely home behind my own door, I find myself smiling foolishly at the walls. The combination of Scotch and Pam has been enough to turn a stronger head than mine. To sober myself, I pull up a chair to the sitting-room bookcase and, as Cuthbert urged, begin one after another to take out and shake open every book, on the off chance that a will may obligingly drop out. In a Victorian novel, of course, it would do that after a delay of only a few hundred pages, but I have little hope anything of the kind will happen in the real world. My mind, as it keeps doing these days, drifts off into trivial reflections instead of busying itself with serious questions (e.g., what is the relationship between language and truth, and does anybody's last will and testament ever really express it?) – speculations I would have if I were a more impressive woman. Instead I think about the cat Wittgenstein, who seems to like me. I hope the Wrights will remember to invite me over again, and that they won't be annoyed when they find my unfinished drink.

It is kind of Tom and Cuthbert, too, I think, shaking open a Greene thriller, to take such an interest, specially since in the past, as Edwin's friends, they never before seemed much aware of either my identity or my gender. In fact they've always treated me rather like a piece of furniture too familiar to be even vaguely interesting, whereas now ...

What an eclectic collection of books ours is. It consists of worn-out paperbacks or shabby out-of-print hardbacks picked up at church bazaars. Marion's childhood copies of *Alice* and Grimm jostle Edwin's do-it-yourself manuals on plumbing and a rain- or tear-soaked copy of *The Wide, Wide World*. There's little here to tempt even such a browser as me, but, yawning, I go on dutifully opening even such unlikely sources of a will as Edwin's prayer book. Once my heart gives a jump when a square of paper flutters out of a borrowed copy of Orwell's *Down and Out in Paris and London*, but this turns out to be an old shopping list. The last item on the shelves is a coverless *Bleak House*, which, for all it is about a lost will, also yields up nothing. Here, though, flipping through the pages, I am seduced into reading about Mr. Guppy's visit to the Dedlock mansion, where he gaped with such interest at the portrait of a Dedlock ancestress "with large round eyes and other charms to correspond." There, I think, I must show that to Pamela.

Just then a rap at the front door makes me start. Who can that be, calling after dark like this? To ignore it seems the prudent thing to do. Then I think it might be Marion, dropping in on impulse, perhaps having lost her key. But no, I remind myself, Marion has no impulses and never loses keys. When the knock comes again, I approach the door in a dither of indecision. Then to my alarm the letterbox flap is raised. A voice muffled by stooping says, "It's only me, Rowena – Cuthbert."

"Oh! Just coming. Hold on a second." I wrestle the chain free of its slot and let him in.

"Sorry, I should have called you first," he says, once more stepping neatly onto the mat where he wipes his galoshes with care before removing them. "Hope I didn't startle you. But on my way out to get a bite of supper, I suddenly remembered something I meant to mention this morning, only what with everything, it completely slipped my mind. It's about cash – Edwin's bank account."

"Why don't you take your coat off, Cuthbert? And if you haven't eaten yet, will you stay and have something with me? It won't be very exciting, but I've got eggs, and we could have some kind of omelette, if that's all right for you."

"Well, I'd love to, if you're sure it's not too much trouble."

"Not a bit. Give yourself a glass of sherry while I get organized." What Edwin would say to this reckless expenditure of alcohol I can't imagine and don't much care. Normally a single bottle of sherry and another of port saw us from one Christmas to the next. Well, it's his own fault for dying and creating the demand. But, aware that my own breath is redolent of Scotch, I hastily munch a soda cracker at the kitchen counter.

A moment later, Cuthbert comes in, glass in hand. He has something folded small in his free hand, which he furtively shoves under the tea caddy when he thinks I am too busy beating eggs to notice.

"Yes," he says, "I can't imagine how I could have forgotten to mention it this morning; but of course you realize because your bank account was in Edwin's name, it will be frozen now. Obviously, though, you'll need some money to go on with, so I'm advancing you some ready cash, Rowena, to meet current expenses and pay any outstanding bills."

"Oh, but Cuthbert –" It's not really surprising that this significant detail should have failed to occur to me, but it surely should have occurred to Marion. Odd that it has not.

"Now that's an end to it," he says firmly. "What's an old friend for if not to give a hand."

"Well, but I really feel –"

"Enough," he says. "Just don't bother yourself one bit about it. As a matter of fact, you know, I've been quite rich ever since my father passed on. He left me some nice lakefront property up there in cottage country near Barrie, which I sold and converted into T-bills. And when Mother goes – which I hope will be never – there'll be a portfolio of pretty good stocks as well. So unless the bottom falls out of everything, I'm quite nicely, thank you. And what have I got to spend money on? Basil's my only dependant, isn't he?" He sits down, adding prudently, "Of course if you insist, and if we have any luck with our application for support and assets, you can pay me back some day out of the estate." He pauses to sip his sherry. "It really is the most frustrating thing we can't find a will later than the one that fellow showed us, because if only we could, you'd be entitled to seventy per cent of all Edwin had. And I say again, it simply wasn't like the man to leave you unprovided for."

Not trusting myself to comment on that, I say simply, "Well, I've looked through every book in the house, and there's no sign of anything."

"Now, you cheer up, Rowena. Such a dear, nice person as you are, somehow or other I just know things are going to work out all right for you."

I look up sharply from the tough heel of Cheddar I am grating. "Do you really believe that whether we're nice or not has anything to do with what happens to us? What a sunny philosophy."

"Well, I don't mean physical things, of course, like diseases. Even then, ulcers don't happen to tranquil people, do they, and teetotallers generally have nice healthy livers. Even with accidents – how many accidents are there with no human factor involved? No, I really believe just about everything that happens to a person relates to his inside self somehow. Or hers, of course."

"If that's true, then Edwin killed himself. After, of course, killing me."

With something like horror I hear myself (or the Wrights' Scotch) blurt this out. The naked, devastating truth of it seems to break the air between us into long, destructive shards of glass. Without warning I then burst into noisy sobbing, the bowl of egg mixture still gripped in my hand.

Calmly, as if neither surprised nor shocked by this outburst, Cuthbert first switches off the heat under the omelette pan, and then wraps his short arms tightly around me. He presses my head into the front of his soft sweater and rocks me to and fro exactly as Nana used to do. He pats my back and murmurs the sort of word-less comfort appropriate for babies. And indeed I feel as outraged and disoriented as any newborn. Eventually he provides a clean handkerchief. Then he says, "There now. That's better, isn't it? You needed that. Have a sip of this sherry, Rowena dear. You'll feel much better now."

I blow my nose. "No, I won't, Cuthbert. This isn't grief. You don't understand – and neither did I, really, till just now. It's so obvious once you put it all together. He got involved with me in the first place against his better judgement – against his con-science – and against the law, come to that. And he resented me for it – how could he not? Punished me for it, too, in various different ways, all those years we were together. Destroyed me, you could even say. As for his death, you might say he ran to keep himself young for me. That would be touching if it were true. But what he did was run to get away from me. And dying the way he did – that was not only the one way of escape for him, it was revenge as well, do you see that? Well, probably not. But I do."

"Rowena, let's go in and sit where it's comfortable. You're just very shocked and tired." He guides me into the sitting-room where, after turning off all but one small table lamp, he draws me down beside him on the sofa. There I lean against him, closing my eyes. In the dim light I all but forget he is there; my own wailing voice seems to be the only real presence in the room.

"Of course I resented him, too. But that's nothing to how I feel about him now that I know the lie he lived, and made me live with him. Mrs. Edwin Hill, indeed. But that wasn't the worst of it. *He* was the worst of it. When Marion was conceived, for instance. He was furious, as if I'd impregnated myself . . . For a whole week he barely spoke to me. It meant, among other things, that instead of spending what my grandmother left us on a car, we had to make a down payment on this house, and saddle him with a mortgage as well. So I carried all this guilt around for the rest of the nine months, plus the fear he'd resent me even more if it weren't a son. Oh, I was so pleased and relieved he turned out to be delighted with a daughter. Of course he was. He already had a son. After that he focused more and more tenderness on her, and less and less on me. That was another surprise, though not so nice a one. After that, without of course denying himself anything, he vetoed any more children, though I badly wanted more. Couldn't afford it, he said. But he could afford to pack me off to the doctor to be fitted for a thing I loathed using . . . After that it was the pill, never mind that it gave me headaches and depression. After all, it was only me. And I didn't exist, except as Mrs. Edwin Hill, did I? And then even my name – if you call it mine – turned out to be a fraud. What a dirty thing betrayal is. It taints the victim, too, because what happened was that I betrayed myself. I collaborated with him. I was even more or less loyal to him. And that's the worst thing of all."

A short silence follows.

"Blow your nose, dear," he suggests gently.

I do that, then settle back inside his arm with a long sigh. After another silence I say, "Your sweater's all wet. Sorry."

"Well, I must say when you cry, you don't fool around."

"Do you want that omelette?"

"Not really. Do you?"

"No."

"Why don't you just lie down here and get comfortable."

"All right. But please don't go."

"No, no. I'm going to lie down right beside you. How's that, now. Comfortable?"

He clicks off the light, removes his glasses, then takes off my shoes and his own. After that he tucks himself close against me with a matter-of-fact cosiness, as if we do this sort of thing every day. A smell of damp wool comes from his cashmere sweater, and from his skin a spicy aroma of aftershave. His proximity feels perfectly natural and so reassuring that in seconds I begin to drift towards sleep. But then his voice in the dark tugs me back.

"As a matter of fact, you know, even before you told me about yours, the whole idea of marriage has always scared the heck out of me."

"Has it?"

"Well, my parents were what people call a devoted couple, but I lived with them, and that doesn't quite describe it . . . That's one reason I've never . . . I mean, finding somebody you actually want to spend your whole life with . . . And then I guess I've got some hang-ups besides . . . Just the same, I'm as hetero as anything, you know, Rowena, though plenty of people think otherwise. Girls – women – turn me on so sometimes I can hardly . . . Well, you know what I mean. But because I don't look macho, women just aren't interested. The fact I've never actually – that's beside the point. It's simply that casual sex is not something I can possibly . . . well, part of it's upbringing, of course. My mother, sweet and kind as she is, has very strict notions, and . . . Anyhow, the truth is sex without commitment just isn't for me, and that makes me a real freak these days, I know."

"Never had a girl-friend?"

"Not really. Once, years ago, I was sort of engaged to a girl in my last year at Osgoode – that is, I wanted to marry her, but she never would give me a definite answer. Anyhow, one night we were – sort of necking around, and things got – I thought – she seemed more than willing and started to undress me, which I found pretty embarrassing but nice – anyhow, when she saw me – that is, my – she burst out laughing. I found out later she'd done the whole thing as a bet."

"Not nice."

"No. And you can imagine that didn't do my various inhibitions one bit of good."

His voice shakes a little and I fumble one hand free to lay it on his cheek. "She was stupid, on top of everything else, Cuthbert. Not to know that the size of a man has nothing to do with his manhood."

"Well, the problem is, where are the girls I could ever – I mean these smart, tough career women I work with have no time for anybody bald and short and half blind. I go bird-watching with a nice group, but all the women in it are married, except for a couple of sad, cranky singles like myself."

"Somebody will come along one day." But hoping this is true is no real excuse for saying it, I know.

"No, Rowena, they won't. I know that."

He nuzzles closer and clumsily as a child begins to drop kisses on my face. Half by accident one of these lands on my mouth and instantly ceases to be childish. After my brief courtship days with Edwin, kisses ceased to play any part in our relationship, and now, with astonishment, I feel (for the second time today with Cuthbert) a whole series of mild, delightful stirrings. Since he is, by now, lying half over me, I am aware he is having them, too. For a few minutes, bemused with growing pleasure and half-stunned with fatigue, I accept it all with gratitude. It is very soon clear that, mother or no mother, inexperience is no real problem for Cuthbert; in fact he has plenty of natural aptitude for this kind of thing. Then, abruptly, he gets up.

"Sorry, Rowena," he mutters. "Forgive me. You're so sweet, but I mustn't . . . The money isn't really why I came back here tonight. It's so lovely to touch you. But I mustn't."

I murmur something drowsily.

"Tell me you're not angry."

The truth is that for the first time in forty-eight hours I am free of anger, but I have no energy left to explain this to him.

"It was wrong of me," he goes on, "to take advantage . . . Of course it's far, far too soon, I know; but would you consider marrying me some day? Don't say anything now. You're worn out and I'm going home. But think about it, will you?"

This unforeseen proposal does not seem much more preposterous than most of the other things that have happened to me recently. I murmur something noncommittal. Sleep is closing thickly around me again. With a faint but audible groan in the dark he resumes his shoes and glasses.

"Go to sleep now," he whispers, touching my head. "See you tomorrow." I feel him gently cover me with the afghan Nana crocheted years ago; but I do not hear him go.

CHAPTER FOUR

❧

Next morning a square of radiant sky, blue and immaculate, confronts me like the first day of creation. I blink at it, bewildered. For a minute or two I recognize nothing in the room, including myself. The bright light dazzles my eyes. I hear the chirp of sparrows somewhere outside with a kind of amazement, as if they are exotic birds in a fable. It is some time before I can connect or focus the commonplace impressions that drift around me like pieces of dreams: a long arrow of sunlight on the wall; the postman's whistle as he retreats down the street; the mantel clock, which now politely chimes nine times.

What on earth has possessed me to fall asleep on the sofa in all my clothes? But the answer to that, when it drifts along, is not one I care to dwell on. It is strange how weak, almost light-headed I feel, as if drained by a long illness. It is a real effort to disentangle myself from the afghan and get clumsily to my feet. The mirror over the mantel reflects without mercy my dishevelled clothes and tangled hair. Fumbling, I collect my shoes. My throat feels hot and dry, so I pad into the kitchen and drink down a large glass of cold milk. Beyond the window the yellow leaves of the maple glow. It occurs to me this whole day is mine, to do what I like with. There is nobody now to defer to, consult, consider or placate. Only yesterday that thought would have been intimidating; now I find it satisfying.

I head upstairs for a bath, unbuttoning as I go the old grey cardigan and rumpled skirt. These I drop like a discarded skin on the tiled bathroom floor. In the tub filled deep, I find naked immersion in the hot water less an ordinary bath than a sort of baptism. Closing my eyes, I lie full length and let the water lap round me in ritual purification. *Cleanse the thoughts of our hearts*, as one of the collects puts it. "And as a matter of fact, Mrs. W.," I confide, as the delicate steam rises around us, "in spite of my behaviour last night, this morning I feel peaceful and purged. Odd, isn't it."

"You know," she remarks in her inconsequential way, "I once saw an ad in the personal column in which someone classified herself as a Serious Widow. If there really are such, do you want to be one of them?"

"Well, but Ethel – you don't mind if I call you Ethel? – after all, it's been years – you must admit that all that cuddling with Cuthbert – pretty shameful, wasn't it. At our age, too. Also unbelievably silly. Could lead to all sorts of complications. And that would be entirely my fault, because it was all really just to spite Edwin." After a moment I add, "Well, not quite all, maybe."

"Everything worthwhile is complicated, and what a good thing, really," she says, idly blowing a hole in the steam. "There are, for instance, two or three sexes, good and bad angels, and the easiness of lies. Makes life amusing and full of surprises."

"But it was terrible of me to encourage him. Whatever must he think? Don't answer that."

"I rather imagine neither of you did much thinking at the time. Surely there are places and positions where thinking is a waste of time."

"But what am I going do about it? He actually proposed."

"Whatever you feel like doing, my dear. Go fishing like Maggie Vardoe, for instance. Fish for the truth. Not hers, necessarily. Fish for your own."

And with this Mrs. Wilson blows me a kiss and disappears.

Refreshed by this encounter, I wrap myself in a towel and cross to the bedroom to dress. But a survey of the cupboard (half empty, now, with most of Edwin's things packed away) does nothing to encourage the idea of rebirth. My clothes are all depressing reminders of many things, in particular my dressmaking inadequacies. The brown checked skirt that never did hang quite straight. The grey dress I made three years ago that looks even more boring whenever I try to brighten it up with a new scarf or belt. The beige skirt, baggy at the seat with age. Fretfully I push these dreary articles about on their hangers. Catching my eye in the mirror, it occurs to me that I look better in the bath towel pegged under my arms than in any of my clothes. The ruby colour and the soft pile are both pleasing. Turning first one way and then another, I look at my reflection thoughtfully.

The towel is one of a set given to us by Marion last Christmas. She apologized at the time for the colour, explaining that they were on sale. Of course few people in this cautious country would care to pay full price to dry themselves on anything so vivid. Certainly it would take a bolder spirit than mine to wear such a rich red any place where other people could see it. But just to lounge around in at home . . . The longer I look at myself the better I like the way that ruby colour makes my hair look darker and my shoulders whiter.

After a minute, I pull the matching towels out of the linen cupboard. There is enough material for a wraparound skirt and a sort of tabard top. Half furtively I uncover the sewing machine and sit down. A few hours with scissors and thread . . . Why not? It's not exactly fishing, Ethel, but maybe it's not far off.

Marion's key scrapes in the lock downstairs just as I am leaning towards the mirror to remove a last pin from a shoulder seam. Before I can dart out of sight and strip off the whole ensemble, she has slung off her coat and come swiftly up the stairs. I back myself in haste halfway into the cupboard, where I pretend to have legitimate business among the shoes.

"Mother? Oh, there you are. You'll never guess what's happened." Here she pauses impressively. "Gloria McNulty has resigned."

"No," I say feebly.

"Yes, actually resigned, after twenty years. Polly phoned me just now with the whole story. It seems at the commissioners' meeting yesterday, Margaret-Ann Carslake from Manitoba told her she was an obstructionist. There was a sticky kind of silence and when nobody denied it, she just up and resigned, then and there."

"Well, well. I suppose that's good. You sound pleased."

"Mother, you know who McNulty *is*."

"Actually, no."

Marion sits down vehemently on the edge of the bed. "Honestly, Mother. She's our area commissioner."

"Oh, yes. I see."

"Do you? It just means for the first time in about a whole generation something will actually get done here in Guiding. And who's next under area commissioners? Divisions, that's who. And after Connie Ball and Babs, I'm senior in divisions. And that means there's a good chance I'll get the job. Heaven knows I'm the obvious choice. Babs Harrington can't decide what to have for lunch, never mind anything else; and everybody thinks poor old Connie has Alzheimer's."

"Well, dear, I hope it comes your way if you want it. The job, I mean."

"Of course I want it. Not just because of the rank, either, or the raise. There's so much that needs doing – the whole organization for years now has been in the hands of these dear old ladies who knew Baden-Powell back in '37. Infatuated with him, if you ask me, most of them. They're sure nobody could ever possibly improve on his ideas, though it's obvious that since then – Mother, what on earth are you doing in there? And what, for pity's sake, is that you're wearing?"

Half sheepish, half defiant, I come out of the closet.

"But that's – but Mother – those are your towels!"

"That's right. I decided to make them into a nice little leisure outfit. Isn't the colour great?"

"The skirt is much too skimpy. In fact, the whole thing looks ridiculous," says Marion.

Law Number Four: A Guide is a friend to all, I think bitterly.

Downstairs the door knocker gives a smart tattoo, and with something of a flounce Marion goes to peer through the small landing window from which large-headed, tapered callers can be seen on the porch below. "It's Canon Tom," she says. "I'll go. Change into something decent."

"Won't," I mutter when she is safely out of earshot. Instead I put on a long-sleeved white blouse and on the shoulder of the tabard over it pin a pretty old gold brooch of Nana's.

"Rowena, my dear," booms Tom as I come down the stairs. "What a delightful frock. Your clever needle at work again! Most becoming!" His blue eyes move appreciatively over the skimpy skirt. Marion fails to repress a faint snort. "I hope you'll forgive me for dropping in like this, but my friend's grandson – you remember I mentioned the Whittakers the other day – they've commissioned me to ask whether you'll agree to an interview."

"An interview!" says Marion. "Whatever for?"

"Tell her about it, Tom, while I get the tea."

From the kitchen I hear the rumble of his voice alternating with her incisive questions. In a leisurely fashion I set a tray with cups and find some ginger biscuits to put on a platter. Wittgenstein is out in our yard sharpening his claws on the maple tree. I rap on the glass by way of greeting, and he instantly runs up our back steps to yowl at the door. "Abandon hope," I tell him, muffling the teapot in its cosy. Cheerfully he shoots off in pursuit of a squirrel.

". . . and when Margaret-Ann Carslake called her an obstructionist at the meeting, there was a sticky kind of silence and then she simply up and resigned," Marion is saying as I carry in the tray. "So you see this may open the way for me."

"Bless me," says Tom comfortably. "Well, I daresay it may be time for a little young blood to find its way onto that board. I wish you all the luck in the world, my dear."

"But about these Whittakers," Marion says, turning to me with a frown. "You can't be seriously considering it, Mother? Turning out six days a week in all weathers, and taking orders from a stranger – how would you ever adjust to all that? You don't realize how spoiled and sheltered you've been. And four children – all boys – I can't imagine it."

As a matter of fact I can't imagine it, either, but after all only days ago she was hectoring me about practical plans for the future, and it irritates me to find her so dismissive now. So I say, trying to sound confident, "Well, you never know till you try, do you? After all I dealt with you when you were two . . . Once you kicked quite a big hole in the wall with temper. Besides, all my reading, specially in Victoriana, might come in very handy in a job like this. Gin is what they used to tranquillize babies, you know, and if that didn't work, you held their little heads over the gas stove. Anyhow, Tom, I'll be glad to go and talk to them about it," I add, though I know Marion understands as well as I do that this talk is mostly swagger.

Another rap at the door brings Marion to her feet. Casting a repressive glance at me over her shoulder she goes to the door. There is then a bustle of coat and boot removal in the hall, and Cuthbert comes in carrying a sheaf of yellow roses half as tall as himself. He walks up to me with a fixed, self-conscious smile and presents them with an awkward flourish that suggests guilt rather than gallantry.

"Oh, thank you, Cuthbert. How lovely."

"You're looking very nice," he says, blushing as he glances at the new outfit. "Is that a new dress? Very attractive."

A noticeable bleakness of expression has settled over the faces of Tom and Marion during this exchange. When I go out to put the roses in water, Cuthbert would have followed me, but Marion seats him with authority, and soon her voice floats out to me: ". . . and when Margaret-Ann Carslake called Gloria an obstructionist at the meeting, there was a sticky kind of silence and she up and resigned on the spot."

I replenish the teapot and take it back in with the vase of flowers. Set on the coffee table they seem to drink all the light in the room, and in return they shed such a voluptuous perfume into the air that conversation about sensible things like jobs falters to a stop. Tom moodily crunches the last biscuit. Outside the sky dims, then the street lamps bloom green, officially proclaiming nightfall. Wittgenstein strolls into the room and sniffs at my shoes.

"I'm afraid he squeezed in when I arrived," Cuthbert says apologetically. "Would you like me to put him out?"

"I will deal with it," says Tom. Masterfully he scoops the cat up and carries him away. A moment later he is back, sucking a long scratch on his wrist.

"Here, I'll look after that," Marion says briskly. She brings in the kitchen first-aid kit and from it produces antiseptic and a Band-Aid, with her usual air of faintly scornful competence. Over her shoulder Tom casts me a glance in which reproach and wistfulness are the chief ingredients. "You'll hardly believe this," she remarks to no one in particular, "but I found three hundred dollars in cash just now on the kitchen counter. Under the biscuit tin. Really, Mother, I don't know what's going to become of you."

I clear my throat. Cuthbert is looking attentively out of the window at nothing. Luckily the others show no interest in either of these reactions.

By now it is nearly dark, and Marion gets out her coat, asking rather pointedly, "Can I offer anybody a lift? – Canon Tom?"

"No – no, thank you, my dear. As you know, I live not too far away to walk. Make a point of my four miles a day. I'm still good for more than that, thank the Lord."

"And I have my car, thanks, Marion."

After perfunctory farewells she leaves, closing the door behind her with rather unnecessary firmness. Conversation then idles from Meech Lake to Eastern Europe, and thence to Toronto's garbage-disposal problem. I begin to feel hungry, but there is nothing in the house to offer two guests for dinner. I cross my legs; then think better of it and uncross them. Blinking and stiffening my jaw, I try not to yawn. Why on earth don't they go home? The clock strikes six; still neither takes the hint. Tom's eyes keep straying to my legs.

Cuthbert's face has taken on a wooden look of obstinacy. I pull down the red skirt. Marion is right about it, of course. She has an exasperating habit of being right about such things.

At last Tom mutters something about a vestry meeting and stands up. "I'll be glad to drive you over to the Whittakers' tomorrow, Rowena," he says. "Would four o'clock suit you? I'll be here in good time. Good night, Cuthbert." He accepts my help with his coat, holding up his wrist with a brave air of concealed suffering, and leaves with a last rather languishing look at me.

The door has barely closed when Cuthbert joins me in the hall, rubbing his short hands together in satisfaction. "I thought dear old Tom would never push off," he says, "but I just had to have a quick word . . ."

I have retreated swiftly to my chair in the corner, where I sit with both feet primly together on the carpet. I avoid even looking at the sofa with its now neatly folded afghan. But to my surprise, Cuthbert reappears winding on his muffler. "I must be off myself, Rowena," he says rather breathlessly. "It's my night to visit Mother. And no doubt you'll be glad of a quiet evening to yourself. You've had a . . . Well, what I mean is that yesterday – last night – was – well, best all round if we both just forget all about that . . . whole incident. I'm sure you agree that's best all round. There are times when one says things . . . You understand, I'm sure."

Before the last of these words is out, I have cut in (trying to keep the relief out of my voice), "Oh, absolutely. You're quite right, Cuthbert."

"That's all right, then. Bless you. So I'll be off. See you again before long. Now take care."

Our mutual embarrassment hangs in the air like some powerful, not very pleasant smell – the odour of sanctity, perhaps.

"**W**ell, my dear, that went off very well," says Tom, heaving himself into place behind the wheel of his little sports car. Before putting it in gear, he gives my knee a congratulatory squeeze. Did it? I want to say, but instead murmur, "Yes, it seemed to."

"I could see they were impressed by your maturity and – if I may say so – your excellent calm. Now their last home-help was calm, to be sure, but she took it to extremes, rather. They found her snoring in the family room last week while the children tore all over the house squirting each other with Sprite. How she could sleep through that –"

Maybe through despair, I think, but dutifully say, "Amazing."

"Spirited children," he remarks, stealing a sidelong look at me. Certainly the two who skateboarded in and out of the room throughout our visit did not seem to lack spirit. The youngest, it's true, hid behind the sofa, but from that vantage point he growled and yapped at the family dog until it had hysterics and puddled on the rug. These details have not escaped Tom's attention any more than they have mine, but for some reason he seems very anxious to put the whole tribe in the best possible light. I can't help wondering why.

"Miriam's great-grandchildren are very dear to her, naturally. And she herself is one of my most valued parishioners."

You mean richest, I think, my question answered.

"At any rate, the Whittakers were delighted that you accepted the job," he goes on.

"Provisionally," I put in. It surprises me that he could have seen any delight in Toby Whittaker, an exhausted-looking young man who, after shaking hands, said not a word from first to last, but whose silence emitted a faint air of disaster and gin.

"I could see that they were delighted," he repeats firmly. "Of course it's a stroke of luck for them, as they must be well aware, to have a trustworthy person like you to take over."

"On a trial basis."

"Yes, of course, my dear. Tell me, just between the two of us, what was your impression of Wilma? I get the feeling, from various things Miriam has let drop, that there's not much love lost between those ladies. Perhaps that's because they're so much alike."

It's a sobering thought that there might be someone else like Wilma Whittaker. She frightened me even more than her children did, which was quite a lot. She was a large, square girl with the swaggering walk of an SS officer. Her hair was dragged back off her face with an elastic band, thus giving full exposure to a prominent jaw and a steel-blue, aggressive stare. The couple were barely out of their twenties, but she seemed to have behind her a lifetime of authority and self-esteem.

"Finding the right person to interface with the children," she said to me, in the resonant voice God might use if He ever felt like conversation, "that's the bottom line for us here. But you don't strike me as the kind of person interested in establishing a dependency relationship, and that's a plus. You'll help them deal with the learning experience on a day-to-day basis is what I guess I'm trying to say."

"Yes, I suppose it is," I said, trying not to sound ironic. But I was at the same time mesmerized by that metallic gaze and by her clothes – a black leather mini-skirt and a magenta satin blouse with food stains down the front. This outfit actually gave me a certain new respect for my old grey dress. With one bare foot (the toenails also magenta) she fended off one of the skateboarders who would otherwise have overturned the standard lamp.

"Then we'll expect you at noon Monday," she said briskly.

"Yes. On a trial basis."

Now the thought of Monday, on any basis whatsoever, makes my stomach contract. What a ridiculous position I've put myself in, simply because I can't bring myself to utter the word no, even to an old acquaintance like Tom. However, as it is he can enjoy the belief he's done a good day's work for all concerned. We are by now nearly home and he swings cheerfully off the Don Valley Parkway.

"I suppose I will be able to cope," I say dubiously.

"My dear Rowena, think of the money. I mean, in your position at present, this is a godsend. As for the children – why, you simply must have more confidence in yourself. You know, don't you, that you're a person with many rich resources that have so far never been tapped. Don't you know that?"

The car has stopped with a jerk outside my door. "Well, but Tom, it's going to be tough trying to be even a part-time parent to those kids. I don't know what it is about children – their egos, maybe – that makes them so scary."

"I don't know about that. My father was a whip-the-offending-Adam-out-of-him parent," Tom says rather gloomily. "And that was even worse than it sounds, because he enjoyed it. Almost makes me a believer in permissive upbringing. I say almost, of course."

"Well, the grandparents who brought me up – they went to the opposite extreme. They were so sweet and gentle I grew up think-ing everybody was like that, and what a shock to find it wasn't so. And they adored me too much . . . they tried to protect me against absolutely everything."

"That was bad luck for you," he remarks. I glance at him, star-tled by this point of view. "Because," he goes on, "that's probably why far too many things frighten you now."

With reluctance I admit, "It wouldn't matter what job I was going to on Monday, I'd be scared rigid. Not really much help, is it?"

"That's where the resources come in." Tom's light-blue eyes look intently and kindly into mine.

"Well, maybe. The thing is, have I got the right ones?"

"Of course you have, you little goose." He takes me by the chin and gives my face a little mock shake. "Courage, my dear!"

For a minute I think I am going to be kissed – again – but evidently he remembers in time we are more or less in the public eye. He helps instead to extricate me from the seat belt and reaches across me to open the car door.

"I'll drop by Monday evening to see how you got on," he says. "All right?"

"Of course. And thanks, Tom, for everything."

Some spiritual emergency or other must have called Tom away on Monday evening, because it is well after nine, and I've given him up before he appears at the door. A high wind is booming through the dark streets, and his face is ruddy from his walk. Tired as I am, it is good to see him.

"Excuse my dressing gown, Tom . . . do sit down. Let me make you some coffee."

"No, my dear, don't bother; you look a bit tired. How did it all go, then? Come sit here and tell me all about it." He plumps himself down on the sofa and pats the cushion beside him invitingly. But, remembering the aphrodisiac effect my widowhood seems to have had lately on more than one occasion, I wrap my old gown close and sit discreetly nearby on a straight chair.

"Well, Tom, I'm afraid . . . After all the trouble you've been to . . . Just the same, it was – I mean in our wildest –"

"Here, here," he says, looking at me in some alarm. "Was it that bad, then, my dear?" Midway through these remarks he perceives that my bent back is shaking not with sobs but with laughter. Then he says with rather less warmth, "Tell me about it."

Wiping my eyes, I try to pull myself together. "Well, after the parents left, I caught the two older kids smoking in the bathroom, and I'd rather not mention what they called me when I took the cigarettes away. I asked the seven-year-old then if it wasn't time for him to go to school, but he said he wasn't into all that lesson crap and his mother lets him stay home. I made pancakes for lunch and that was all right, but they got into a fight over the syrup jug, and by the end of it we were all pretty sticky. So was the kitchen."

Tom draws a sigh.

"I offered to take them to the park to play, but they preferred to stay home and shoot cap pistols at each other. Well, by five o'clock my legs were feeling sort of trembly and my head was aching fit to split. The parents showed up at six-thirty. It turned out they'd stopped off for a drink after work. They'd had a tough day, they said. I am leaving out, Tom, the only adjective the whole family seems to know, because it's not a word I can say out loud, even when I'm alone."

Tom clears his throat.

"Anyhow, I spent all afternoon working on a speech to Mrs. Whittaker that went something like this: 'Your kids have turned me into a believer in the cane – the dark cellar – the head held over the gas ring. For the first time in my life I find the idea of child abuse attractive. I'm sure you wouldn't approve of that, so I am resigning as of now.' Of course what I actually said was, 'I'm sorry, but I'm afraid this job calls for a much younger person, so would you please send the day's pay to my home address.'"

"Oh, dear."

"Well, yes, for me that was terrific assertiveness. It was quite a thrill, in fact, to find I could do it. Maybe you were right after all about those resources."

"Hm. A pity it had to work out that way. Miriam will be really disappointed, I know. Most regrettable." He steals a glance at his watch.

"I'm sorry, too, Tom."

"Of course I do admit those boys are a bit unruly, but with a firm hand . . . Oh well. No help for it, I suppose. I mean I don't suppose you'd feel like giving it another . . . No, I guess not. Only trying to help, bumbling old duffer that I am. My intentions were of the best."

"It's not that I don't appreciate it, Tom."

"No. Quite. Well, I must get along now."

"Sure you won't change your mind about coffee?"

"No, thank you, Rowena."

"Good night then, Tom. And thanks again."

"Not at all." But his voice is cool, and he takes himself off with a faint air of injured dignity.

As soon as he is gone, I step into the hall cupboard among the coats, close the door on myself and into the darkness whisper the word *fuck*.

After a twenty-minute wait in line, I finally reach a girl in the tellers' row who gives me an encouraging smile. As soon as I mention Edwin's safety deposit box, however, she waves me to the opposite side of the bank. "They'll look after you over there," she promises. But after I have stood another ten minutes at the counter, nobody there seems at all keen to do that. Many of the desks in this area are empty, it being the lunch hour; but there are young men here and there talking into phones or gazing intently at computer screens. At the desk facing me a large woman sits frowning at some papers. I try without success to catch her eye, though she seems to me to be busy chiefly in seeming to be busy. Eventually, though, she does get up and approach me with a heavy sigh. She is the possessor of a quite enormous bosom that projects in an almost menacing way.

"There was something," she tells rather than asks me.

"Well, yes. You see, my husband – he died last month – and his safety deposit box –"

"You the co-signee?"

"The what?" (All very well for Cuthbert to say, "Just tell them who you are" – for me, that's a lot easier said than done.)

"I'm Mrs. Edwin Hill. The box was – is – in his name, but I – that is, my lawyer – we need some of the papers in it, and he told me to come here and – I have the key here . . ."

"We'd need some official notification of the death, and also proof of your identity, Mrs. – um – Hall, before we could give you access to the box."

"It's Hill. And as for official . . ." (here a sense of unreality steals over me in a sort of vertigo) "I mean, he was buried at Pinewood Cemetery on October third . . . I haven't got proof of that, of course, but surely I wouldn't make up a thing like that; and as for proof of identity, I'm afraid I . . ."

"Driver's licence? Credit cards? Citizenship card?"

"Sorry, but I haven't got any of those –" Here I scrabble nervously in my handbag and after what seems an hour, unearth my dog-eared library card. The large woman looks at this with suspicion and contempt before flipping it back to me. I am about to turn away and go, so total is my sense of non-existence, but a customer standing behind me at the counter speaks over my shoulder.

"My mother died last summer and I was given access to her S/D box here without the slightest bother. You've had this lady's ID, and that's all you need." She adds, turning to me, "You have the key with you, Mrs. Hill? Then –"

Sulkily the big-bosomed one moves to open a wicket at the side of the counter and let me through. Before following her to the vault, I turn to say thanks to my rescuer. With envy and admiration I discover she is a jean-wearing girl of not more than twenty.

"**M**other says do please come over and have a drink – she'd like you to meet some amusing people. It's not a party, she said to be sure and tell you." Young Maxwell Wright gives me a disarming smile, but I back away from him defensively, drawing around me the old grey cardigan. A cold wind whirls at the open door, tumbling his fair hair.

"Oh, please thank her so much, but I'm afraid it – you see I'm not dressed and –" I can hardly after all explain to this pleasant boy that my evening plans are to read through the classified ads for domestic help, and complain to Prince Charles about the defection of both my former admirers. Then I remember that Pam has promised to introduce me to her friends in the chicken-pie business who might have work for me. This leaves me no choice: I'll have to go.

"She also said to tell you that people will be wearing just any old damn thing, so not to give that a thought."

The candour of this and the echo of Pamela's verbal style make me smile in spite of myself. "Yes, well, thanks, then. Let's go."

"Great," says the boy cheerfully. Seconds later he flings open their front door for me and shouts, "Ma!"

I shrink into my cardigan for protection. What would anyone call this throng, if not a party? The brightly lit hall is full of people who have spilled out of larger spaces. All of these strangers are talking at once. Quite a few others are sitting on the stairs, thus cutting off access to the bathroom, that home from home for social misfits like myself. Job or no job, I long to back out quietly and go home; but Pam now emerges from the ruck, flinging her arms wide in welcome.

"I'm absolutely delighted to see you, Rowena," she tells me. And some overflow of her delight with herself really does seem to include me. She is wearing black jeans and a green T-shirt that pictures someone hugging a tree over the caption, "I'm environment-friendly."

"Now we won't bother with any of those people up there, Max's old schoolmates are bores to a boy. Come in here with me and meet Steve and Arlene, they've been living together for three years and have a poppet of a little boy, but they're having a huge white wedding in June, isn't that wonderfully absurd of them? – Steve, this is Mrs. Hill, the charming neighbour I told you about. (John, dear, a drink here – Scotch, isn't it? – and a tiny smash more gin for me.)"

Steve's bride-to-be is a pretty Japanese girl as little and neat as a paper doll. "How do you do?" I say to them.

"Pam says you're a master chef and cut up chickens like a veritable wizard," the young man says, his lips close to my ear as if imparting a secret.

"I'm afraid she has rather a creative imagination."

"Who has?"

"Pamela."

"Well, maybe; but she never – you must have noticed this – she never actually lies. If you're half as good with chickens as she claims, I can offer you a job at my place starting Monday. Five bucks an hour and no fringe benefits. Dream Pies, it's called, in the plaza – you know it? Here's our card. Give me a call if you're interested."

"Thank you." I pocket the card with a ridiculous sense of accomplishment. Somehow or other, with a little help from friends, I may just wind up self-supporting. And cutting up chickens all day, while not exactly fun, would be preferable to facing the Whittaker family or vacuuming Marion's apartment. Now perhaps I can slip away, I tell myself, edging quietly towards the door. But just then John appears with my drink. "Nice seeing you," he says. "Frightful crush. Come this way. Meet Pam's –"

I lose the rest of his sentence but allow myself to be steered into the kitchen. It is relatively quiet here, the room being chiefly occupied by a silent, hand-locked couple, and Arthur, who is too busy gulping his dinner to bark. Young Max, at the sink opening a bottle, waves the corkscrew at me in a friendly manner. He then presents both me and a glass to an old man on a bar stool. "Here you are then, Seb – nice malt whisky. This is our Revered Ancestor – our neighbour Mrs. Hill." Balancing a rubber-tipped cane across his lap, the old man turns towards me a long face creased with melancholy and says in a sharp voice, "Pointless contiguity."

"Excuse me?"

"I said, 'Pointless contiguity.'"

"Oh, I see. Yes, it is rather."

"Inconsequential jabber. No communication whatever. Just syllabic diarrhoea." He grasps the cane lying across his bony knees and stares past me into the crowded hall with age-bleached, fierce eyes. He is a scrupulously clean old man, thin as a thread, his nails scraped white and pink scalp showing under his scant white hair.

"Wittgenstein," he adds angrily.

I look around. "The cat?"

"Of course not. The philosopher. *Tractatus Logico-Philosophicus.*"

"Oh. Is that who he was?"

"Only philosopher of the century with the intelligence to shape a brilliant theory and then the guts to repudiate it. Think of the intellectual energy that took, eh?"

"Yes." Abandoning my glass on the counter, I climb onto the stool beside his. "I'm interested in philosophy – up to a point.

Specially lately. But it's so abstract; it seems to have little or no connection with real life, don't you think?" Yet even as I say this I'm
aware that it's ghosts, memories and speculation, ethical, moral
and theoretical, that have preoccupied me for these past weeks.

"Think so, do you? Well, ponder this connection. I was
Philosophy Chairman at York till '75. Then, just when I was begin-
ning to know something about my subject, they kicked me out.
Mandatory retirement. Emeritus pat on the back. The scrap heap."

Well, you're scrappy enough, I think, and as if he can read this
message on my forehead, he gives an uncouth snort of laughter.
Then he goes on, "Never mind, he was the greatest thinker of the
age, Wittgenstein. He was about the first to understand that language is central to every system of thought. Now that ass McLuhan
couldn't even write English. Old Ludwig should have lived into the
age of TV; he'd have told 'em."

"Told 'em what?" I ask, interested.

"Well, for example, that a sentence that says something must be
a picture of reality."

"Oh, yes. Especially in fiction. Good fiction, that is."

His hooded eyes contemplate me with suspicion.

"You trying to take the piss out of me, young woman?"

"I wouldn't dream of it."

"So you say. Wouldn't trust you. Profound introvert, sticks out
all over you. Subterranean fantasy life."

I feel my face grow rather hot. But then he thrusts forward a
cold, bone-white, liver-spotted hand. "Sebastian Long," he says, as
if we are meeting for the first time. It is like shaking hands with a
skeleton. "Pamela's father," he adds. "Such are the accidents of
conception."

"I'm Mrs. Ed – my name's Rowena Hill."

"Never heard of Wittgenstein, eh? Shame on you."

"I'm an autodidact. Lots of holes in my education."

"Mine, too. I've never read much fiction." We look at each other in a friendly fashion.

"Rowena, you must come with me at once and meet Miriam Whittaker – she's trying to line up a housekeeper for her grandson." And as Pamela hustles me away she mutters, "Sorry you got stranded with the old walrus. Dire, isn't he?"

"I like him. He called me a young woman. Now, Pam, I'm afraid you'll have to excuse me – I really must go home. Mrs. Whittaker wouldn't find me satisfactory – I know this in advance. Tell you all about it some day, maybe. Meanwhile, thanks for the nice party. Don't bother – I'll see myself out. Oh, and please say good-night to your father for me."

"No, I really can't understand why Cuthbert hasn't been in touch . . . It's been a whole week now. And after I managed to get those things from the bank he asked for, you'd think –"

But ever since that night on the sofa, Prince Charles has not been particularly keen to discuss Cuthbert. His face now takes on a rather huffy, Royal look and he gazes off into space. "I don't think about him at all," he says. "Do you?"

"You needn't imagine there's anything like that in my mind," I tell him with some severity. "It's simply a matter of business." I pull free a long strand of blue wool and knit busily away. It is the same rather unusual purply blue of the waistcoat Edwin wore on our wedding day. Those are purls that were his eyes, I think crazily. Nothing of him doth remain. *If only*. Then I jerk myself back to the subject at hand.

"Now don't let your imagination run away with you, Charles. You must have been eating too much fish lately or something. For pity's sake, the last thing on earth I want is another man, for a start."

"You didn't give that impression on a couple of recent occasions we can both recall."

It is now my turn to be huffy. "I was not myself at either of those times, as you very well know. Whatever myself is, I mean. A passing impulse . . . it could happen to anybody. You've had one or two yourself."

"It's not like you to be unkind, Rowena."

"I wish people wouldn't keep on saying what's not like me."

"I could say what a lot of thought to waste on a man who looks like a gerbil, but I won't. Don't let's quarrel."

"No, don't let's. Cuthbert's just a dear old friend, that's all, and I wonder why I haven't heard from him. No doubt he's busy with all sorts of things besides my affairs. I wouldn't think of calling him, with all he probably has on his mind."

"I should hope not. He'll call you when he's ready."

"It's true I have those papers from the bank now –"

"He'll ask for them when he needs them."

"Of course. I have no intention of bothering him."

"It would be very inconsiderate."

"You're absolutely right, Charles."

"Of course I am."

"I'm so glad you called me, Rowena. And how nice of you to invite me to dinner." Cuthbert tucks the napkin into the V of his tartan vest and looks around with approval at the embroidered place mats and polished candlesticks. When I bring in the meat on its platter, he draws up a deep, appreciative sniff of it – as well he might, I think, since it cost so much, eating it is going to be almost an act of sacrilege.

"I'm afraid, though, Cuthbert, I'll have to ask you to carve. I cut my finger yesterday."

He leans forward to look with concern at my bandaged forefinger. Any kind of illness or injury (particularly, of course, his own) always interests him – so much so that once Edwin, after a slow recovery of Cuthbert's from flu, said he had the soul of a school nurse.

"Poor girl. How did you do that?" he asks, and I find it endearing that he really wants to know.

"Well, you see I've been working at Dream Pies – you know that take-out place in the shopping plaza? Cutting up things, chickens, mostly. Five dollars an hour."

Cuthbert stops whetting the carving knife. He turns his thick glasses on me in real dismay. "My dear, you haven't."

"Why, yes – why not? I have to be practical, Cuthbert. It means over twenty dollars a day after tax." The businesslike sound of this pleases me, but it only seems to increase his discomfort.

"But Rowena, that's barely over the minimum wage. And besides, work like that –"

With this, self-pity washes over me in a sweet, warm wave. The cloying smell of chicken steamed in big pressure cookers, the plastic apron I have to wear, the bloody guts and pimpled flesh of the birds – it's been obvious why Dream Pies has trouble getting – and keeping – help. But Steve and Arlene have been so kind and patient with me that so far I haven't had the courage to let them down.

"No," continues Cuthbert warmly, "you know as well as I do that's not suitable work for someone like you. Not at all. Haven't I told you not to worry about money for the time being? I'll look after all that, until your court hearing comes up. So we'll regard that matter as settled." Resolutely he flourishes the tools and begins to carve.

I swallow with difficulty the qualm of pure fear invoked by the word *hearing*. "Cuthbert, you don't mean I'll actually have to appear in court."

"Yes, but you probably won't have to say anything, Rowena. Don't worry about it."

This is roughly tantamount to advising me to stop breathing. With an effort I drag my mind back to what we were originally talking about. "Well, it's very sweet of you, Cuthbert, to subsidize me, but you must see I can't keep taking – I mean it may be months before –"

He wags the knife at me warningly. "This is beautiful meat. Have you got plates there? Ah, gravy, as well. What a delicious feast you've prepared."

Here I am tempted to tell him (but do not) what a struggle I had with old habits at the supermarket meat counter. Many years ago Edwin invested in a tall aluminum pot with a vented lid. Into this fitted several smaller vessels with pierced bottoms. In just a little water a whole meal could be cooked – a cheap cut of meat, with potatoes and other veg. – thus saving both money and energy. The result was that our food bills were wonderfully low and all our dinners tasted of wet flannel. It was defiance and reckless rebellion that sent me home with this expensive cut of veal, which I then cooked wastefully in a slow oven. A pity, really, and one in the eye for prudence, I think now, pouring gravy, that all that self-discipline and thrift should produce this kind of backlash. But there it is. I even allowed one extravagance to lead to another, as witness the bottle of Beaujolais Cuthbert is now lifting.

"Chin-chin," he says, beaming at me. "Absolutely delicious."

"Help yourself to vegetables. I hope you like broccoli."

"I have had," he says, after a moment's devout attention to the food, "one or two phone chats lately with John Hill's lawyer."

"Oh, have you?"

"Mm. Superb veal. Yes, quite a pleasant man. The lawyer, I mean. So often they're nicer people than their clients, if I may say so. And our friend Hill is a case in point, I'd say. Quite comfortably off, he turns out to be, you know. Something in lumber. He's not married or anything, either. There's a house in Ottawa where he and, er, the mother live. Mortgage paid off, too, which is more than we can say for this one. Hill knows your position, but he seems determined to claim absolutely every cent he can, right down to the cash in Edwin's account."

My first reaction is to think grimly, A true son of his father. But the second comes as a surprise: I feel flattered. It's a tribute of sorts, after all, to be so strongly resented. John Hill's desire for vengeance makes me feel important; even, in a retrospective sense, dangerous. My smile manifestly puzzles Cuthbert, who has paused with the gravy ladle suspended. "I call it a very poor attitude," he says with severity. "And so would you, if you weren't so sweet and good."

With an effort I prevent the smile from extending itself in a grin. "Oh Cuthbert, you can't really blame the man for claiming what's legally his, can you? Also, of course, he wants satisfaction of another kind. Just as I did at first, till I began to realize it can't be had. Anyhow, it's all just one more reason I've got to face earning a living on my own."

"Rowena, I'm confident you have a good case under the terms of the Succession Law Reform Act. Your claim is perfectly clear-cut; I have no doubt about that at all."

"God knows I hope you're right. If I could just be sure of a roof over my head, it would be . . . But it might easily be a year before anything is settled, isn't that right? And meanwhile I have to live somehow, which I can do, thanks to Dream Pies and some help from you. Now I hope you have some room left for the crème caramel."

"But I can't let you do a menial job like that, Rowena. I suppose it's terribly old-fashioned of me, but I can't help feeling that people like you and my mother are *ladies*, and should never dirty their hands with sordid manual work."

Without comment I hand him a helping of the pudding.

"Now making pretty things like this –" and here he puts his nose down close to his place mat, one of a set Nana and I worked in drawn thread many years back "– made these yourself, didn't you? Exquisite. Couldn't you find a shop somewhere that would sell work like this on consignment for you?"

"Well, I suppose I could try," I say tepidly, because my thoughts have wandered again to satisfaction, compensation, revenge and John Hill – topics Cuthbert left behind minutes ago. "Fill up your glass," I urge him.

"Nobody does beautiful needlework like this any more, and yet I know there's a market for it – all these yuppies with no time, but pots of cash. Children's clothes, for instance. My secretary not long ago paid nearly two hundred dollars for a little smocked dress for her one-year-old! Come to that, I spent eighty dollars myself yesterday for a nice silk knitted tie, the kind of thing you could probably make in an afternoon."

I wrench my mind away from a dream vision of John Hill being nailed up in a coffin – something in lumber. "More pudding? No coffee, I suppose."

"Pure poison to me, my dear. I won't spoil your beautiful dinner."

"Take your glass into the sitting-room, then. I'll join you in a minute. It won't take me a second to clear this stuff away."

"We will clear it away together and wash it all up in tandem," he says gaily. So we don aprons and tackle the job side by side, while he tells me all about the pair of golden hawks he saw on Sunday with the bird-watchers, and I give him an account of my day with the Whittakers. Unlike Tom, he laughs.

"To me, the only good thing about children is that they eventually grow up and become human beings," he says. "I don't know how you stuck it out, even for a day." He hangs up his apron and rolls down his white shirt-sleeves. "Now virtue can be rewarded. I'll finish my wine now, if I may. And where's your glass – you must join me. No, I insist."

Before I can stop him, he has found and filled a clean glass for me. He brings it over with his own and sits beside me on the sofa. I edge unobtrusively a little aside to give him plenty of room. Somewhere, audible only to me, Prince Charles clears his throat.

"Your mother is well, I hope," I say.

"Oh, not too bad, thanks. Except for her diverticulosis. I'm a bit worried, because she's been having trouble with it lately, and at her age, surgery would be – well, I hope it won't come to that. No point borrowing trouble, is there?"

"No." I think suddenly of the cold, thin hand of Pamela's father. "Poor old people. They've run out of chances – for sure trouble's ahead, and they're in for it."

Cuthbert looks thoughtfully into his empty glass, then reaches for the rest of what's in the bottle. "Not for me," I say hastily.

"You know sometimes I think quite seriously that when I'm old and start going downhill, I'll just find some dignified way of finishing myself off."

With interest I see that he is serious about this. "Really? Which would that be, then, do you think – cowardly or brave?"

"Neither one. Just intelligent. Because I'll be alone. Nobody to be involved, one way or the other."

Somehow – impossible to tell on whose initiative – my hand finds itself in his. "That's never completely true, you know. Anyhow, I'd never have the courage. Scared as I am of everything to do with living, I'm even more scared of dying. Unfortunate position to be in. No dignity there."

"But you are very brave, Rowena. Look at the way you've coped since Edwin's death and all the rest of it . . . it's been quite heroic.

I've really admired you. I said as much to Marion last time I was here, and it surprised me that she looked surprised."

"Did it?"

"I believe you're blushing."

And now quite naturally somehow his arm is around me and my head rests in the hollow of his shoulder. When I half-close my eyes the wine makes the room sway around me not unpleasantly, like deep water. In a crack between the drawn curtains a bright star peers in at us. Get lost, I think peacefully. What's happening here is nice but not cosmic.

"I feel so relaxed with you," he says in a sleepy voice. "So comfortable."

"Me, too."

"Isn't it strange? Because before neither of us really . . ."

"No."

He turns and begins to place a number of small kisses at random over my forehead and cheeks. In what seems like seconds we are lying flushed and closely entwined, full length on the sofa. My skirt has pulled up thigh-high. His glasses have fogged over and he pauses briefly to pull them off.

"I have never felt like this with anybody before, you know," he tells me earnestly.

"Come to that, I never have either. But why do we bother talking?"

"It's got to be right for us, though, hasn't it, Rowena?"

"But what has right or wrong got to do with –"

"Everything," he says firmly. "For people like us, everything's to do with right and wrong. Unless you think everything physical between the sexes is meaningless, like hiccups. No, I was right in the first place when we . . . perfectly right. Only later, you see, I sort of panicked. That's where I was wrong. Now I'm asking you again to marry me. This time I really mean it. I'm going home now, and I want you to think about it. Seriously. If I stay here one minute longer – well, that would never do."

"I don't really see why marriage has to come into this at all, Cuthbert. For one thing, I'm just beginning to recover from mine. And for another –" But I don't like to add that though we are nearly the same age, I feel immeasurably older.

Now he is getting slowly to his feet, where he brushes and shakes himself tidy and resumes his glasses. "I understand all that," he says calmly, "and of course I realize you need more time. But we're the same kind of people." (Oh, dear, I hope not, I think.) "And that's all that really matters, isn't it?" Once in his street clothes, he pauses, briefcase in hand, to look at me. "I don't dare go near you again," he says. "If you invite me, though, I'll come to dinner again next week. Take your time and think about what I'm asking you. Nobody needs to know a thing about it yet, of course; but I want to consider us engaged. Meanwhile, please be sure to give those pie people your notice. Good night, Rowena dear."

The front door closes gently behind him. I hope he has not heard me sigh.

CHAPTER FIVE

In the next few days, as if to illustrate tranquillity, the sun beams down from a windless, smiling sky of postcard blue. Because the habit of passivity is still strong and the line of least resistance is so attractive, I have resigned from Dream Pies, and one midday, rich with my new leisure, I set out for the library. Just as I pull the front door shut behind me, Pamela rushes up the steps on her side of the porch. She is hatless and looks harassed.

"Oh, hi there, Rowena – so glad to run into you, because I've been wanting a chat. The fact is life has become utterly frantic ever since Pa broke his toe, which I'm sure he did on purpose to get back at me, and of course Mrs. Blot, for quitting on him . . . She was his daily till he called her a flatulent old sow. That's exactly what she is, you see, so of course she was furious. But what it all boils down to is that now I have to rush over there twice a day to feed and water him, and it is driving me totally desperate." She fans herself with one end of her silk scarf. The sun warms our heads like a blessing, and a little breath of air lightly frills the skirts of the pine tree on my patch of lawn. Wittgenstein is under there, emerging from time to time to pounce on fallen maple leaves.

"Now, I seem to remember you once said you might know somebody who could cope with Pa," Pam goes on, "because if this goes on much longer –"

My attention focuses itself sharply. "Well –" I begin.

"I mean, it's just caretaking, really, there's no actual nursing involved, all anyone would need is the time and ability to endure him, though of course this last is the stickler, because he really is exasperating to the last degree. Well, you've met him, so you know."

"Yes, but actually –"

"And I don't think it's being related that makes me find him so impossible, though that probably doesn't help. He's depressed lately, I know that, hence more bloody-minded than ever, and it's effect not cause that's the point here, because *I* don't know how to cheer the old devil up. In fact I just seem to get up his nose more every day. He says to stay away, I constipate him, but how can I just leave him there to starve? I really am utterly desperate, do you think it would be any use to advertise? I mean we'd pay practically anything –"

"Well, actually, Pam, I –"

"This afternoon, for instance, Rowena, is typical . . . I've just given him his lunch. In half an hour I have to be downtown with Colin for his shots. Then just as he's beginning to get a reaction – he always runs a temp afterwards – I'll have to rush over to the house again. It really does make me feel I might as well douse myself with gasoline and light a match. Sorry. Did you say something?"

"Pam, I'll go over there and get his supper tonight, if that would help. In fact, if you really need long-term . . . I could – Anyhow, he lives near here, doesn't he?"

"Oh, my dear, if you could just fill this gap till I can lure Mrs. B. back, I'm negotiating like mad, so – that would be marvellous. Yes, he's quite near; it's that big house at the corner of Garland and McKenzie – green roof, gingerbread front balcony. It started out as a farmhouse, and of course it's absurd of him to hang on in that big place alone, but – well, here's the key, and bless you. I'm so grateful. Just soup and an egg or something will do him. My God, I must fly. Thanks again, just pay no attention to anything he says."

It's rather exasperating that Pam hasn't seemed to hear my hint about salaried help, but so graphic is her account of the old man's frame of mind that I may have had a lucky escape. Even on a short-term basis, I'm not much looking forward to confronting him. However, I stride along toward the library, telling myself stoutly that a promise is a promise. Ahead of me a car is parked squarely on the sidewalk. Setting a good example of aggression, a teenager kicks it hard in the bumper with his Greb boot. A quite respectable woman about my own age actually picks up a clot of mud and smears the back window with it. But I pick my way meekly round the obstacle and carry on, wondering how best to deal with a cantankerous old man. No doubt he'll make it difficult, but surely I can put up with him for an hour or so. And I've been feeling (foolishly, of course) rather guilty about leaving Pam's friends at Dream Pies, so doing her a small, neighbourly favour is a sop to my conscience.

Bolstered by thoughts like these, I put the key in the farmhouse door at six, tell myself to be a woman, and walk into the hall. "Mr. Long?" I say with caution.

There is no answer. Though dusk is thick outside, not a single light is on anywhere in the house. After some fumbling I find the switch of an overhead light and peer into the sitting-room. It is a space made glum by the faded upholstery of overstuffed furniture and dingy wallpaper dating back at least a generation. One hem of the sallow window curtains has torn down, and everywhere there is a smell of carpets thick with dust, old toast crumbs and solitude.

Finding no one downstairs, I timidly mount the creaking stairs. This part of the house, too, is in darkness, but I turn on a hall light, and after a moment find the right bedroom. There, propped on crumpled pillows, the owner of the house lies snoring lightly. The instant I approach the bed he opens his eyes and says, "How the hell did you get in?"

"Pamela's busy, so I offered to come over and get your supper."

"Typical of her. Be off. I don't know you from Adam."

"Yes, you do. We met just a few weeks ago, at her party. My name's Rowena. Remember – you told me who Wittgenstein was."

His frown eases off slightly. "Ah. So I did. You're the reader of fiction."

"Except for really heavy stuff like *The Brothers Karamazov*, say."

"Well, the Russians. Always going on about their souls. Not that we haven't all got one. Bothersome bloody things. But souls just aren't something that can be discussed. One of those things language is no good for. Wittgenstein had it, as usual. 'Unsayable things do exist,' is how he put it. He also said, 'Whereof one cannot speak, thereof one must be silent.' How right he was." He stares at me as I switch on a bedside lamp and draw up a chair beside him. "Yes, that's right – we met at Pamela's. At first, though, I didn't remember you at all: there's old age for you."

"That's all right. People rarely do remember me. And I don't mind. Just to get by without bothering or offending anybody – that's my aim."

He heaves himself higher on the pillows. "It's a hell of an aim to have, if you ask me. Oh, damn and blast this toe."

"What would you like for supper?"

"The hell with supper."

"Some nice hot soup and a scrambled egg, maybe?"

"Cat food. Get out," he adds abruptly. "Got to go to the bathroom." He flounces about, groping for a pair of crutches by the bed, and then struggles to extricate his bony legs from the tangled bedclothes. I turn away tactfully while he slowly levers his tall frame upright. As soon as I am sure he can manage, I go downstairs to the kitchen.

This room has not been renovated in any way since about 1940, to judge by its worn linoleum and faded wooden cupboards. Mrs. Blot, whoever she is, evidently keeps it more or less clean, but there is a faint, suspicious smell of mice about, none the less. A calendar for the year 1979 hangs on the wall beside a framed diploma from the University of Heidelberg, and a yellowing photo of Sebastian in a wing collar with his bride. Even on his wedding day all those years ago, his long face had a melancholy cast. With an effort I tear myself away from these relics and go to the fridge for eggs. Soon after that I carry a steaming tray upstairs, feeling competent.

He is back in bed now, but still breathing hard, and sunk in a kind of brooding gloom that seems to intensify with my arrival. His knotted throat rises, bristling with white hair, out of his pyjama jacket, which has been dragged crooked by the exertion of getting back into bed.

"Take that stuff away," he says. "Told you I didn't want it. You and your aim. It's failed. You're annoying me."

I set the tray aside on the dresser. "Well, forget the food if you like. But there's a drink here for you – malt whisky, isn't it? I found the bottle in the kitchen cupboard beside a trap, meant either for you or a mouse."

"Ah," he says, and reaches out a shaking hand for the glass. "Now, that's different. Why Pamela should think alcohol is bad for a broken toe – but it's all part of her quite lunatic mental processes." He takes a long swig of the drink and says "Ah" again.

Knowing as I do nothing about whisky, I have poured him a small wineglass-full, and it now occurs to me this might have been over-generous. But after all, I think, does it really matter at this point? The parchment skin of his cheeks has flushed up, his hand is steady, and his blank, glaucous stare has gone. He glances at me with life in his faded eyes.

"What did you say your name was? Mrs. Something?"

"Call me Mrs. Nobody, if you like."

"No, that would not be at all appropriate."

"Glad you think so."

"Fancy thinking of yourself as nobody," he says crossly.

"Even if it's true?"

"It's never true."

"Well, names don't help much anyway. Take yours – are you a saint stuck full of arrows then?"

"The goddamned arrows are true enough," he mutters, with a relapse into gloom.

"Now how about just a nip of this soup."

"Certainly not. Don't you try your female tactics on me."

"*Philosophical Investigations*," I say, settling comfortably into the bedside chair. "I looked up Wittgenstein today in the library. What an interesting life he had. Imagine giving away a big legacy because you don't like luxury. It's not the sort of moral problem that would bother most of us, is it?"

He gives a loud sniff of amusement. "Did you know he loathed being an academic all those years at Cambridge? Talk about most of us – he wasn't like most of us. Professor of Philosophy with all that pomp and deference – he called it 'a kind of living death.' Wise man. No, not like me. I liked the gown . . . too much. He quit, too, before they threw him out. Had cancer at the end but it didn't bother him, dying; not a bit."

"Why was that, I wonder."

"More than I can tell you. Scares *me*, that's all I know. Standing here looking at midnight." Without warning he begins to sing in a cracked voice:

> *Standing on the bridge at midnight*
> *Throwing snowballs at the moon –*

But he breaks off here, clearing his throat. "The rest," he says, "is not decent."

"Maybe Wittgenstein was serene at the end because he'd given up looking for absolute answers to everything."

"No, no; he never gave up looking for *das erlösende Wort* – the solvent, the clarification of all our stupid human confusion . . ." His voice trails away and for a minute he seems to drop into a light doze. Then his eyes snap open and he says testily, "Well, where's my supper, then?"

Trying not to smile, I put the tray across his knees. He tips down the last of his drink and begins untidily to fork up the scrambled egg. When every dish is clean he says, "There – take it away. I remember your name now; it's Rowena. Nice old name. Got to go to the loo again, damn it. Hand me those crutches, will you? Oh, a hideous curse on this bloody toe."

Laboriously he creaks off down the hall and I take the opportunity to make up the tumbled bed. His return is slow and evidently painful. He drops back onto the pillows, his breath rasping. Eyes closed, once more he appears to pay no attention while I set his water carafe and the telephone within reach and pick up the tray. But just as I turn to go, a bony hand shoots out to pluck at my sleeve. "Come back tomorrow, Mrs. Something," he says. "You're not bad company. I'll educate you about Wittgenstein."

"All right," I say cheerfully. "See you tomorrow then."

I walk home briskly under a sky festive with millions of twin-kling stars. I'm glad I've left his curtains open so he can see them, too. Poor old boy, the nights must be very long for him. I hope quite earnestly that Mrs. Blot may refuse to come back, because in that case . . . Now what would he like to eat tomorrow that could not be called cat food? A nice little steak, maybe; though spending Cuthbert's money on meat for a man he's never met seems vaguely immoral. However, it's probably too late now for me to qualify as a good woman, so I decide not to worry about it.

When I walk into my bedroom a few minutes later, whom should I find curled in the very centre of my bed but black Wittgenstein, who must have slipped into the house somehow when I left. He stretches luxuriously and curls his pink tongue up at me in a yawn that says he has come to stay.

On impulse, I look up the recipe for *béarnaise* sauce and make some to go with the steak. Then I have the satisfaction of watch-ing Seb polish off the last of it with a bit of bread. For the past ten minutes the conversation (one-sided, about Bertrand Russell) has been totally suspended. Finally he lays down his cutlery and remarks, "Quite eatable. You have hidden depths, Mrs. Who. Somebody's obviously taught you the psychic satisfaction of a good meal. Your husband, presumably."

I think of Edwin's tall aluminum steam pot and smile faintly.

"Do you know, my earliest memory is of a bowl of warm bread and milk with brown sugar, fed me by my mother in some infant illness. She died when I was just over four."

"That's too bad."

"My father had popped off a few years before that, so from then on I was handed from one relative to another like an awkward parcel nobody wanted. I can't remember my mother's face or voice or anything specific about her at all – just a general kind of softness and warmth, and a smell of sandalwood from the scent she used. Not much, is it, to create this enormous sense of deprivation I've had ever since? Russell's biographer, you know, makes a big point of his orphanhood – even links it to his insatiable appetite for women. Four marriages and any number of affairs, as you probably know. I never went quite that far myself, though far enough to support the theory."

He fumbles among the bedclothes for the book he tossed aside earlier to make room for the tray. "Here's a letter Russell wrote to one of his mistresses: 'The centre of me is always and eternally a pain – a searching for something beyond what the world contains – something transfigured and infinite – I do not think it is to be found – but it's like a passionate love for a ghost.'" Here I think grimly: and what about a ghost you hate? But he is still talking. "Ben-Ami Scharfstein actually finds orphanhood a common factor among many philosophers; he says it's to compensate for that loss that we grope for truths others wouldn't look for." He glances up at me with a mischievous grin. "And now I've given you the key to me, Rowena, what are you going to do with it?"

"I'm going to wash your hands and face and tuck you in."

"*Touché*, damn you."

Next night when I get home I find Marion on the sofa with a cup of tea.

"Hello, dear," I say, surprised. Surely she hasn't come over to tell me more about Babs and the area commissioners. "What brings you here so late?"

She tosses aside her copy of *Canadian Guider* and looks at me with disapproval. "Late! I should think it is. Where on earth have you been, Mother? It's nearly eleven!"

"Oh, is it? Any tea left? Give me the pot, then – I'll make some fresh." But Marion follows me out to the kitchen to demand, "Well? Where were you, then?"

I bite my tongue and say mildly, "I've been sitting with a neighbour – Pam Wright's father. He's laid up with a broken toe and I've been getting supper for him the last few nights."

"Oh." She immediately appears to lose all interest in my evening. Studiously she begins to realign the canisters on the counter, ranging them in a precise row.

"And come to that," I say, "what brings you out at this time of night?"

"Well, I thought I'd better tell you. I've just come back from Ottawa."

"Ottawa!" I echo foolishly, as if I've never heard of the place before. "Whatever took you there?"

"I wanted to talk to that man John Hill."

Suddenly my legs feel weak. I am devoured with curiosity, but Marion does not seem at all eager to tell me more. It touches me to see that she looks strained and overtired. "Let's go in and sit down," I suggest, and to fortify myself I swig down a gulp of strong tea.

"Well, there were several things I wanted to know," she begins, tucking her skirt neatly round her knees. "By the way, Mother, I didn't tell Cuthbert I was going, and there's no need for you to mention it, either."

"Why – did it have something to do with our case, then?"

"Not exactly."

"Then why not tell Cuthbert about it?"

"Because he would have advised me not to go."

I look at her, surprised by this admission of human weakness. "Then what did you actually go for, dear?"

There is a brief pause. Marion recrosses her ankles and looks down, frowning, at her squarish, capable hands. "I just felt I needed to talk to him – that man Hill. There was no chance, was there, at the funeral, to do anything more than digest the facts. There was so much more I wanted to – So I just looked up his address in the Ottawa phone book and took the afternoon train."

Today is Friday – Edwin's regular day for that journey. I wonder if she has thought of that, or whether she realizes it is her father she is really looking for.

"I wanted to talk to him," she repeats. And I think, Yes, poor thing, maybe you do realize it.

There is another small silence while I form a mental picture of Marion in her neat navy coat standing at her brother's door like Nemesis. The more I think about this confrontation with her father's double, the more like something out of Maupassant it seems. No practical purpose could have been served by this meeting, and it is so unlike Marion to have any other aim. "Talk about what?" I ask warily. It is strange and disturbing to see her suddenly as a woman just as confused and vulnerable as myself.

"Things I wanted to know," she says curtly.

"Such as?"

"Trying to get a handle on what made him *do* it. I mean, bigamy! Dad, of all people."

"Isn't it better not to know the answer to questions like that?"

"No doubt you'd think so. But you were always sort of . . . aloof with Dad. As if you weren't really with him. Off somewhere in your own world, in books or wherever. But he was my father. He mattered to me. I had questions to ask John Hill, and I'm glad I went after them."

My heart has begun to beat very hard. The answers I've been finding for myself, without ever leaving Don Mills, are disquieting. I hope hers are less so.

"Tell me what you asked him."

"For facts, of course. Like when did this commuting of his between here and Ottawa begin? It turns out it started the year I was born. In other words, Dad was separated from – that man's mother – for at least two years, though it wasn't a legal separation. That's when he came and settled here, and met you, and all that. Then she had to have some kind of major operation, and he went up to see her. There was apparently some kind of reconciliation. After that he went up regularly. So you see it wasn't what it looked like at first. In fact what took him up there was kindness – even decency – that's what made him spend time with her every month. And that was exactly like Dad. He always had a terrific sense of duty."

And did that legalize our marriage – legitimize you? I want to shout. Did it justify humiliating me – keeping us both in the dark about the whole thing, all those years?

As if these questions have jumped out of my mouth like the toads in the fairy tale, Marion says quickly, "It was kinder not to tell us. He was doing his best to do the right thing by everybody, that's the point."

After a long pause I find my voice.

"Marion, do you remember telling me – it was just after you began Grade One with a literal-minded teacher called Miss Watson – you said to me at bedtime one day, 'I don't want those dumb fairy stories any more, Mum. Dragons and witches – there are no such things. Miss Watson says they're silly.' Well, I think it's high time you changed your mind about that. There *are* dragons. And spells, and witches who practise white and black magic. Tell me why else your father would have lived such a life? And then tell me whether you met Mrs. Hill the First. That's where to look for answers; surely you know that."

She shifts a little uneasily in her chair.

"Well, I just saw her for a minute. She has heart trouble, you know, so he sort of hustled me away. Very protective, he was, of both of them. But he did introduce me."

"And?"

"And what?"

"What was she like?"

"Oh, just an old woman. White hair and all that."

"What was she *like*, Marion?"

"She was just ordinary."

Marion's face is studiously blank. It's evident that she will not tell me what I want to know, either because she is incapable of it or because she doesn't know herself. Then suddenly, she turns to look at me with the half-shamed glance of someone who cannot resist the forbidden pleasure of giving pain after receiving it. "Actually," she says, "the mother's a good-looking old lady. She had – a sort of odd smile. Almost mischievous. She must have been . . . a bit of a beauty once."

I get up from my chair abruptly and take my empty cup to the kitchen. My jaw is trembling and I feel cold all over. I have the liveliest reluctance to go back and continue talking to Marion. I now want to know less, not more, about this visit of hers. I am not enjoying this confirmation of an old suspicion – that Marion was more married to Edwin than I was. It explains many things – among them her attitude towards me from childhood on. But there is little satisfaction in perceiving that there have been two witches, not just one, involved in all this. It means, for a start, that there may be real dragons in the path of any further conversations we may have about Edwin. Nevertheless, I go back slowly to my place in the sitting room, where the clock is now chiming twelve. I am suddenly, overwhelmingly tired, and see with relief that Marion is getting into her coat.

"Anyhow," she says briskly, "that's over with. I'm glad I went. It's sort of settled my mind. He was sorry for her, and doing his best. That's what it all boils down to."

"You think so, do you?"

"That's right. Well, see you soon. You'll be going to Tom's church bazaar next week, I suppose? I'll pick you up around three."

"Yes."

"Don't forget to lock up after me."

"I won't."

"Good night, Mother."

"Good night, Marion."

The door closes behind her. I stand there looking at it for some time.

After a while I wander to the kitchen and stand at the counter for another indefinite interval. I stare blankly at the canisters and the teapot, thinking about the potency of spells and seeing in the air before me, detached from any specific presence, a mischievous smile. Then I pick up one of the empty cups and throw it with all my strength at the wall. It breaks with a crash, and shards of china rattle to the floor. A thin trickle of tea rolls down after them like an anticlimax. Feeling slightly better, I leave it all there, turn off the light and go up to bed.

But depression with no particular focus or definition hangs about me for days after this encounter. At night my sleep is thin and plagued by bad dreams. By day I feel almost too tired to move. Rain falls persistently from a grey sky. The light is wintry, and cold draughts seem to invade the house from every direction, making me shiver. I go nowhere and see no one. Even Wittgenstein fails to drop in. Cuthbert's mother has been scheduled for surgery, and he is spending all his spare time at the hospital. Pam Wright has phoned to thank me for my help and tell me she has managed to persuade Mrs. Blot to go back and look after Sebastian.

"And let me tell you, my dear, Metternich, or whoever it was, simply also ran as a diplomat. I have to say it was nothing short of brilliant, the way I managed to fix this up. Bribery on the one hand – a raise for Mrs. B. – and quite shameless appeal to principle on the other. We simply can't go on imposing like this on Rowena, it isn't fair, she has her own life, where's your pride, I asked him, and he simply had to agree. So now that's over, and I must say I feel absolutely born again, though not in the religious sense, far from it, for well I know my motives have not been the least bit pure – for one thing our sex life had sunk to a truly dreary level with me being so exhausted all the time, so it was pure selfishness on my part getting us both off the hook like this, anyhow you've been so sweet, Rowena, and I'll never forget it."

Instead of cheering me up, this news depresses me further. Not only has a job opportunity vanished, but I find I miss Sebastian and our talks over the evening tray, which were beginning to extend to a later and later hour. I have a feeling, too, that he may miss my company as much as I do his. The more I think about it, the harder it is not to resent Pam's interference. I also think it inconsiderate of Cuthbert's mother to need an operation at this juncture, thus depriving me of his promised visit. In this low state, I forget all about Tom's annual church bazaar until Marion turns up at the door to take me there.

"You're surely not going like that," she says with a scathing glance at my old grey skirt and sweater, which is even older than my beige skirt and cardigan. "Hurry up and change – the best things will be gone if we don't get there early."

Obediently I toil up the stairs and change into the beige outfit. Ignoring the glum eye of that all-too-serious widow in the mirror, I pull a brush through my hair and cram an old beret on top of it.

Outside the grey rain is still falling drearily, spreading broad puddles everywhere and dripping coldly from the bare trees. Scarcely has Marion started the car when she discovers a flat tire, and the delay while it's fixed at a nearby service station makes her cross.

"I do wish you'd been ready on time," she grumbles. "Tom is going to wonder what on earth is keeping us."

"What does it matter?" I say, trying not to sound irritable. "You can't be all that keen to buy other people's old stuffed toys and battered paperbacks, can you?"

Something seems to have happened, not to her, which itself is discouraging, but to me or our relationship, because today she makes me feel edgy, even slightly tearful.

"That's you all over, Mother – you always miss the point. We're going there to help Tom, not to – oh, what's the use? By the way, I suppose you're all right for money at the moment?"

This is not the time or place, I feel sure, to tell her Cuthbert is supporting me. So I mumble, "Oh, yes. Fine. Quite all right."

"Well, I suppose those Wright people have been paying you something to look after the old man."

"No, they haven't. For goodness sake, I was just doing them a favour for a few days."

Marion makes an impatient sound with her lips, but perhaps reminding herself in time of the First Guide Law, says nothing more.

By the time we arrive it is so late that the parish hall is half empty. The booths with their dubious, pawed-over goods have a forlorn look, and the attendants droop wanly in their chairs. Voices echo under the roof and there is a strong smell of wet umbrellas. The only people enjoying themselves are some children in stocking feet sliding with shrieks of glee along the margins of the polished floor.

"Ah, the charming Hill ladies," says Tom, approaching us with dignity. He runs a finger under his dog collar to loosen it and mops his forehead with a white handkerchief. He always expends much energy at these affairs, bustling to and fro to greet everyone and bully them cheerfully into buying articles they don't want and can't use.

"Now, my dears, you must see the delightful things Mrs. Carraway has here in the china booth. What about this grand old moustache cup with the roses on it, eh? Or this cake plate with slots for a ribbon? They don't make things like that any more, do they?" (I'm glad they don't, I think gloomily.) "And here's a vase with water-lily handles, you'll like that, Rowena."

Marion dutifully buys the cake plate and I the moustache cup. We also buy a toasting fork with a loose handle, a velvet cushion with the painted motto "Rest," and some beribboned sachets that smell of medicine. By now the hall is nearly deserted and most of the booth attendants have disappeared. Marion twitches up her sleeve and steals a restless look at her watch.

"Well, Mother, I'd better get you home. I've got my first-aid group tonight."

"There now, my dear," puts in Tom, "don't you bother about Rowena – I'll run her home as soon as we close up here. You young people are always so busy – thanks for coming along, Marion dear; I do appreciate it."

With evident relief Marion says goodbye and speeds off.

"A thoroughly good girl," he says, looking after her with approval. "What a comfort she must be to you."

After a pause I say, "Yes."

"And now," he goes on, rubbing his substantial hands together, "let's count the loot. I believe we've done particularly well this year." From a battered cash-box he pours out a cascade of change and small bills. When totalled it comes to nearly five hundred dollars. Tom breaks into a little jig of delight.

"This is glorious," he says. "Now we can get those eavestroughs fixed and have a bit left over towards the vestry carpet. Glory be! The best take ever!" He fumbles in a pocket and produces a key to the door giving access to the church. "I shall give thanks," he says. "Will you wait here for me?"

"No, I'll come with you."

What prompts me to do this I cannot say, because though I go occasionally to a service, it is purely for literary reasons, the language of the Jacobean prayer book being a sort of religion in itself. But the physical interior of churches always oppresses me with a sense of some impersonal presence far beyond my comprehension or reach, and makes me feel snubbed. The discreetly ornate decoration of this Anglican space is no exception. The ruby sanctuary lamp presides over a chilly white altar. The one stained-glass window depicts Abraham about to sacrifice Isaac, in obedience to one of those cruel and arbitrary edicts the Old Testament God used to specialize in. Clearly, I think, such a deity is someone who does not want to be understood or even liked, and what kind of a Creator is that?

Tom drops to his knees after genuflecting to the altar and without the least self-consciousness says in a ringing voice, "Thanks be unto thee, O Lord, for thy great goodness and bounty to us and to all men. Amen." His lifted face is full of a very sweet and simple joy. Rather awkwardly I kneel, too, and try to formulate an appropriate prayer, but no words will come. Not until we are on our feet again and filing out do I think, Help me to forgive Edwin and Marion, whether they deserve it or not. Perhaps it is sheer happenstance, but the pall of depression that has weighed on me all week now begins to lift.

"And now, my dear," says Tom, taking me cosily by the arm, "the evening is ours. In fact, I've planned a little surprise for you. Just look here."

From under the crëpe-paper skirt of one of the booths, he produces a carton of what looks like groceries. Nestled in one corner is a bottle of cognac. "Donated by Miriam," he says, "and purchased by me, for our enjoyment. Now we'll adjourn to my house and have a nice little picnic supper together – how does that sound?"

"Very nice," I say, my spirits rising. As if to encourage this trend, we find when we go out to the parking lot that the rain has stopped at last, and a rising copper-coloured moon is glorifying the dispersing clouds.

The Fosters' house was furnished some time in the thirties, and Tom and Marjory thereafter never saw any reason to change the stamped velvet armchairs with bowed legs, the cut-glass ashtrays or the swags of befringed curtains. All these things combine, in fact, to create a restful air of permanence reassuring to anyone over forty. It all reminds me comfortably of Clive and Nana's apartment. I find something appealing in the extreme ugliness of the wall sconces with their crystal droplets, and the pagoda shape of the silk lampshades. As soon as he has disposed of our coats and stowed the food in the kitchen, Tom pours us each a glass of brandy. Then he goes to the long walnut cabinet that houses a record-player. Moments later the husky rhythms of "I Won't Dance" pour from the clothbound mouth of the speaker.

"Your health, my dear."

"And yours, Tom."

"Life is good," he says comfortably. "It pleases me that monks were the inventors of brandy. Why should love of God mean distrust of pleasure? A contradiction in terms is what that is."

The pensive strains of "Blue Moon" now give way to a bouncy rendition of "Let Yourself Go," and seizing my hand, he pulls me out of my chair. Before I can protest he has clasped me firmly to his front and set us both revolving round the room. His dancing style dates from about the same uncomplicated era as mine, and I find it easy to follow him. Like many big-boned people he is remarkably light on his feet. Very soon I am enjoying myself. It is not long, though, before I find he is pressing me extremely close and his breathing, redolent of brandy, becomes heavy.

"Tom, I think –"

"You dance like a sylph, my dear."

"But, Tom, I –"

His grip tightens. His hand moves from my shoulder-blade down to a much lower location. When I open my mouth to protest, he kisses me with such vehemence we both nearly lose our balance. But instead of being outraged or disgusted as might be appropriate, I am without warning swiftly caught up in a chain reaction of sensations that dazzle me. Seconds later he has pulled up my skirt and, bracing us awkwardly against the wall, without further ado proceeds to astonish me even further. Long before I want it to end, it does. There is no sound in the room but our hurried breathing.

"Thank you," he says simply – though whether addressing me or God is not altogether clear. "That was lovely."

With this I entirely agree, though some sort of pride makes me conceal my surprise that such pleasure is possible in any circumstances, especially these. But even so preoccupied, I have time to wonder that there is no contradiction at all between Tom's prayer an hour earlier and his remark now, after what must surely be the most secular of acts. It makes him seem much more interesting a man than he has ever appeared before; so much so that I feel almost shy with him, and attempt a small joke.

"Well, Tom, I don't know what the ladies of the parish guild would say about this —"

"What the parish ladies don't know will never hurt them. Besides, Rowena," he adds with a grin, "you might as well know, if you haven't guessed before – quite a few of them wouldn't be the least bit surprised."

Rather sheepishly pulling up and pushing down various items of my clothes, I still have to smile at this. Tom is zipping his trousers in a matter-of-fact way as he adds tranquilly, "God would never have made this act such a pleasure if he hadn't meant us to enjoy it." And I am in no mood to argue with that. It is hard now to remember how depressed I've been lately, and why. When I do, it is only to think, Well, Edwin, what have you got to say now? But I can remember almost with pity those prudish, tormented hangups of his. Nothing in the past seems to have any real relevance to the remarkable experience I've just had.

A familiar smell is stealing into the room, and Tom beams at me proudly. "Dinner's nearly ready, my dear," he says. "Dream Pies."

CHAPTER SIX

Twenty-nine dollars and eighty cents. With reluctance and dismay I count it up again. How could my funds have sunk this low? Of course, I tell myself, trying to be calm, it was paying the fuel bill last week that has so depleted the money Cuthbert left with me; but how can I possibly mention this to him now, worried as he is about his mother, who is hanging on, but only just, after her operation? Indeed, I almost resent poor Cuthbert for providing for me so generously, because without him, I would have been forced some time ago to face up to my situation. It would of course make more sense to blame Edwin for it, as for everything else, because it was his endless preoccupation with money that has made me react by being disorderly and even reckless with it since his death.

On the other hand, I tell myself sternly, you're in charge now. The very thought of turning to Marion for help makes my mouth harden. I will not do that unless there is absolutely no alternative. I will deal with this somehow on my own.

To help me concentrate, I pace the length of the house a few dozen times. How can I earn money? What can I do that anybody would pay for? Eventually the dining-room table catches my eye. What was it that Cuthbert once said about place mats? Smocked dresses for toddlers?

Ten minutes later I am making for a children's clothing shop in the plaza I've often noticed in passing. A cold wind is bouncing hard little pellets of snow along the pavement and I turn up my coat collar. Past the supermarket, the library, the wool shop; and there is the sign: Yankee Doodle.

The shop window displays a number of absurd and charming small garments: a T-shirt with a large red-felt heart sewn on the front, a jogging suit made to fit someone aged six months, a brown velvet frock falling from a yoke over a deep cream-lace petticoat frill. I stand in the cold wind looking earnestly at these for some time, while the pavement whitens around my feet. At last I gather up my courage and approach the door. It confronts me as blandly as those impenetrable doors Alice faced in Wonderland. You read too much, I tell myself sternly, and taking a deep breath I walk in.

Two bars of Yankee Doodle announce my arrival, but the shop is quite deserted, except for a disembodied voice grumbling in some distant stock-room. This is a relief; it gives me time to rehearse my spiel once more: "I do hand-smocking and embroidery, and I wondered whether you ever take orders for that kind of thing, or sell hand-made things for babies, on commission, by any chance."

No one appears, though the deep voice from the stockroom can be heard more distinctly now. It sounds considerably annoyed. I inspect a rack of little dresses in denim, rayon and cotton, interested to note their prices range from fifty dollars up – mostly up. I do hand-smocking and embroidery and I was wondering whether you ever –

"Completely god-damn irresponsible," says the hidden voice, causing me to jump slightly. A faint, querulous second voice can now be heard as counterpoint. "If I've told you once I've told you a million times!" shouts the baritone. I do hand-smocking and embroidery, I repeat to myself, inspecting a tie-dyed denim dress with stud fastenings priced at sixty dollars. "The fact is, you're nothing but a stupid bitch," the deep voice shouts. The invisible second now bursts into tears. I edge defensively a little nearer the door. Excuse me, but I do hand-smock . . . A ponderous silence now falls. From the back regions a tall woman in a yellow leisure suit appears, frowning. She approaches me in a menacing manner, her professional smile only heightening the effect of the scowl on her forehead. "Can I help you?" she snaps. It is obviously the baritone of the stockroom. She eyes me with hostility and repressed rage.

"Ah, well – I – er – was just wondering . . ." Fumbling, I cram the little dress back onto the crowded rack. "I was wondering if – if you – have any small toys."

With a scornful wave of the hand she indicates a shelf six inches away crammed with small toys. I seize a miniature teddy bear and mutely hold it out to her.

"Six ninety-five," she says furiously.

I produce the money, mutter thanks, and make for the door. Outside the snow stings my hot cheeks. I do hand-smocking fades hopelessly from my mind. A block away the sign for Dream Pies swings in the wind, and with a sigh I head for it. Probably Arlene and Steve will have me back; they said as much when I left. As for the teddy bear, I'll give it to Tom at the first opportunity, for his next bazaar. It's not something I'll want to keep around as a reminder.

"The thing is," I say next morning to Mrs. Wilson over early breakfast tea, "if I'm this bad at wage-earning, how am I going to survive? Five dollars an hour – it's better than nothing, but not much."

"Providence," she says vaguely. "Whatever that may be." But she is in one of her dreamy moods and keeps glancing past my head at a row of sparrows having a conference on the telegraph wire.

"I'm not aggressive enough, that's the trouble. But how can you be aggressive if it just isn't your temperament? I do think it's so unfair, because after all I do quite nice needlework."

"French knots and good manners are both out of style these days. It's nothing personal."

"Maybe not. But what am I going to do? Dream Pies may be all very well, but it doesn't pay enough to live on. And that undertaker's bill – I mean it was twice what I ever – how can anyone afford to die? So that insurance money I sort of thought of as a cushion will just about vanish by the end of the month. I don't know . . . at first I was so numb, what with one thing and another; none of it seemed real; but now I wake up at night in a panic."

More and more birds are flying in to the convention. The wire sways as they teeter together, twittering with gossip and fluffing out their feathers importantly. Mrs. Wilson smiles at them.

"Please pay attention," I tell her. "This is serious. The mortgage payment will soon be due again. You don't seem to realize –"

"There's a sort of rhythm to these things," she says. "Good times and bad; bad times and good . . . And then Providence weighs in from time to time, often when you least expect it."

"Providence takes no interest at all in people like me."

"Ah, that's just it. Applies to everybody. That kind of detach-ment is the whole point about Providence."

"Well, I can't wait around for miracles. Is that all you can suggest, for heaven's sake?"

"I suppose you could always marry Cuthbert."   ·

"Nonsense. Even if I wanted to, it would be a bad idea. We're far too much alike."

I rather hope she might disagree, but instead she murmurs, "True." Then she adds idly, "Well, what about Tom, then? He can't be sixty-five yet. And you must admit he's young for his age, what-ever that is."

"Come on, Ethel. The last thing on earth he's going to do is marry anybody. Why on earth should he? And besides, marriage isn't the answer to women's problems any more – haven't you noticed? I wish I had, thirty years ago, I can tell you."

"Well, things were simpler then, weren't they? In my day, women married the most unlikely people. And quite happily, too, on the whole."

"Not that Tom hasn't got charisma, of a kind. He's certainly got skills I never . . . well. Anyhow, of course that was nothing but a crazy sort of episode – it has nothing to do with anything. I can hardly believe it happened at all. And it certainly won't happen again. That much I'm sure of."

"Are you?"

"Come on, we're forgetting the point here. I do wish one of us had a tidier mind."

"Neat as a new pin, they say," she remarks, more to the birds than to me. "But there's nothing in the least attractive about a pin, in my opinion."

The phone rings. Suddenly all the birds rise with a flutter and wing busily off, leaving the wire to swing empty in the wind. Mrs. Wilson seizes the opportunity to disappear with them.

"Rowena," quacks the voice in the receiver. "Pamela here. Could I possibly pop over for a minute, or is this a madly inconvenient time?"

"No, come right along." My heart has given a little skip of expectation. Sebastian has insulted Mrs. Blot again, I think, and they want to pay me – didn't she once say practically anything? – to take over. Oh, I'll never again say a bad word about Providence.

Pam is evidently on her way to work. Scarlet trousers under her fur coat would give her the air of a guardsman if it were not for the silver earrings big as handcuffs that swing from her ears, and the Shalimar with which she is lavishly perfumed.

"We're off at noon today for bloody Hamilton again," she begins, "so this is my only chance to ask you the most terrific favour."

"Glad to help," I say, trying to sound casual.

"Well, we'll be gone all weekend, you see, because John's mother, who is ninety-one and crazy as a hoot owl, is finally going into a home, and we have to pack up the stuff in her apartment and get her settled in, what a hideous job, old people have such tons of tat, old photos and hats left over from various wars, and all of it *sacred* to them. Oh, well, it has to be done, I shall pack an enormous bottle of lovely gin. Anyhow, Max is back at Queen's now and Colin and Arthur will have to come with us, so I wonder if you'd be an angel and pop in twice a day to feed Wittgenstein." Here she fumbles rather distractedly in her coat pockets.

"Oh. Yes, Pam, of course I will."

"It never pays to get chummy with the neighbours," says Edwin sourly from beyond the grave. Before I can so much as ask how

Sebastian is – and I really would like to know – Pam has looked at her watch with a faint shriek and thrust into my hands her house key and several foil packets of cat food. A second later she is gone.

A fortnight later I'm walking home from Dream Pies, breasting a bitter wind from the east that makes my eyes burn. Saturday is always our busiest day at work, because people want to escape weekend cooking; and then after hours we all have to give the kitchen a thorough scouring to be ready for the coming week. It is nearly seven; the sky is black and starless. At the corner my own empty street stretches away under the cold, greenish eyes of the lamps. I meet no one but a lean dog going purposefully some-where, as lonely a wayfarer as myself.

Out of the corner of my eye I become aware of a large car nosing along close to the curb. Nervously I begin to walk faster, but the car keeps pace; then toots its horn softly. With alarm I see the driver switch on the interior light and click open the door on my side. Then I recognize Cuthbert.

"Just on my way to your place," he says. "Hop in."

"Thanks. Nice to see you, Cuthbert. How is your –?"

"She passed away early this morning. Exactly at four o'clock."

"Oh, I'm so sorry, Cuthbert. Poor you; that's very hard."

As we get out of the car, the street light catches his glasses, giving him a blind, bewildered look. "Well, the doctors really didn't seem to expect anything else, right from the start; you'd wonder, wouldn't you, why they operated at all. To relieve discom-fort, they said to me. Well, I don't know what you'd call what she went through afterwards, with that incision and all . . . It's hard to figure out their logic, I must say."

Glad of something practical to do, I whisk off our coats (mine smelling faintly of chicken) and hurry to plug in the kettle. It is reassuring to see that Cuthbert, clean-shaven and neatly buttoned into his three-piece suit, seems to be his usual calm self. "I actually came by, Rowena," he says, slipping three fingers into a breast pocket, "to give you this – your funds must be very low at this point, and I apologize for that – but you understand how it's been these last weeks; I've been at the hospital every spare minute." Deftly he tucks a little packet of bills under the biscuit tin.

"Oh, please, Cuthbert – of course I understand. I'm back at the pie place now, but the mortgage was three days overdue yesterday and I couldn't bother you with it, so I asked Marion . . ."

(An uncomfortably vivid memory here intrudes of Marion's frown when I had to explain my dilemma. "Of course I'll pay it, if you can't," she said sharply. "I can manage. Been putting something aside for a vacation. But I wish you'd told me before. Overdue payments can affect your credit rating, you know." "Sorry," I said. She wrote the cheque with an offended air and added, "Next time, let me know well in advance. Don't let this kind of thing happen again." It won't, I promised not her but myself.)

"Well, I knew if necessary she'd help out," he says comfortably.

"I was afraid they'd turn me out in the snow, you see, or I'd –"

"They wouldn't have done that," he says, and gives me a sharp glance. "But you pay her back now, do, and keep what's left over in reserve. From now on, I want you to turn over big bills like that to me. No need to bother Marion. I'll deal with them."

"Well, it's sweet of you, but I mean to keep on looking for a proper job."

"That's right," he says vaguely.

"And until something better turns up, the chicken place isn't a bad stopgap, though I know you don't approve of it. They've even given me a raise. Only it's put me off chicken, probably for life. Come, our drinks are ready – let's sit in the other room."

Pam's hooting laugh comes muffled through the wall, and I think as I sit down, pressing my tired back against a cushion, how solitary that would make me feel if I were alone. But Cuthbert has now lapsed into silence. Even as I look at him, slowly stirring his cocoa, grief seems to dwindle and wizen him. In the big chair his feet dangle just short of the floor and his pale face looks forlorn as a lost child's. I try to find something comforting to say to him, but can find nothing. Instead I lean forward and take his hand in mine. It evidently conveys the message, because he says, "Yes, people try to make you feel better, but everything they say only makes it worse. They say, 'Well, she had a grand, long life,' or 'She is resting now.' It doesn't help one single bit that these things are true. Not one bit."

"No. Nothing does."

Of course I am not thinking of Edwin's death, which deprived me of so much, and yet so little. I am remembering how Nana drifted away from me after Clive died, and my desolation when she joined him. Cuthbert's sad, numbed face brings it all back as if I'd lost her three hours, not thirty years ago.

"I suppose it's ridiculous to feel orphaned, at my age," he says, "but that's how it is."

"You have to be a lot older than we are – or much younger – to face this kind of thing without damage. I was three when my parents were killed at a level crossing, and I was perfectly cheerful about it. Nana told me they'd gone to Heaven, and to me that was just as if they'd gone to Calgary or Niagara Falls. But when Nana died long after that . . ." My throat closes here and I have to stop. There was something clean about that grief, though. My much more recent loss, on the other hand, has left behind it a crippling debris of mostly ugly emotions and confusions that still from time to time overwhelm me. There are days (and nights) when, like the Old Man of the Sea, Edwin rides my shoulders and I wonder whether I will ever be free of him. But Cuthbert, leaning his head on one hand, is listening to his own sorrows, not mine.

"I'd gone home, you know," he says, "because it was so late, and she was sleeping after something they gave her. But about three in the morning I woke up just as if somebody was shaking me, and I got dressed right away and drove to the hospital. On the way there I heard her call, 'Bertie' – she called me Bertie – it was her voice, just as if she were in the car with me. In a way I guess I knew right then what was happening. And sure enough the nurse came down the hall to meet me. "Just on my way to call you, Mr. Wesley," she said. "I'm sorry, but your mother passed away fifteen minutes ago." I went in and sat by the bed – they'd taken away all those awful tubes and wires, thank heaven – and when I took her hand it was still warm. She looked exactly as she did when I left her just a few hours before, as if she were asleep. But it was different, because she wasn't there any more, Rowena. She'd gone – somewhere. For good. No mistake about that. Nothing could possibly be more empty than that room."

Fumbling a little, he puts his cup and saucer aside and stands up. "Well, I'd better get on home," he says, and with a forefinger pushes the heavy glasses up more firmly on his nose. "Thanks for the drink."

"Could you eat anything? – no, what you'll want now is to get some sleep."

"Yes. Only how can I possibly sleep? She called me, Rowena, and I wasn't there. I should never have left her all alone. She called, and I wasn't there."

He turns his face helplessly away and begins to sob. Tears blear his glasses before spilling out and rolling down his cheeks. Silently I put my arms around him. My stomach gives a loud rumble of hunger. The weight of him makes my back ache harder. After a little I draw him down to sit with me on the sofa where, holding me fast, he gradually weeps himself out. It is strange as he quiets to hear Pam's laugh again from next door, and the clock ticking indifferently on. His breathing slows and thickens, and, mouth a little open, he finally sleeps.

With care I draw off his glasses and tuck the afghan around him. Outside like another voice the November wind shakes the windowpane. Wiping my own eyes, I turn out all the lights and leave him sleeping there. Sooner or later, one way or another, I think, we're all orphans. It should make us kinder to each other than it does.

The envelope is addressed simply "Rowena Hill," with no preliminary tag of Mrs. or Ms. The handwriting is unfamiliar – a small, crabbed script. I examine it carefully, intrigued to have mail from someone unknown, and bemused by the novelty of seeing my own name (at least some of it is mine) on an envelope. A heavy cold has kept me away from work for several days and given me a good excuse not to attend the Wesley funeral. But it has also given me a feeling of isolation and immobility. I feel like that static toy figure inside a glass ball full of whirling snowflakes. But now this letter . . . Instead of tearing it open, I fetch a knife from the kitchen and slit it open with care.

"Dear Mrs. Whatshername," the note says, "Where the hell have you disappeared to? Mrs. bloody Blot is back, to be sure, but is that any reason to deny me the pleasure of your company? I herewith invite you to tea any afternoon around four when it may suit you to come. Wittgenstein (Ludwig, not the cat) pointed out that there is a connection between the signs on paper and a situation in the world. There is a connection here. Do come. Yours – Sebastian Long."

This piece of paper gives me a pleasure out of all proportion to its simple message. It tickles me that so few words can convey so much of their writer's personality, and at the same time endow me with quite a vivid identity of my own – because he knows I will enjoy the tease of his "Mrs. Whatshername." I read the note over and over again. I even read the envelope again. His handwriting, though small and untidy, is bold, but the stamp has been applied haphazardly, crooked and upside-down, as if by a shaky or impatient hand.

With a sense of luxury I sit down at the desk where till now nothing at all interesting to write has ever taken me. A phone call is obviously not the right response. Yet once confronted with a square of blank paper, I struggle in vain to find words. "Dear Sebastian," I write; then come to a dead halt. "I'd love to come"? Too gushing. "Thank you for your –"? Too stuffy. "How good to hear from you"? Sickening.

The empty page stares up at me and I stare down at it. Can this be what they call writers' block? Hopelessly I look out at the winter day for inspiration. Snow is coming down, gusting upward from time to time on vagrant puffs of wind. Ground, air, snow and sky – there they all are, communicating without vocabulary of any kind. They are no help to me whatever.

Sneezing, I walk up and down the house; come back and contemplate the square of paper once more. Somewhat desperately I consider, "Your nice note came this morning"; but the dictionary confirms my suspicion about the word "nice." I tear up the page and am still biting the end of my pen when the phone rings.

"Mother," Marion begins in her usual abrupt fashion.

"Yes. Hello, dear."

"About receipts. I've been meaning to remind you. You're keeping everything, I hope. Dad had a file for them somewhere.

You'll need them all when it's time to send in your tax return."

"Yes. All right."

"You're keeping them all – hydro, fuel oil – everything?"

"Er, yes, that's right." (Actually I don't know where the last paid fuel bill has gone to.)

"You're sure, now."

"Yes, quite sure." Try as I will, I cannot keep a slight edge of irritation out of my voice. But then, I think, she doesn't even try to keep it out of hers.

"Mother, when are you going to learn! The other day when you were here about the mortgage, I found your last fuel bill – stamped paid – on the floor. It must have fallen out of your purse or pocket somehow. You see what I mean."

"Sorry."

There is an ill-concealed sigh at the other end. Poor Marion. Suddenly I sympathize with her. No doubt I'm a very trying and unsatisfactory parent for her to have.

"How was your weekend up north with Bernice?" I ask, trying to change the subject to something we can discuss agreeably.

"Oh, quite nice. We got in some good skiing."

"That's good. I'm glad."

"One thing happened you'd have liked. I was out by myself early one morning and in a field just a few yards away I saw a big red fox trotting along in the snow. I was downwind of him and he didn't see me at all. Just trotted along about his business. He had a rabbit in his jaws. There, I thought, that's the kind of thing Mother likes to hear about."

"Yes, dear. Very true; I do. Wish I'd been there to see it with you."

"Well, I've got to go now. Remember about those receipts." And she rings off. For some reason this call lifts my spirits. The snow spins and whirls past the window gaily as a celebration. I go back to the desk and without any pause for thought write, "Dear Sebastian, I have a bad cold just now which I'd rather not pass on to you, though I don't care what befalls Mrs. Blot. It will be gone by Monday – my day off – and then I'll come for tea. Yours, Rowena."

There is something familiar about the bulky figure approaching me along the snowy street; and sure enough, on closer view it turns out to be Tom. His girth is increased by the big sheepskin coat, and he wears a woollen toque pulled well down on his forehead. With a polite token gesture he indicates he would remove this headgear if it were not so cold. His smile is broad with pleasure.

"Greetings, Rowena. Splendid day, isn't it?" His breath puffs an exuberant plume of white into the frigid air. He takes my mittened hand into his gloved one and gives it a chummy little squeeze. We have not seen each other since the day we danced to "Let Yourself Go," and I am glad the cold air can be blamed for my red face. Low in the sky an orange sun hangs, but the light wind has such an arctic edge that it has frozen the tears on my eyelashes.

"Would you really call it splendid? I wouldn't."

My hand, which I try to extricate, only receives another ingratiating squeeze. "Nice to run into you, my dear," he goes on. "I hope you'll be home a little later – I have a couple of parochial calls to make hereabouts, but after that maybe you'll give me a cup of tea."

He allows his blue eyes to travel significantly over my own bundled form, and in spite of myself I have to smile. How marvellous at his age – or any age – to have the energy to think about such things in weather like this. "Sorry, Tom, I'm invited out to tea myself," I tell him, trying not to sound too cheerful about it. I stamp my feet lightly in an effort to keep them warm.

"Pity," he grunts. "Shall we make it next Monday, then?"

"Well – yes – come for tea."

With reluctance he releases my hand. I give him a noncommittal smile and hurry on my way, wondering ruefully how I am going to find a tactful way to let him know that one freakish indiscretion is not going to lead to another. Just how I am going to manage this without offending or hurting him is far from clear; but pondering the problem passes the time and helps me forget the cold until I ring Sebastian's bell.

A broad middle-aged woman with a bush of frizzy black hair and a flat face like a pie plate opens the door. She wears a pair of once-pink bedroom slippers and a surly expression.

"Good afternoon. I'm Mrs. Hill. I've come to see Mr. Long."

"He sick in bed. No see anybody." She would have closed the door and the discussion here, but I add rather loudly, "He invited me to tea."

Her small eyes narrow. "No see anybody," she repeats mulishly.

"My name is –"

"You go now."

"But Mr. Long invited me to tea, Mrs. Blot."

"That not my name. You sell thing. No want."

"No, no. I'm a friend of Mr. –"

"You go now, lady."

This impasse might have gone on indefinitely, but a bellow at last reaches us from upstairs. "Is that Mrs. Hill? Let her in at once!"

At this, with reluctance, Mrs. B. removes her bulk from the doorway and allows me in. She immediately slops off to the kitchen, leaving me to pull off my boots and coat and put them wherever I please. Quickly, my heart still beating fast after this encounter, I mount the familiar, creaking staircase.

"Stupid woman," Sebastian grumbles. "Blot, not you." The bed is made up and he is sitting in an armchair, his plastered foot extended on a hassock. A faded cardigan hangs open over a tieless shirt that exposes his ropy neck, but his white hair is meticulously brushed and he smells of aftershave.

"What is her name, then? We really ought to call her by it, don't you think? She's entitled."

"Of course. But you might not be so keen when you discover it's Blovantasakis. She is indisputably a valuable part of our cultural mosaic. Actually, she has the beautiful first name of Calliope, though there are reasons why we don't call her that, either. Do sit down. I'm glad to see you."

"Glad to be here." I sit down and smooth the old beige skirt over my still-cold knees. I wish now I'd obeyed the impulse to wear my red towel outfit. There is something infinitely sad about this dim and stuffy room with its old-fashioned furniture, and the crutches and Aspirin bottle established familiarly by the bed. The window, which needs washing, frames a bleak outlook of icicles, clotheslines and telegraph wires – not a very satisfying outlook for a philosopher, or come to that, anybody. Here, in the anteroom of his own termination, the old man sits alone by the hour with only his thoughts for company. He is gazing out of the window now in silence, as if preoccupied, thin shoulders hunched, eyes hooded.

"How's your toe coming along?" I ask, to remind him I am there.

"We won't discuss that. Boring."

"All right. My cold's better. Now we've got health out of the way."

"Your nose looks red."

"It's hellishly cold outside, that's why."

"Ah. Bloody country, this."

"What made you settle here?"

"Depression. Second marriage. Land of opportunity, we were told."

"And was it?"

"Yes; more or less."

"This was your wife, then?" I indicate a photo in a tarnished silver frame on the bureau. He glances at it in surprise as if he's long forgotten it's there, or even perhaps who the woman was. "Yes, that's my first wife, Enid. Pretty woman. Brain like a peahen."

I get up to look at it more closely. "But this isn't the bride in the picture downstairs. How many wives have you had, then?"

"Ah, that was Gwennie, my second. Pamela's mother. Another cardinal error. We were divorced in 1950, after committing two children. After that I gave up matrimony."

"Where's your other child then?"

"My son was killed in Korea in '52. Nineteen years old. You'd wonder what he was begun for, wouldn't you?"

"Oh, what a pity." I cast around for a more cheerful topic of conversation, but can find none. I remember the melancholy face of the bridegroom in the picture downstairs, and as if he remembers it, too, he says, "There can't be much to be said for a man who makes the same mistake twice, can there? Marriage is not a rational arrangement, of course. Too big a divergence in expectations. Men want emotional partnership with a mental equal. Women want sex and all that goes with it – brats and so on."

"Most people would say it's the other way around."

"Would you?"

I think this over. "Well, my own case – I hope – is hardly typical."

"One's own seldom is. What was so different about yours?"

"Well, I married for security . . . protection. And Edwin . . . crazily enough, I think he wanted adventure. Romance. Something like that. It wasn't me he wanted; it was just the idea. Terrible motives, anyway, on both sides." This is the first time I've articulated these thoughts, and the sound of my own voice surprises me, as if a stranger has spoken. But having begun, there seems no reason I should not add, "Anyhow, it settled down, like most unions, into a sort of holy deadlock."

He gives a snort of appreciation. "Trouble is, by the time you've defined who wants what, it's too late, and the lawyers move in like jackals on a corpse."

"Well, that could be preferable to . . ."

"That's what I thought. Divorce like surgery. Better than the disease." Without warning he throws back his head and shouts, "*Mrs. Blot!*" When a mutter from below answers, he shouts again, "Bring up the tea, please. And the whisky."

"Anyway," I go on, because the subject interests me, "why should getting married be any more rational than all the other things we do? Surely none of our relationships are logical. And I'm glad they're not, really. Otherwise there'd be no surprises, would there?"

He looks at me under his wrinkled eyelids with a wry smile. "Wittgenstein would agree with you. He thought logical truths are meaningless. Tautologies, he called them. Claimed they say nothing. So you like surprises, do you?"

"Well, I've had a few lately that . . . They're sometimes pretty devastating, though some turn out to be rather nice." (Tom here foxtrots lightly across my mind.) "Anyhow, I'm getting rather used to them."

"It takes a lot of self-confidence to like surprises."

"Does it?" I say, flattered.

Noisy breathing and the clatter of china herald the arrival of Mrs. Blot with the tray. She sets it down with a light crash on the table beside him, gives me a bitter glance from her small eyes and slops off again downstairs, all without a word. The pot of tea proves to be strong but not hot. There is no lemon and not enough milk. The digestive biscuits on a cracked plate are crumbling with old age. All in all, Mrs. B. has without question won this round on points.

"Muse of epic poetry indeed," mutters Sebastian, pushing away his half-empty cup. "Debased, in this case, into the modern keyboard steam whistle. Here, get yourself a glass out of the bathroom and have a drink with me."

I do that and find that malt whisky, while a new experience – another surprise, in fact – is not without its attractions. We sit in silence a little while over our drinks. The sky outside deepens to a dense and beautiful blue. Sebastian draws a long sigh of satisfaction. "I like you," he says. "You don't talk too much."

"I'd rather listen. To you, for instance. You studied at Heidelberg. I'm not even a graduate of the Don Mills Public Library."

"Well, I drank a lot of beer there. That was just after the war – the old war. Unfortunately I was just too young for that one, and too old for the next. Another planet, anyhow, that world. Soon after that I married damn-fool Enid (can you believe it, in spite of studying Strindberg), and went to work for an advertising agency in London. Perfectly good sense in all that; but I couldn't even be consistent. Met Gwen, who had academic ambitions for me. She pushed me into a M.Litt., married me and then decided we should emigrate. Not that I blame her for any of it, you understand. She's not responsible for my failure."

"But you were a professor at York."

He grins sardonically. "You call that success? No, I've written nothing, that's the point, except a few little penny-ante articles in the lesser journals. Nothing of any significance whatever."

"But writing things isn't enough to make anybody a success. Look at all the junk that's written. There are people who think Kahlil Gibran or Jonathan Livingston Seagull are great philosophers, but that doesn't make them right, does it?"

"You may pour us another drink, Rowena."

"No, not for me – I'm afraid I must go – look, it's quite dark. I've stayed far too long. But I have enjoyed it. Thanks for asking me."

I'm afraid he may press me to stay into the dinner hour, and thus create another stressful encounter with Mrs. Blot; but he has suddenly drifted into one of his half-dozes and hardly seems to notice when I say goodbye and slip away. Downstairs I get soundlessly into my outdoor things and ease the front door open with caution. In the kitchen, pots clash and cupboard doors bang dangerously, and I step out into the cold with a sense of escape.

The crystal night contains one brilliant star. It pulses overhead, bright, remote, but not entirely unfriendly.

"Thank you, darling," says Tom into my neck.

There is no appropriate answer to this, coming as it does only minutes after I have kindly but seriously explained to him that what we've just done must not and cannot happen any more. It is a considerable shock to discover that only a few expert gestures on his part have been needed to sweep away every one of my scruples. What began half an hour ago over the teacups has led to the bedroom with the most effortless ease and speed.

Now I lie here under him as the pleasure slowly ebbs and wonder whether I can be quite normal. Surely susceptibility like mine must be highly unusual. It is a surprise, too, to find that another aftermath of this encounter is a kind of fleshly tenderness I have never felt before. As for Tom, the blue eyes looking down into mine are so loving that to ask for a definition of exactly what it is he loves seems ungenerous. Is there anything wrong, after all, with simple animal gratitude?

"Must go, my dear – there's a vestry meeting," he murmurs, and heaves himself off the bed. Cheerfully he whistles into and out of the bathroom. After climbing into his trousers, he pauses to drop a kiss on my forehead. Seconds later he has disappeared down the stairs and banged the front door exuberantly behind him.

Wittgenstein then jumps on the bed, his fur fragrant with the cold outside air. The two of us are just settling down on the pillows when Prince Charles walks in.

"Well," he says, with a cold glance at the dishevelled bed, "I must say both you and the Church of England surprise me. Surely, at his age and in his line of work the Rev. Foster ought be above this kind of thing. As for you –"

"As for me," I say, stung to defiance, "you could say I'm making up for lost time."

"In Edwin's bed. How tasteless."

"It's my bed now." But because he is an old friend, and looks sad rather than angry, I feel I owe him some kind of explanation. "This is not an inappropriate place for it, as you know. Helps to exorcise a lot of other occasions."

"But where's your dignity, Rowena?"

"Nowhere, I guess. But does that matter a lot?"

"To me it does. But the point really is, I thought you'd made up your mind quite definitely that –"

"I know. Well, I changed my mind. Or something did. The thing is, you see, that first time, at his house – well, that sort of – er – detonation was something I honestly didn't think could ever happen again. It was so – it was so – it actually scared me."

"That's typical of you, heaven knows."

"And now it's happened again, with even more . . . Well, I mean, is that – does it always –?"

"You mean you didn't know you could have that feeling again?"

"Charles – Sir – I had no idea. Good Lord, then I wonder how people ever bother doing anything else like earning a living, and so on. As for self-abuse, if this is what it does, well, no wonder it's so popular. Nana called it that, you know, I suppose to put me off – *her* mother told her it made people crazy or blind, and while she didn't quite believe that, she warned me against it anyway, just in case. So I never . . . Why, if that were true this whole city would be full of lunatics going blind this very moment."

The Prince shakes his head in a deprecating manner. "But a man of the cloth like that. What an outrageous old pagan."

"But that's the best of it. If he were furtive about it and full of guilt afterwards – but he's not. After all, it was Paul, you know, not Christ, who was so anti-sex. I think I agree with Tom that nothing that feels so good can possibly be bad. Anyhow, what harm are we doing anyone? Neither of us is married any more, and as you hinted yourself, at our age there's no risk of pregnancy."

He gives a sniff of disapproval, the Battenberg nose being specially useful for this purpose. "And what," he says, "about those ladies of the Parish Guild? Promiscuous old trout."

"Well, that's his affair. So to speak. It makes no difference, really. No, there's no use trying to doomsay, Charles."

"That's all very well. But these things never happen in a vacuum, you know. What about Marion? Have you thought about that at all? What if she ever found out that you and Tom –"

I stare at him. "Thanks. You've made your point."

With dignity he stalks away, hands behind his back, and for once I am not sorry to see him go.

"Still, it was a really beautiful funeral," Cuthbert says bravely. He juts up his chin in a not quite successful effort to look less sad. "And Tom is always marvellous at times like that, as you know. Here, I'll take your coat. Now you just go in and say hello to Basil there. I'll be right back."

He trots off busily. I walk into the sitting-dining area of his condo, which is a space rather than a room, furnished in bleak, basic, blond-wood style. Everything in it is new and specklessly neat. The broadloom carpet is pale beige, as are the drapes framing a splendid after-dark view of several downtown office blocks and the hypodermic needle of the CN Tower. Bright modernistic prints framed in metal emphasize the general air of sterility. The one living thing in the place is small, yellow Basil swinging on his perch. When I go over to greet him, he flutters about in such real or pretended agitation that a feather and some droppings shower to the bottom of the cage.

"You'd hardly believe what a comfort he's been to me," Cuthbert says, carefully edging into the room with sherry decanter and glasses on a tray. "Somebody to come home to, it just makes all the difference. Aren't you good company, sweetie; aren't you Daddy's boy, then?" Basil replies by flying at the bars of his cage and clawing his way up the side of it, eyeing us coyly from a bright black eye.

"I'm sorry I couldn't be there, Cuthbert. But I'm sure Tom took the service very well. That big voice of his – he almost makes you believe those incredible promises, doesn't he? 'Though he die, yet shall he live,' and all that. Sheer power of language, I suppose. He's so right to have no truck with the new prayer book."

"Well, I believe it all – while he's talking, anyway. And whenever I go to church. It's in between times – that's the hard part. But nobody's a believer one hundred per cent of the time; Tom once told me that, and it made me feel a lot better."

I sip my sherry cautiously. What with the bottle of brandy Tom has installed on my sideboard, and the occasional malt whisky at Sebastian's, I am becoming quite an experienced drinker.

"My, it's nice to see you again, Rowena," he says comfortably. "Such a pity I had to go down with flu right after the funeral. Settled right down in my bronchial tubes, too, till the doctor bombed it with Aureomycin. You knew that Tom's had it, too?"

"Yes, I knew."

"Anyhow, it's ages since we got together. And you were so good to me that day after Mother –"

"You did the same for me, if you remember."

"And how is Marion these days?"

"Oh, she is in good form," I say, trying not to sound discouraged about that.

"There's no date set yet for your court hearing, but I hope there will be soon. Meantime, as I keep on saying, I'm sure Edwin left a will somewhere to provide for you – if only we could find it. Then most of your troubles would be over."

Those dire words *court hearing* give me such a pang of fear it is a moment before I can reply. What will be heard, and by whom? and what will become of me if –? But I wrench my mind back to what Cuthbert is saying.

"Yes – well – I've looked everywhere in the house, Cuthbert. The other day I even flipped through the kitchen cookbooks, but no luck, of course."

"Never mind, Rowena, I just feel in my bones that things are going to be all right. Blind faith, I guess you could call it."

I raise my glass to blind faith and wish I could share it. Cuthbert pushes up a striped shirt cuff to look at his watch. "The Black Pearl man ought to be here by now. I hope you like Chinese food. Perhaps I should give them another call."

"Oh, they'll be along. This is nice sherry."

"It's Montilla, actually. Yes, it's nice and dry. Well, since we have the time –" and he tops up our glasses.

"How are things in your office?"

"Oh, a bit hectic . . . much gossip about. One of our Law Society members has apparently been swindling a client of his – a poor old lady in a wheelchair."

"That doesn't sound very nice."

He gives a faint chuckle. "No, but the fact is, this particular old lady is literally hell on wheels. She came as near as dammit to hitting me with her cane the other day when I was getting her

affidavit. I can't help sort of sympathizing with anybody who –
now where are those people with our meal? You must be starving."

"Don't worry about it." Tropical air smelling faintly of machines
pumps into the room from the ceiling registers. I unbutton my
cardigan.

"Nothing much else is new on Bay Street. Except for my poor
secretary Elaine – the one with the baby, you know? Her husband's
left her. Not for another woman, which poor Elaine says she could
understand, even if she didn't like it – but because he wants to go to
India to study Hinduism. He converted to Catholicism a few years
ago, but this is a bit much. It's really rough on Elaine, poor kid."

I murmur something affirmative as the buzzer sounds. Cuthbert
hurries to the door and opens it to a deliveryman who sways
lightly to the unheard music in his headphones. Cuthbert carries
the stack of cartons out to the kitchen, calling back, "This stuff is
barely warm – I'll just stick it in the microwave. Won't be a
minute. As you know, I can't cook, and I was sure you'd rather eat
quietly here than go to a restaurant."

Well, you were wrong, dear, I think genially.

"Now a drop more sherry while we wait," he says, bustling
back. He refills both glasses before I can stop him.

"Anyhow, I'm acting for Elaine to be sure she gets support
money for the baby and so on. She's in an awful state about it,
though if he really feels like that, she's better off without him. I can
hardly tell her that, though, can I?"

"How old is Elaine?"

"Just twenty-nine. Pretty girl, too."

I finish off my sherry thoughtfully. "Easier to adapt at her age
than at ours. As for sex, I'm developing a new respect for it, you
know. I mean it's connected to so many other things . . . to almost
everything, in fact. Like the human condition. I'm becoming quite
a philosopher in my old age, which is surprising, isn't it, even for

an introvert like me. Maybe it's the sherry talking, but d'you think perhaps one reason we're here at all – if there is a reason – could be to figure out the connection between sex and all the rest of it?"

Something beeps in the kitchen and Cuthbert excuses himself to hurry away again. Possibly he is not sorry to have this particular discussion cut short. I wander around the table, which has been neatly set beforehand with Danish cutlery and blue linen place mats. Looking more closely at these, I see that they are handwoven. An oval sticker under one corner reads "Handmade for Devices and Desires, Queen Street West." I pry it free and slip it into my cardigan pocket.

"Now here we are at last," announces Cuthbert, bustling in with several steaming bowls on a tray. "Could you just grab a couple of paper napkins out of that drawer, Rowena? Great. Now I have something nice to go with this." And he produces a long-necked brown bottle. "Lacrima Christi. I don't think Tom would disapprove, do you?"

"No, but I'm afraid I'd better pass, Cuthbert; I've really had –"

"Mustn't be a cowardy custard," he chides me, and firmly fills both wineglasses. "It's mild as milk, I promise you. All through poor Mother's illness, I found I could hardly eat a thing unless I had a glass or two of this to help it down. Maybe it's the road to ruin, but if so, I don't really care that much. Now cheers."

The various Black Pearl dishes taste of nothing very much except fried rice and the cartons it all came in, but I think it prudent to blot up the sherry with as much food as I can manage. By sipping my wine, only at widely spaced intervals, I find I can keep the room more or less in equilibrium, but Cuthbert more than once cheerfully refills his own glass.

"Have you had enough to eat? Another fortune cookie? Mine says, 'You will move forward with confidence.'"

"Mine says, 'You will be direct in romance.'"

"Rosy futures, eh? I never know whether they're meant for warning or advice. Let's listen to some music."

He goes over to a bank of expensive electronic equipment and pushes some buttons. At once a sprightly Vivaldi concerto springs into the air.

"Odd, with all that exuberance, it's hard to remember he was actually a priest," I say. "Though maybe that's not as contradictory as it sounds. He's celebrating life. Am I talking rather a lot?"

"Will you have a bit more wine? Well, I'll just finish it off, then."

I sit down carefully on the blond-wood, sparely upholstered sofa. "It was sweet of you to ask me over, Cuthbert. Thanks for the treat."

"Dear Rowena, you deserve a little treat, if ever anyone did. Here, I'll just cover Basil's cage. I think he should have an early night. These last weeks have been a strain on him."

"Naturally," I say, trying not to smile. He sits down beside me, opening the top button of his jacket. When he leans aside to put his glass on an end table, the bald crown of his head glitters in the light from the overhead track lamps.

"Well, if we get what we deserve, Cuthbert, you ought to be in line for something pretty good yourself. Crowds of beautiful women fighting over you like wolves, for instance."

He rubs his forehead ruefully. "Well, the uproar sure hasn't broken out yet."

"You just hang in there. It may, any time now."

"Why now, when it never has before?"

"I don't know, but upheavals like death create all kinds of peculiar waves. Strange, unexpected things happen."

"Do they?" He glances at me sidelong.

"Yes."

"To you?"

"Yes."

"Really?" He pulls off his thick glasses and polishes them on his handkerchief.

"Believe me."

"Well, nothing like that is going to happen to me."

"That's what I thought, Cuthbert."

"Did you?"

By way of reply, I give his hand a friendly little squeeze, and as if absent-mindedly, he puts his arm around me. There is a silence during which Vivaldi continues to celebrate life. Then, still with an air of detachment, as if to convince himself or me that nothing of consequence is happening, he kisses my cheek. I turn his face to a convenient angle and put my lips to his. This act of assertion surprises me even more than it does him; but he responds with enthusiasm. Then, seconds later, he mutters, "No – I promised myself –" and draws away.

"Sorry."

"It's only that – dear Rowena, I mustn't do this. You know we –"

"Cuthbert. Sh." We have clearly reached a point where one of us has to make a decision, and there seems no reason why it shouldn't be me. I open a button of his shirt and slip my hand inside. His chest is quite amazingly hairy. He groans and, turning, hastily unbuttons me in turn. We sink into a reclining position. He says breathlessly, "Look – we've got to – remember last time – say you'll marry me."

"Anything," I mutter.

"You'll marry me. We're engaged."

"Whatever. Don't stop."

"Ah. Yes. Oh."

"Easy, love. Not so fast."

"Now. Slowly."

"Oh."

"That's right. Easy does it. Lovely."

The priest's music flows on serenely. Basil, protected from trauma behind his cover, sleeps. Eventually, so do we.

"I'm waiting," the Prince says grimly.

"What for? I don't have to explain myself to you."

"Oh, yes, you do. Either that or explain me to yourself. You needn't be afraid of boring me – not after all the speeches I've sat through. Come on, I haven't got all day."

I kick the bedclothes rather sulkily. He has woken me up, and a faint taste of Lacrima Christi lingers sourly at the back of my mouth. A pale winter sun is just whitening the window blind; it is barely seven o'clock.

"Well?"

"Well what? I do wish you wouldn't nag, Charles."

"You *seduced* that little man."

"Well, yes, but he was a consenting adult – to put it mildly."

Charles sits down on the end of the bed, pushing his hands into the pockets of his double-breasted suit. After the silence has gone on for some time, I add with dignity, "Anyhow, it's a private matter. Nobody's business but ours. I refuse absolutely to feel guilty about it in any way."

"And I suppose you're going to tell me that drink had nothing to do with it?"

"Well, it didn't. Not much, anyway. Come to that, it's not our fault if we have inhibitions to overcome."

"And Tom's recent absence? Are you going to tell me the fact that you've missed his, er, attentions recently had nothing to do with –"

"That is not true," I say loudly.

"Knickers," he says.

"Look, it was simply a small, harmless act of loving kindness. Cuthbert's such a dear. I'm truly fond of him. And it was high time he –"

Suddenly his normally pensive face breaks into a smile. "Rowena," he says, "call it a celebration of life or an act of kindness – call it what you like – as long as you're completely honest with both of us. And that means facing the whole truth about this little episode, including good old Tom's tutorials, and the wine. More to the point, admit there's profound satisfaction in the vision of Edwin somewhere up there in a state of outrage . . . You've tied the score, haven't you?" And with that he tosses me a royal wave and disappears.

CHAPTER SEVEN

❧

Shifting the black bulk of Wittgenstein slightly, I push the Wrights' doorbell. A beribboned Christmas wreath, its tinsel blinking in the sun, is already rather crookedly tied to their knocker.

"Rowena!" cries Pamela, flinging the door wide. "Come along in. So glad you're here – now I can stop doing this. What a revolting way to spend a Sunday, but needs must now I have a job." She kicks aside an entanglement of vacuum-cleaner cord and hose, and glancing briefly at the cat says, "Is this our Witty, then? Has he been bothering you?"

I put him down and he immediately shoots under the sofa with a hiss.

"He keeps coming to my door, Pam, crying to be let in, and in this weather I hate to say no, since you're out so much. But please don't think I mind. Actually I'm flattered he seems to like me that much. Only I didn't want you worrying where he might be."

"Yes, well, I'm working part-time now in a dress shop. And he's feeling very sorry for himself these days, is Witty. Give me your coat; we'll have some coffee." Here she pulls off the crimson scarf tying back her hair and leads me to the kitchen where I climb onto a bar stool. Sitting in the sunny window washing its face with a white paw is a fluffy, peach-coloured kitten.

"Somebody gave this creature to Colin a few weeks ago," she says, scooping coffee lavishly into the basket of a large percolator. "We really couldn't resist her, she's so fetching; but Wittgenstein has taken fearful umbrage. He's pretending to be insulted and not speaking to us, but the shaming truth is he's frightened out of his mind of LaVerne, she bullies him dreadfully, isn't she attractive, though, with all those frills and ruffles, but tough as old boot under it all. We think she belongs in some feline chorus line, hence LaVerne. How do you like your coffee, I think there's some cream somewhere, I adore cholesterol myself, and what have you been doing these days anyway?"

This doesn't seem to be quite the right time to go into detail about what I have been doing, though I have a feeling Pam would not only be fascinated, but would highly approve. Instead I say, "Not much, actually. Tell me, how do you think your father's doing these days?"

"Oh, he seems about the same – you know, depressed and tiresome, grumbling about everything. The damn toe is taking forever to heal or knit or whatever bones do, I suppose at his age it's natural, and it's boring for him, not being able to get around, poor old bugger. Not that anybody in their senses would want to go anywhere much in this weather, I often wish I could break a hip or something and just stay cosily in bed all winter."

"I've been to see him a couple of times this last week or two."

"Have you? – Yes, he's mentioned it, actually. How noble of you. A pity he doesn't care for dogs, maybe a pet would take his mind off things, though they are madly inconvenient sometimes, look at Arthur at the vet for ages now, running up the most enormous bill and giving us awful pangs because he looks so pathetic with his yellow tum – he has hepatitis, of all things. For a while we thought he was going to die, John nearly cried, and as for me, floods."

I shift a little on my stool. I have not come here to discuss pets, but Pamela's personality – or her persona – has a certain irresistible force.

"About Sebastian –" I say hopefully.

"Ah, this is ready at last, do let's go through where we can sit like ladies of pleasure off duty, you know those Lautrec paintings of half-dressed whores in plushy parlours, whatever one does at night, it's deliciously depraved to be idle in the morning, it's almost my favourite thing."

I fall in behind her, glad to conceal the self-conscious grin prompted by this remark. Pamela clears an armchair for me by removing three books, a sweater and a Coke tin from the seat. "Why are men so madly untidy," she grumbles, "is it testosterone or what, women never create such litter, not that I prize neatness all that much, it's rather a dreary virtue."

The black nose of Wittgenstein emerges cautiously from under the chintz skirt of the sofa, then withdraws abruptly as the kitten strolls into the room. LaVerne glances around with a calm air of ownership and begins to sharpen her claws on the rug.

"As a matter of fact, Pam, I wonder – I hope you won't mind my mentioning this, because of course it's not my business at all, and the last thing I want to do is interfere in any way, but –" I stir my coffee, trying to muster the courage to go on.

"You're going to tell me something unpleasant," says Pamela. "That kind of preamble always means trouble."

"Well, forgive me ahead of time, then."

"Oh, all right. Let's have it. Something about my wretched old parent, I suppose."

"Yes, well, actually it's about his housekeeper."

"What about her? She's repulsive, I know, but necessary – a bit like a truss."

"Well, yes, but she really – I mean, it –"

"Do spit it out, Rowena."

"What I mean is this. I'm allowing for the fact she doesn't like my visits, so it's not her rudeness that bothers me . . . I don't know just how to put this without sounding . . ."

"Look, you are making me really nervous. Get on with it."

The kitten has curled up to sleep on the sofa and Wittgenstein's whiskers reappear. With infinite caution his head and shoulders ooze forth from his retreat.

"Well, Pam, it's just that last time I was there, I got the impression that Sebastian was – I know this sounds a bit far-fetched – but it seemed to me he was afraid of her."

"What, Dad? Afraid of Mrs. Blot? You must be joking!"

"I know it sounds –"

"Oh, my dear, wildly improbable, don't you really think? I mean he's so fearsome himself, an ogre with fangs is simply nowhere, I can assure you, when he's in form."

"But these days he isn't really in form, is he?"

"Oh, come, now, what could he possibly find to be frightened of in Mrs. B., unless you count those ghastly slippers and the things she does to the English language."

"I can't put my finger on it, Pam, but it's there, I really think, just the same, and –"

"Well, you haven't seen her slapping him about the head, have you?"

"No, of course not."

"Or starving him or anything?"

"No, no, but . . ." I think of the lukewarm tea produced on my last visit, and the torn-open packet of biscuits on the ring-marked tray, and my voice trails away in defeat.

"I mean it's sweet of you to take an interest and all that, Rowena, but you do realize he can be pretty impossible, don't you, and nine people out of ten wouldn't put up with him for any money, so Mrs. B. has to be regarded as something of a treasure. This has been the story of his life, you know. He's not only difficult in every way, but absolutely unpredictable as well. You never know where you are with him, you simply have no idea what it was like as children having him for a father, one minute roller-skating with us (which we actually found dreadfully embarrassing), and the next raging like Attila the Hun about some minor lapse like saying lie when you meant lay, or the other way round. I've seen him create the most frightful hoo appropriate to murder or treason because one of us said 'between you and I.' Actually it was my brother who received the blast that time, though Dad adored Geoff, practically idolized him, and never really got over him getting killed like that in Korea, so you see it's no wonder both his marriages broke up, and in fact the truth is, if it comes to fear, I've always been mildly terrified of him myself."

"Yes, well, I do see your point. It's only that the last time I was there I had the feeling he was going downhill, somehow. He had nothing much to say, and . . ."

Soundlessly, belly to the floor, Wittgenstein inches forth. His baleful eyes are fixed on the sleeping LaVerne, who curls a paw over her nose and dozes on.

"Well, what exactly happened to give you this feeling?" Pam sets down her coffee cup on an end table with a sharp little clack, and Wittgenstein freezes once more.

"It sounds like nothing much, I know. She brought up the tea and dumped down the tray, and he asked her – in a perfectly polite way – if she'd mind bringing up the whisky later. And she said, 'No good for you.' He said, 'Please bring it up anyway, Mrs. Blot,' and she went off without answering. A bit later when he called down and asked for it again, she didn't answer. He tried again. No reply. Then he actually got up on his crutches to call again from the head of the stairs; and this time she yelled back, 'You be quiet!' and he came back to his chair and sat down, all out of breath and a bad colour, and he didn't look fearsome then, Pamela, he looked afraid."

There is a short, uncomfortable silence. Then she says rather stiffly, "Not that I've given any orders, but he's far too fond of drink, you know. Could easily become a lush, in my opinion. He'd probably be into the sauce before ten in the morning if allowed."

Wittgenstein has now inched his cautious way to my foot. He leaps into my lap with a triumphant little bleat and curls himself up there.

"The thing is, I don't think it was his welfare Mrs. B. had in mind. Not at all. It was a war of some kind, and she won it."

But Pam has turned her head aside momentarily and does not seem to hear this. And it occurs to me how convenient it must sometimes be not to hear – or appear not to hear – some things. "Anyhow," she says rather vaguely, "sweet of you to be concerned. Poor old brute, I suppose he can't help being such a pain at this stage, but he certainly is, I suppose even to himself. I'm doing the best I can in the circs., and that's really all I can do, isn't it?"

"Of course it is. Please don't think I'm –"

"It would really be so much better if we could be born at, say, Colin's age, which is quite sweet, really, all that drooling and crying stage nicely done with, and then die with tidiness and dignity at about sixty-five, before we go dotty and get awful things wrong with

us. On the other hand I'm rather looking forward to being a terrible, wheezing old hag nobody dares to cross, think of the power."

Behind the waterfall of this chatter, I perceive two things
clearly enough: she wishes I would go home, and she doesn't want
to know anything more about Sebastian's fear. I make a move to
get up, and half-contritely she leans forward to touch me on the
arm. "Look – do take Witty home with you, if you like having him
around. I'm sure he'd be much happier with you; this kitten really
does make his life miserable."

"Oh, do you mean that? I'd love to have him. But he's your cat –
how can I take him away from you?"

"Call it a permanent loan," she says, giving his black head a
careless stroke.

"Thanks," I say, clutching him firmly to me. Just the same, I do
not feel my visit has been a success.

The kitchen window of Dream Pies overlooks a garbage-haunted
city alley. But this afternoon it also frames a western sky gloriously
on fire. Huge clouds of russet, gold and purple burn there like a
celebration. I stand at the work-table gazing out, the chopping
knife slack in my hand. I should get on with feeding chunks of
carrot and onion into the food processor, but Steve is on the
phone and Arlene is daydreaming, too, one hand over her belly. I
think she is pregnant again, which will certainly add interest to
their June wedding.

At the very least I should be busy planning a quickly prepared
dinner for Cuthbert tonight, because his embrace on arrival often
leads to immediate further action. Unless the meal is ready at once,
we may well not sit down to eat until the middle of the night.

"No doubt you take a dim view of all this," I say to Mrs. Wilson,
dutifully dropping vegetables into the processor's tube.

"What, sky watching? Certainly not. I'm a great looker-out of windows myself. You poor Torontonians, though, with no sea or mountains – what poverty. I don't know how you manage."

"No, I mean this relationship with Cuthbert."

"Oh, that."

"You think it's insignificant?"

"Of course not. Nothing is insignificant. Trivial, maybe. Take those neat little squirrel tracks out there in the snow. If we were God, we'd know everything they mean; as it is, just being you and me, we only know that they're nice to look at, they somehow complete the snow, and they indicate the squirrels will be around in the spring to eat up our tulip bulbs."

"Yes, but about Cuthbert, Ethel?"

"What a lot of questions you ask nowadays. You ought to know by now the only ones worth asking have no answers. Cuthbert? – he's like all growing people – a wayfarer; a transient. And that's all there is to Cuthbert."

"Growing? Yes, he is. Only I –"

"You wonder about complications. What next and how and why and so on."

"Yes."

"Well, try to keep out of all that. Clingers," she goes on with some severity, "come to no good, as you should know. Look at what you clung to in the name of stability and safety all those years. Edwin. Almost as bad a name as Eddie. Such birds never migrate. Or mutate. To mate with that kind is like being embalmed while you're still alive. And for some people not to mate at all may be the best of all possible worlds."

The sun, emerging from under the cloud bank, briefly turns the window glass to gold and then disappears.

"**I** must be off to a baptism, my dear. Wish I could stay, but there it is – duty calls."

I turn on my side to watch Tom buttoning his shirt. The blue of his eyes is bright and clear, and his still-thick hair and square clipped moustache are daisy-white. His cheeks are still rosy from recent exertion. My eyes rest on him with affection.

"It doesn't bother you to go from this to that on a Sunday afternoon, does it?"

"No, why should it? It's you that has the Puritan conscience, my dear."

I can hardly explain, though, that what troubles my conscience is not our sexual activity at all, but the rather squalid little strategies involved in making sure Cuthbert's visits and his own do not coincide. Which shows pretty devastatingly how far gone I am in moral corruption. Still, Tom's serenity intrigues me. "Just the same, Tom, you're the one who has to stand up an hour from now and hold forth about the sins of the flesh."

"Rowena, it's a matter of relativity. We are carnal creatures, but we must try to live by the spirit. Get the two in proportion somehow. The Almighty gave us both sides, for reasons of His own, and all He asks is that we put the spirit first. Seems perfectly reasonable to me."

Fat, soft flakes of snow are drifting past the window. "Well, it's always bothered me, that part about being conceived and born in sin. Remember Marion at her christening – two months old and fast asleep – all us sinners gathered round her – but she wasn't one of us, surely."

"In that, like the rest of us, she was human, of course she was a sinner."

I sigh. "Christian doctrine is too much for me altogether. Though, to be fair, it's not too much for Marion, apparently. Sunday school, confirmation – she's sailed through it all. Never questions anything, as far as I know. She still goes to communion regularly, I believe. But then, I don't know; Marion doesn't seem to have any hormones to contend with."

Rightly judging that these remarks call for no comment, Tom thrusts his arms into his jacket and takes out a pocket comb to tidy his hair.

"It makes me a bit giddy, in fact," I go on, "all that mystery in the universe. As a child I can remember turning sick with fear one Sunday because some creed or other proclaimed that the Holy Ghost 'is neither made, nor created, nor begotten, but proceeding.' For some reason that made everything solid seem insubstantial – made of air – and abstract things the only real ones. I had the same feeling, only worse, when we took Marion to the planetarium years ago. You know how they darken the place and you look up into this vault and see the planets, while a recorded voice tells you all about light years and the dimensions of space that can't even be defined. I actually had to get up and go out onto Bloor Street to get rid of the panic."

"I'm sure that did the trick," he says, smiling.

"It did."

"Well, I'm only a steward, my dear," he says, coming to the bed to kiss my cheek. "We're told that the Lord in His own time will bring to light the hidden things of darkness, and make manifest the counsels of the heart, and that will have to content us, won't it? Bless you. Till next time."

When he is gone I stretch out peacefully. I feel everything drift away – money worries, the Holy Ghost, strategies and all spiritual perplexities. I yawn largely and give myself up to pagan sleep.

Notwithstanding such interludes, I spend most of my time actively worrying over how to make ends meet. With increasing zeal I brood over the help wanted ads. Surely some time soon I will find a job that pays better than Dream Pies. But it's profoundly discouraging to find that even nannies seem to be required not only to be loving and reliable, but to have certificates, references, experience, a driver's licence, creativity and a positive attitude. Office help, however humble, is even more demanding: applicants must offer communication skills, career orientation (whatever that is) and the ability to operate an Apple Macintosh word processor.

Desperation, as bill-paying looms at the end of the month, sends me to the local wool shop where I've been a customer for years. Perhaps they might buy some of my work. This time I do no rehearsing and pause only a moment to glance at the window display of handsome hand-knit sweaters.

The bell pings loudly as I enter. Two elderly women stand at the counter conferring with a salesgirl over a heap of wools. Pretending to inspect a table piled with balls of green angora on sale, I glance around for the friendly fat lady who owns – or used to own – the shop. There is no sign of her. Instead her place at the cash desk is occupied by a sharp-looking youngish man with a Vandyke beard that makes him look faintly sinister. I study the green angora display, trying to muster the courage to approach him. I wish the women at the counter would go, but they seem in no hurry; indeed, one of them sits down on a stool and loosens her coat.

". . . and I said to him, I said Herbert, if you would take tran-quillizers, I wouldn't have to. I'm going out, I said, you get your own lunch, if I stay in this apartment with you one minute more, Herbert, I said, anything could happen. Suit yourself, he says, nothing gets through to that man. I said to the doctor, I said, have you got some kind of pill I can take for matrimony, I said, because it's killing me, I can tell you. The purple is nice, but who can wear that colour, I'll have this peach instead and then let's have a coffee somewhere; I'll have to be home by five, though, to take my pills.

And when I walk in, there Herbert will be, laying on the sofa with a book, and he'll say, sweet as pie, Well, there you are, have a nice day? I tell you that man, ever since he retired, it's read, read, read, enough to drive you crazy. If you would take a tranquillizer, I wouldn't have to, I say to him, but does he listen, never."

I would gladly hear more about Herbert, who sounds like my kind of person, but the two women finally collect their parcels and leave. I look longingly after them as the bell pings them out. My heart gives a little jump of alarm when the Vandyke man comes towards me and says, "Good afternoon. Something I can do for you?"

Swallowing hard, I force myself to speak. "Well, yes – I mean, I hope so. The thing is, I'm afraid I'm not actually here to buy anything; in fact I was wondering if by any chance – if you'd consider – you see, I'm a fairly good needlewoman, that sort of thing – probably you don't handle embroidery or anything like that, but I wondered – I see you sell a lot of baby wool, I knit and crotchet, too, and these sweaters you have in the window – that kind of thing – do you ever buy articles like that and sell them on commission?"

"No," he says.

"Oh. I see. Well, I just thought I'd ask."

"Good afternoon," he says coolly.

"Thanks anyway," I add politely. It is such a relief to get out of there that I might have bought myself a coffee to celebrate, if it weren't for the fact that I recognize this is another defeat – and I can't afford many more of them.

"**M**other."

"Yes, dear."

"When are we going to do our Christmas shopping?"

"Oh. Well, surely this year – I mean, I have no cash to spare for presents, as you know."

"Never mind that. I'll pay for everything. Meet me downtown tomorrow after work."

"But dear –"

"Continuity is important, Mother."

To whom? I want to ask, but refrain. "We always did our shopping near home," I remind her instead.

"The big department stores have some good sales on. Meet me at the south end of the Eaton Centre at six-thirty, all right?"

I stifle the many objections I have to this plan, because I find something touching about this wistful clinging to Christmas rituals. Nostalgia for her childhood, I suppose. Yet Marion seemed to be a child only very briefly. I was the child in our house – timid, dependent, immature. Yet until she moved into her own place, she always insisted on a tall tree at home, overriding Edwin's objection to the cost and mine to the dropped needles. But I'll not deny her now. Next evening I stand obediently among the jostling shoppers at the Eaton Centre, peering about for her navy coat.

"*There* you are," she says, darting into view. "Honestly, Mother. I told you the *south* end. Well, come on; we haven't got all night."

I fall into step with her, trying not to plod in my heavy boots. I unbutton my coat because the throng of people round us creates heat as well as a surflike, roaring sort of din. Through it all filters gusts of pop music from hi-fi shops and "Silent Night" pumped into the air courtesy of Muzak.

The broad indoor concourse linking two department stores teems with teenagers eating fast food on benches, affluent young people feverishly buying things, and the unemployed, who sit and gaze pensively at the fountain that periodically shoots a jet of water fifty yards into the air, like some gigantic mercantile orgasm.

"I thought a CD for Cuthbert," Marion says, peering at her neatly written list. "He likes baroque music, right? Vivaldi, perhaps."

"Um – I think he already has quite a bit of Vivaldi."

"Mozart, then."

"Aren't these new discs awfully expensive?"

"Not if you know where to go. Besides, I told you, Mother, I'm buying everything this year." Meekly I fall behind while she pushes our way into a record shop where, after a thorough search, she finds a set of Mozart horn concertos on sale. "Now for Tom," she says, as we struggle back to the concourse. My feet are already aching. My coat feels as heavy as a suit of armour, and I long to sit down. Yet Marion looks fresh and invigorated; I can barely keep up with her long strides.

"I've made Tom a nice big Christmas cake full of brandy," I say hopefully. "Won't that do for him?"

"They have some lovely Italian sweaters reduced at Eaton's," she says firmly. We choose a rather sophisticated black cardigan with pale-blue trim, and after that, riding up two people-clogged escalators, we choose a yellow blouse for Bernice. After that again, struggling fiercely into and then out of a stationery shop, we buy rolls of Christmas paper and ribbon.

"I'm afraid I really will have to sit down soon, Marion. Could we maybe find someplace for a cup of tea?"

"Oh, all right, if you're tired. There's a little snack bar over there." She seizes a tiny table just vacated by two other shoppers, and we sit down on the railed side of the gallery, which affords a view of hundreds of foreshortened people below. Trying not to groan with relief, I wriggle out of my coat and stuff our parcels under the table. Marion orders tea, which eventually appears in those stubby little pots seen only in restaurants, with the kind of spout that pours tea all over the saucer and place mat. I sup the part that lands in my cup with gratitude.

"Well," says Marion, dropping a cube of sugar into her tea. "It's been quite a while since I've seen you, Mother, what with one thing and another. How have things been?"

"Oh fine – just fine." Thank heaven for platitudes, I think, and to forestall her asking just what is fine, and how, I ask, "What's developing with that commissioner's job, dear? Anything new?"

"Well, Babs Harrington is going after it, too, as you know. Running around charming people left and right. It makes me sick. As if charm had anything to do with the job."

My poor Marion, I want to say, but of course do not. I feel like reaching across the table to touch her hand, but don't do that, either. What can be said or done to help someone who despises charm?

"I've been thinking lately, Mother, that it's high time something happened in that case of yours. Surely Cuthbert's being terribly slow. It's been more than two months now, with no sign of any action whatsoever. In the position you're in, it's really – I'll have to have a word with him."

"Oh, surely that's not necessary," I say, alarmed. "He's doing his best, I'm sure. The law is horribly slow, everybody knows that. And don't forget he's been helping to support me till this application thing gets settled. Nobody could be more generous than he's been. And I wouldn't for the world hint to him he's not doing everything –"

"That's all very well, but Cuthbert is a bit of a wimp."

"Oh, I wouldn't say that, Marion."

"Come on, you know he has no drive at all."

Here a vivid recollection of a recent example of Cuthbert's drive (which, to me anyway, left nothing to be desired) rises to mind. My cheeks turn hot and I hastily mask my face with my teacup. But Marion's sharp, clear eye is fixing me like a gimlet.

"You've put on some weight, haven't you?" she says.

"Well, I may have put on a pound or two. Not a bad thing, do you think? I was quite scrawny before."

"And your colour's awfully high. Have you had your blood pressure taken lately? Or maybe it's a hot flush. Aren't you on hormones, though?"

"Yes, I am. No problem there. I'm perfectly all right."

She continues to look at me critically. "Twice now when I've called you quite late in the evening, you've been out. It can't be to the library – wherever do you go?"

"I've explained all that, Marion. I had dinner at Cuthbert's one night, and the other time I was over at Tom's."

"Well, I hope they drove you home, that's all. Elderly women out alone after dark aren't safe any more, you know."

"You're not worried about rape, are you?"

"There's no need to *exaggerate*, Mother. Not that it wouldn't be a good idea for you to take a couple of kung fu lessons. I could teach you, if you'd only be serious about it."

"A serious widow," I say, repressing a smile.

"What?"

"Nothing. Well, I suppose we'd better be getting on. There's just one more thing I want to buy."

"Oh? What's that?"

"Just a little bottle of malt whisky."

"Malt – but whatever do you want that for?"

"Not for me. It's for a friend."

"What friend?"

"It's Pam Wright's old father, Sebastian Long. I've been to see him a few times. He's laid up with a broken toe."

"But what's that to you, for goodness sake? Malt whisky costs –"

"I have money put aside," I say stiffly. "I don't expect you to pay for it."

"That's not really the point, Mother."

"What is the point, then?" I look at her squarely and for once she glances away, looking a little uncomfortable. "Oh, all right," she says. "You could make him a gift of a bottle of port or sherry for half the price, but there it is, if you want to throw money around . . ."

I pinch my lips together and say no more. Sulkily she follows me to the liquor outlet, muttering, "I'll wait for you out here. It's a zoo in there."

It takes me a long time amid the crowds milling around the many shelves to find the malt whisky, and, as she predicted, the price gives me rather a shock. By now, though, my blood is up. I join the line-up at the cash desk and carry away my purchase with a feeling of solid achievement.

Someone is following me down McKenzie Street. As if it isn't enough to have had problems first with Marion, and then with putting Cuthbert off for the evening, this has to happen. I step out more briskly. Half the battle, I've heard, is to look purposeful and confident, so I try to put as much as possible of these qualities into the muscles of my back. But the squeak of my boots on the hard-packed snow is echoed by a steady footfall behind that seems to keep pace. The long shadow of the follower swings out under the street light, stretching as if to touch me. Not daring to look back, I hurry on, fighting the temptation to break into a run. Why on earth have I waited till after dark to do this errand? Why didn't I listen to Marion's advice and warning? The answers to these good questions are far from satisfactory. I've waited because I am afraid to encounter Mrs. Blot on duty. And I didn't listen to good advice because it came from Marion.

Meanwhile the steps behind me are quickening. I risk a swift glance back. A tall young man in toque and mittens raises a hand in greeting and calls, "Hi there, Mrs. Hill. I thought it was you." It is young Max Wright. "On your way to Sebastian's, are you?"

"Yes," I say, trying not to gasp. "I am."

"That's nice for him. I'm just here to check the furnace is working – it conked out earlier today."

"Your mother lent me a key back when Sebastian broke his toe, but I've been too busy to get round till now. I have a little Christmas present for him."

"Great," he says cheerfully. With an agile leap up the steps ahead of me, he unlocks the door and ushers me through with a polite flourish. The house is as usual dark inside but for a faint glow on the upper landing, and there is the same odour of solitude haunting the place; the same silence.

"Hoy!" calls Max up the stairs. "Ancestor! It's Max. I'm here with a guest for you. I'll just case out whether he's still alive," he adds in a lower voice. After dropping most of his outerwear in a heap on the floor, he bounds up the stairs two at a time in his socks. I follow sedately, after leaving my own things tidily in the hall cupboard.

In the bedroom I find Max vigorously stuffing pillows at Sebastian's back. "There you are, then," he says. "It's only seven, after all. You can sleep any time. Here's Mrs. Hill to see you."

"Who?" the old man asks crossly.

"Mrs. Hill, Seb."

"Never heard of her."

"From next door. You met her at our place."

"That's no excuse."

Max rolls his eyes at me meaningfully. "I'll just run down to check that guy really did fix the furnace," he says and disappears.

"Interference," mutters Sebastian, following some dream or train of thought we have interrupted. "That plastic credit-card Mulroney and his interference. That furnace," he adds, staring at me, "has been perfectly all right for thirty years, whatever is the boy on about?"

"I've brought you a little present," I say, holding out the gift-wrapped box. He glances at it without interest and waves it away with one skeletal hand, like someone brushing off a fly. Then, peering at me with his faded eyes, he says, "Oh, it's you, is it? Why didn't anyone tell me? Rowena, the best present you could bring me would be a cyanide pill." But his voice is more robust now, and he hitches himself higher on the pillows. "Well, sit down," he adds, "you make the place untidy."

"I just dropped in to wish you a merry Christmas," I say, pulling a chair nearer the bed.

"If you're referring to the birth of Christ, that may be a cause for celebration, though in my opinion it's a highly debatable point. But if you mean this annual orgy of overspending and overeating we call Christmas, I say bah, humbug, and bugger it."

"I can tell you're enjoying yourself from the language," remarks Max, who has soundlessly reappeared. He has a tin of beer and two glasses expertly gripped in one hand, and a bottle in the other. With neatness and speed he pours whiskies for us and pops open the beer for himself. "Cheers," he says. "The furnace is okay."

Sebastian bends his long face over his drink in a prayerful attitude before taking a noisy sup of it. "I could have told you that," he says. "Nothing wrong with it at all."

"Just checking," Max says easily.

"Well, have you learned anything of significance at Queen's this term?" he asks, staring at his descendant critically. "If so, let's hear what it was."

"Sure. I'm definitely getting better at the essays. Not the contents – I mean getting them in on time. Only one was late this month – like penalty-time late. Of course I had to sit up two nights in a row on bennies and coffee to do it, but what the heck." He smiles at us with such charm that even Sebastian's pessimistic face softens a little.

"Universities only postpone learning," he remarks. "As witness that ingenuous confession. What is it you're studying – we used to call it reading, which denotes a more adult activity – but it's some pseudo-science like Sociology or Astrology, isn't it?"

"Political science, Seb."

"You mean P.P.E. – Politics, Philosophy, Economics. I went to a civilized institution where things were called by their proper names."

"Queen's is connected to Glasgow, which makes it half civilized," Max counters mildly. "And did you know, Seb, that some universities in the U.K. offer a package called Canadian Studies these days? Makes you think, doesn't it?"

The old man blows out a snort so powerful he has to push his upper plate back where it belongs. But Max is on his feet.

"Sorry, folks, but I've got to rush off," he says, swigging off the last of his beer.

"You only just got here," Sebastian says, frowning.

"Well, you know. Partying. 'Tis the season and all that." Without self-consciousness he bends down and kisses his grandfather's cheek. Sebastian's thin hand briefly touches the boy's fair hair. "Decent of you to come over," he says. "Now don't get drunk and puke all over your host's place tonight. Try to be a gentleman about it."

"I'll give it a shot," he says cheerfully. We hear him thump two at a time down the stairs. After a brief pause the front door bangs shut behind him.

"That is a very nice boy," I say. "Why did you needle him so, you wicked old man?"

"Because he's young and I'm old, of course. Give me another shot of this. No, he could be worse, that lad. Never been in trouble with the police – so far, at least – and that's about the best you can hope for at that age. Now don't think of going just because he's gone. You're quite safe with me. Unfortunately. Once upon a time you wouldn't have been – but that was long ago. Neutered as an old tom now. That's something you females can never know . . . Once the balls are gone, the whole things's gone – all might, majesty, dominion and power, which is prayer book for virility – all of it gone, and you're left helpless in the hands of the women."

"Well, maybe there are worse fates than that," I say defensively; but halfway through I think of Mrs. Blot, and my voice lacks conviction.

"I doubt it," he says, as if he has thought of her, too.

"You'll be at Pam's for Christmas Day, I suppose."

"Yes. The goose will give me indigestion. So will she. Widow, aren't you? What family have you got? Lots of children? The trick is to have none at all, or dozens, on the off chance that one of them might turn out to be congenial."

"I have one daughter," I say, and leave him to infer whatever he chooses from that.

"It was nice of you to drop in," he says. "Just sweeten this a trifle, will you? And where's this present, then? I'll open it now."

I hand him the parcel and he tears off the wrappings, which drift to the floor to join the *Times*, a pocket chess set and several books. "Ah," he says approvingly. "I was afraid it might be a tie. What an excellent woman you are."

"I thought you might like to keep it up here . . . for convenience."

He gives me a keen look. "Not only excellent but perceptive and intelligent to a high degree. Ah, how you do light up when you smile, Rowena. You should do it more often."

"I'm getting . . . a bit more practice now," I say carefully.

"Like that, was it? Well, enjoy yourself while you can. It all goes soon enough."

"You must have had plenty of good times in your life, Seb. Is it good to remember them, or not?"

"They're gone, aren't they?"

"Yes, but still –"

"No, remembering is a mug's game, unless you enjoy irony. Here I am, a crippled old husk, breathing polluted air, drinking poisoned water (when I can't get this stuff) and existing in a world where there is actually a government that puts its own citizens in front of a firing squad and then bills the family for the bullets. A chamber of horrors, this planet, and it seems to get worse all the time. But tell me this, Rowena –" and he reaches out a bony hand to grip my wrist "– tell me this; with so much corruption and misery everywhere in this rotten world, why are there moments like this when I want so much to stay in it?"

Cuthbert arrives while I am setting out red candlesticks on the white damask tablecloth embroidered by Nana long ago, and used only on festive occasions like Christmas Day.

"You don't mind me coming a bit early," he says, slipping his arms around me. "I was hoping, in fact, we might have a little time to ourselves before Marion comes . . . a little time for . . ." The rest of his sentence trails away as he nuzzles my neck and draws my ear lobe between his lips.

"Dear, I've still got far too much to do – look at this table not set yet – why don't you give me a hand? The silver's in that chest and the –"

"Busy, busy," he mutters. "Give me a kiss."

"Cuthbert, there just isn't time. Now do –"

"Well, I was saving this for later, but why don't you open it now?" And he pushes a small box into my hand. It bears the logo of a famous jeweller, and my heart sinks. His round face is bright with anticipation. "Oh, Cuthbert, what have you done? You know I can't –"

"Go ahead. Open it."

When I shake my head he catches up my free hand and with his fingers over mine pries up the lid of the box. A diamond ring in a pretty setting winks up at me wickedly.

"It took me ages to choose," he says, looking at it with pride.

"But dear, I've told you a hundred times why we can't do this."

"Put it on, Rowena. I want to see it on your hand."

To placate him, I slip it on my right hand. It is much too big, and with relief I put it back into its case. "They can make it fit, you know, dear," he says anxiously. "Don't you like it? I thought it would be the perfect Christmas present." All his happy exuberance faded, he draws away from me with a rather petulant frown.

"Cuthbert, it was a sweet thought, but surely you see –"

"It's too soon, is that it?" he asks, eyes anxious behind the thick glasses. "Too soon after – But I thought –"

"Well, that's part of it," I say hurriedly. "But not all. There's no time to go into all this – Marion will be here any minute. But you do see I need more time . . . As you know, it's not been three months since Edwin –"

As I say this, a sense of unreality overtakes me. Is it possible that all this can have happened in the eleven weeks since that day in the cemetery? "You seduced him," murmurs Prince Charles.

"Everything has consequences," Clive used to say. "You should smile more often," is Sebastian's advice, and I recognize it as wisdom, though three months ago I didn't know he existed. So many truths make me feel besieged. As for this affair with Cuthbert, I've never had much taste for farce, but here I am, living in one of my own making. And at that moment I hear Marion stamping snow off her boots outside the front door. My scalp tightens in the beginning of one of my tension headaches.

"Cuthbert, dear, I'm going to put this away upstairs," I tell him, hastily dropping the small box into my apron pocket. "Remember, now; not a word. We'll talk about it all later." I am halfway up the stairs, my heart drumming, by the time Marion steps inside with a neat plastic carrier full of parcels.

"I thought I'd come early and give you a hand with dinner, Mother."

"Lovely, dear. Merry Christmas. I'll be down in a moment." I push the box out of sight in a bureau drawer and go swiftly down again to forestall any confidences Cuthbert may be tempted to make. When I join them in the dining-room, he is unwrapping his set of CDs and trying to keep a faint, self-pitying reproach out of the glance he throws me. "How nice," he says. "Thank you both very much."

He embraces me and then gives Marion a peck on the cheek. This appears to surprise but not displease her. She is wearing the blue knitted dress I've made for her. As I hoped, it fits well and the colour sets off her pale complexion becomingly. It pleases me that she is wearing it. I give Cuthbert's arm a furtive squeeze, and he brightens a little. Marion's present to me is a huge bottle of herbal shampoo and a year's supply of panty hose, all of the same colour and exactly the right size. "Thank you, dear," I say hurriedly, hoping she will not notice that Cuthbert has apparently brought me nothing. "Just what I wanted. Now then, you two, let's get to work. The turkey will be done before we get this table ready."

An hour later the ravaged turkey has been removed and we sit in paper hats over plates on which only a scrape of plum pudding remains. To my relief the meal has gone off smoothly, with no reference to delicate subjects like formal or informal engagements. Cuthbert has not been as chatty as usual, but he now pours the last of the wine into his own and Marion's glasses, saying with determined good cheer that it might as well be polished off. Just then the front doorbell rings. My heart gives an apprehensive jump. Please, no, I ask the Almighty silently; but when I open the door, there is Tom in his cassock, carrying a big poinsettia. The night is frosty, with a large, bright moon, and his cheeks are red as apples.

"Merry Christmas, Tom," I say, forcing cordiality into my voice. Once in the hall, he gives me a kiss on the mouth, which Marion joins us just in time to witness. Cuthbert, putting his head round the dining-room door, looks rather glumly at the newcomer. My headache quietly begins to intensify.

"Come along," I tell them all, "we'll just leave everything and sit down in here with our coffee. Will you have brandy with it, anybody? I think I will."

"Certainly," says Tom, rubbing his hands together. "Glorious feast though it is, Christmas is pretty exhausting for the clergy when it falls on a Sunday. It means two services after midnight mass . . . and the worst of it is I have a hard time feeling Christian about these people who turn out in force just twice a year. They pack the place so we have to set up extra chairs and drag communion out for two hours, whereas next week at evensong, I may well be the only soul in the place. Yes, I really could use a little fortification. Thank you, my dear."

"I'll have some, too, please, Rowena," says Cuthbert. I give him a meaningful glance, which he ignores. We both know he has had more than his share of the wine. His face has a slightly swollen, shiny look under the pink paper hat he wears, suggestive of an inebriated baby.

"And what news is there, my dear, of that area commissioner appointment?" Tom asks Marion. He notes the new dress and allows his eyes to travel over it in a way that makes her edge her knees together and touch the high neckline defensively. "Sugar for your coffee, anyone?" I ask. Nobody answers me. "No news yet," says Marion. Tom's eyes are lingering on her legs.

"Your coffee, Tom," I say a little sharply.

"Ah, thank you, Rowena."

"Sit here beside me," Cuthbert says, catching inaccurately at my hand as I pass the sofa. To avoid argument I sit down, leaving a prudent distance between us.

"The rumour is that Babs Harrington will get the job," Marion goes on. "Well, if blue eyes and a big smile is what they want, of course –"

Wittgenstein here strolls in, waving his tail in a lordly fashion. Marion frowns at him. "Does that cat *live* here now?" she demands.

"Well, yes, he does," I admit.

"Honestly, Mother. You know he's probably full of fleas – come spring you'll find your whole house infested."

A somewhat uncomfortable silence follows while I control myself. Then Cuthbert leans forward, raising his glass. "Well, everybody," he says, "I'd like to propose a toast. To our wonderful hostess. And while I'm at it, I'd like to make an –"

"Cuthbert," I cut in desperately, "would you please check in the kitchen for me – I think I've left the oven on." Catching my eye, he goes obediently. My headache is steadily increasing.

"What's this you're reading, then, Rowena?" Tom asks, picking up my library copy of *Herself Surprised*. "A novel, eh? Don't know how you can be bothered. Fiction is so frivolous . . . I mean anybody can write the stuff."

"You think there's no art or skill involved?" I ask, nettled on Ethel's behalf.

"Nothing to it. Same romantic formula every time."

"But the trick is to make it seem new, Tom. If it's so easy, why don't you give us an outline for a novel in two or three sentences – one we'd all like to read."

Tom hitches up his gown and throws one leg across the other in a businesslike fashion. "Once upon a time," he says rapidly, "there was a plain girl with glasses. Her boss whips off the glasses one day and discovers she is a raving beauty; they get married and live boringly ever after. You see – anyone can do it."

Cuthbert gives an impolite kind of snort. He has come back from the kitchen looking disgruntled, having of course found the oven off. "That's hackneyed junk," he says. "It's real life that has the best plots. How about this: a pretty girl marries a man who loves her, and they have a baby. Then he leaves her and for extra kicks claims half of the condo and the furniture she paid for out of a legacy. They are now going to court and she is living miserably ever after."

"Elaine," I say.

"Yes, poor kid. Broke down and cried in the office the other day. I had to send her home in a cab. It was her kid's second birthday."

"Well, you never know. There may be a happy ending in there yet. After all, she's only –"

"No, Tom's right," says Marion. "Fiction is nothing but lies. Cinderella stories for people who want to dance with the Prince. In fact, the good old fairy godmother never shows up, and Cinderella is washing dishes to this day. And speaking of dishes, Mother, we'd better get at that mess out there, or you'll be at the sink dealing with it all day tomorrow." She gets up with decision and marches out to the kitchen, leaving behind, as she so often does, an unspoken rebuke in the air. Damn you, Miss Watson, I think crossly. Because of you, to this day all Marion's white horses are rats. The two men, perhaps conscious how far short they come of princeliness, look silently depressed. Cuthbert studies his fingernails gloomily. I sigh.

"And where's your capsule novel, my dear?" Tom asks me, putting down his empty glass with reluctance.

"Oh, I could never in the world write a novel. Not when life's so complicated." My head throbs. I think of Sebastian next door with his indigestion, and wonder whether he will be as glad as I will when this season of peace and goodwill is over.

CHAPTER EIGHT

❧

"Cuthbert?"

"Yes. Who's this?"

"It's Rowena. Just thought I'd call to wish you a Happy New Year, and also –"

"Nice of you. The same to –"

"We haven't talked since Christmas, and we need to."

"Well, things at the office have been –"

"I think we should – I don't want bad feelings between us, dear. Have you got time now for a bit of a talk? I mean there's unfinished business, isn't there . . . That evening was a bit of a disaster, so we really should –"

"Yes, it was."

"Cuthbert, about that ring –"

"Yes."

"I've tried before to explain why it just isn't a good idea, but obviously I haven't done it very well. The thing is we need a civilized, friendly discussion with no sex in it. That's what telephones are for, after all."

"Is it?"

"I'm so fond of you – I want you to understand that – and it's not that I don't appreciate –"

"Well, Rowena, I just don't understand how you can accept me in one way – you know what I mean – and still refuse the ring. Talk about plots in fiction – it's almost like that old chestnut about the heartless lover and the poor girl who trusts him to marry her, only here I'm the maiden, and you can't expect me to like that, can you?"

"No, but Cuthbert –"

"I am simply trying to do the decent thing."

"So am I, my dear, if only you knew it."

"I do realize it's rather soon after Edwin's – but still."

"Yes. Well, that's part of it, but –"

"Well, I know I'm no great prize, of course, but –"

"Now stop that, Cuthbert. You'll be a wonderful husband – to somebody younger – some day. But in the meantime, I think we'd better just be friends. It's been lovely, but we don't want complications, do we?" Before he can answer this, I go on. "You'll understand, I know."

He gives a frustrated sigh. "And it would be best from now on," I continue bravely, "if I manage on my own, financially. As for that ring – it must be worth a lot of money. I think you ought to have it in safekeeping somewhere."

"You want me to take it back, then."

"I'm not happy about this either, you know."

"Oh, Rowena, I can tell you're not. I've been miserable, too, my back's been sore ever since Christmas Day, it's completely psychosomatic."

"Cuthbert dear, try a deep, hot bath."

"I've missed you so."

"Me, too, but –"

"Why don't I come over there right now?"

"Oh, my dear, I don't think that would be a good idea at all. I'm trying to be fair to you. And to myself, come to that."

"But at least you'll keep the ring and think about it. Say you will."

"Well, I'll lock it up in my desk drawer. How's that? Till later – much later. Then maybe we can talk about it. All right?"

He sighs heavily. "If you say so."

On my next morning off, after shopping, I turn up McKenzie Street instead of going straight home with my groceries. Allowing myself no time to think about the consequences, I march up Sebastian's front path and ring the bell.

After an interval, the squat form of Mrs. Blot appears. Her black eyes inspect me with no recognition and even less cordiality.

"Good afternoon, Mrs. – Mrs. Blovantasakis."

"What you want?" she asks with suspicion. Still, her manner is just a shade less truculent than it used to be. Perhaps my struggle to come up with her right name has softened her. It even occurs to me to wonder whether this time she is a little afraid of me. Preposterous to imagine anybody could find me, of all people, intimidating; but it crosses my mind she might possibly be one of Toronto's thousands of illegal immigrants who live with fear. Her thick mouth and heavy chin are as hostile as ever; but for whatever reason she looks tired and there is a stain of darkness around her pouched eyes.

"I was just passing by and I'd like to say hello to Mr. Long, if I could. Of course you remember me – I'm a friend of Mrs. Wright's."

"He sick. He sleeping." And she begins to close the door.

"Oh. I see. Well, will you please tell him that Mrs. Hill called."

"Miss Hell. Okay."

"Or tell him Rowena."

"Ravenna."

"Oh, never mind. Thanks anyway. I'll phone him."

But when I do that, a few hours later, the results are even more frustrating. "Hello, Sebastian," I say. "How are you?"

"Eh? Who's that?"

"It's Rowena."

"Who?"

"Rowena."

"I can't hear. Bloody telephones."

"It's Rowena, Seb. Mrs. Blot says you're sick. Are you?"

"Well, you can't speak to her. Call her lawyer. It's none of my affair. What's her private life got to do with me, or, come to that, with you, Rowena?"

"I don't want to speak to Mrs. Blot, Seb! I'm calling to ask how you are."

"Then why the devil did you ask for her? I'm bloody awful, thanks. But that's nothing new."

"Have you had the flu or something?"

"Of course not."

"Oh. Well, I'd like to see you some time when you feel up to a visitor."

"Don't bother coming to see me out of pity."

"Next week, maybe. Say Monday? I'll call first. All right?"

There is a silence conveying irritability, then he says, "Can't hear a damn word," and hangs up. This conversation – if that is the right term for it – leaves me feeling depressed. When the phone rings a minute or two later, I snatch it up, hoping Sebastian might be calling back in a better frame of mind. Instead a familiar, incisive voice says, "Mother."

"Hello, dear."

"Have you paid the property tax bill this month?"

"Um – well – that's that long bill, is it, that folds in three? It isn't due for a couple of weeks yet."

"Well, will you check it?"

"All right. Hold on." I fumble among the papers on my desk and unearth the bill. "Yes, here it is. February first is when it's due."

"And how much is it?"

"Four hundred and seven dollars."

"Of course you haven't got enough to meet it."

"Well, no. I meant to talk to you about it tonight, actually. Because I agree with you that Cuthbert shouldn't –"

"Well, I've said all along it's not right for him to be giving you money. If necessary I can borrow from the bank. As it is, I can manage this tax thing. Be sure you put it in a safe place; I'll pick it up next time I'm over there."

"Thanks, dear. Sorry it has to fall on you."

"Somebody has to pay it. And Cuthbert certainly shouldn't –"

I am not eager to discuss this topic any further. "Well, how are things with you?" I ask, trying to sound cheerful. "Any news about that commissioner's job?"

"Oh, Harrington got it, of course."

"Oh, dear. I am sorry."

"I wonder when, if ever, Cuthbert is going to get your case moving, Mother. I didn't like to mention it on Christmas Day, but the whole thing could drag on forever, if someone doesn't get after him. Meanwhile how are you managing for daily expenses?"

"Well, as you know, I'm still working at Dream Pies –"

"Yes, Mother. What I mean is, your standard of living seems to have gone up lately, just when it should be doing nothing of the kind. All that wine at dinner, for instance – Dad never –"

"Cuthbert brought that. And it was Christmas, after all."

"And I saw a new nightgown on the back of the bathroom door – slipper satin, no less – where on earth did that come from?

Don't tell me Cuthbert gave you that, too. No, there's no doubt about it, since Dad went, you've been not just disorganized and vague – that I can understand – delayed shock does that kind of thing – but extravagance is something else again, and I must say it worries me. Even little things like the quince jelly from England you had on the table instead of cranberry sauce made at home . . . And the mohair wool it took to make that dress for me – I just wish you'd think, Mother, before you spend money on expensive things like that."

No answer to this occurs to me. I could not have made one in any case, because my voice will not work. She is perfectly right. I am not managing well. In fact, I'm not managing at all. By the time she rings off, tears are rolling down and dropping in wet blots on the property tax bill.

To make up for a brief mild spell, winter returns the next Sunday with a vengeance. Daggers of ice hang from the gutterspouts, and a fresh snowfall swaddles our front yard evergreen in white. While he was home on holiday, young Max kept the Wrights' front path cleared, and mine as well; but now as I peer through the frosted parlour window I can see Pam out there digging. Her lips are moving, and it is not hard to imagine that she is telling God her opinion of snow. I hurry to bundle up, seize a shovel and join her.

"Morning, Pam."

"Morning. Filthy stuff, isn't it?" She kicks a clot of snow fretfully. "And it would choose to come down just when John's away. Bless him, he believes women should never shovel snow – he thinks it damages our delicate insides, and I've done my best all these years to keep him fast to that opinion."

"Not sure he's wrong," I say, puffing. "Incredible, how heavy it is."

"I am just making a tiny channel here for the postman and anybody who wants to come in for drinks. John will be home in a day or two – he had to rush off to Hamilton – poor old Ma had a heart attack, and they thought she might be going to pop off; but no, tiresomely enough, she didn't. I do feel that at ninety-plus she's had her fair share of everything, good and bad, and she must find survival a frightful anticlimax, but there it is."

"Tell me, how's Sebastian?"

"Oh, not in good shape. He had a fall in the bathroom the other day – didn't break anything, the quack says – but it shook him up rather badly and he's all over bruises, which does nothing for his disposition, as you can well imagine. Thank God Mrs. Blot can stay with him nights now, because it's obvious he can't be left alone any more."

"Hasn't she got a family of her own?"

"Oh, yes, tons of relatives, but her husband's turned rather moody lately and started beating her up, so she's getting a divorce, and till all that gets sorted out, which may take years, she doesn't mind living in. Why should she, after all? I've fixed up a nice room for her down the hall from his, with a TV to herself (he never watches), and she can rule the roost over there and keep an eye on him while at the same time keeping out of the husband's clutches. Perfect arrangement all round."

"I suppose it is," I say, trying to sound convinced.

"You know, before we found Mrs. B., he had a housekeeper who seemed to be the absolute in ladylike refinement and all that, and it was over a year before we realized that she was drunk just about ninety per cent of the time. We might never have known, but she set fire to herself one day with a cigarette. And after that we had a sweet, chuckly old dear, all smiles and affability, and she walked out one day with all the silver. So you see Mrs. B. is not without her good points. Do let's stop this now, while our insides are still in place. Come in and have some coffee."

I plunge my shovel into the heaped snow on the lawn and follow her inside.

"Do you loathe instant, I hope not, but I have to help at the shop in an hour. We're having a big sale tomorrow." She fills the kettle with a gush, and the kitten, now much larger and possessing a lush, plumed tail, turns its head to frown at the noise.

"Instant is fine. Liking your job, are you? Does it pay well?"

"No, but the commissions are nice."

"I wonder whether I could do that kind of thing."

"Well, it's better than being stuck at home with afternoon TV. It can be quite amusing, in fact, persuading tall, skinny ladies not to wear skinny clothes, and keeping the fat ones out of frills. Actually you'd be quite good at it, so gentle and tactful." She eyes me briefly and adds, "Of course, you'd have to invest in a few outfits yourself before . . . They do expect you to be with it clotheswise yourself. Anyhow, you're still with Steve's pie shop, aren't you? Are you still hard up? Don't mind me asking, will you, it's curiosity of course, but friendly." With a disarming smile she hands me a mug and pushes towards me a carton of cream.

"I doubt if I'd ever have the gumption to sell anybody anything," I say, evading the question. "Don't you often have to tell someone they look great in a dress just because you want to sell it?"

"Well, but if they *think* they look great, everybody's happy, or does that sound too Jesuit? Actually, though, I think telling the absolute truth about almost anything is a great mistake, all it creates is ulcers and hostility, life is tough enough without total honesty to complicate things, don't you feel?"

"Yes, I do," I say, trying not to grin. Pam swings her long leg over the stool next to mine. She smells richly of Shalimar, and her black stretch trousers and red jersey make her look young and zestful. I glance down sadly at my old beige skirt and repress a sigh.

"Forgive me for mentioning it, Rowena," she says, looking at me with candour, "but I can't help noticing that you have company quite often lately, which is surely a good thing, so deadly to be alone all the time, and the other day I heard a bit of a crash next door and then something that sounded like laughing, though sometimes this aid thing makes odd noises of its own. Anyhow I say splendid, if we couldn't laugh we'd all simply sink into the ground with misery, if not our own then other people's, look at Ethiopia – come to that, look at my wretched parent, he hasn't laughed once since 1952, it's too dismal. Anyhow do tell me what was so funny."

"Well, recently everybody's been trying to frighten me with talk about rapes and muggings, which is pointless, really, because I was born scared to begin with. Well, a friend – he used to wrestle at college – offered to teach me a way of throwing an attacker to the ground. He's not young, but very robust . . ." Here a vivid mental picture of Tom demonstrating a hold presents itself. "And as he was showing me how it worked, we lost our balance and fell down with a crash, and we laughed so much we literally couldn't get up." And here an even more vivid picture intervenes of what ensued before we did get up. Glancing at Pam I find her face wreathed in a broad grin. Hastily I put down my coffee mug and slip off the stool.

"I mustn't keep you, Pam. But about Sebastian – you don't mind if I drop over there to see him occasionally?"

"Of course not. Only too grateful."

"I'm afraid Mrs. Blot doesn't like my visits. That's putting it mildly, in fact."

"I'll have a word with her about it. She can be a bit of a toad, and that's a fact; I guess she's come to think of the place as her territory. Anyhow, pay no attention; go over whenever you like. I think her day off is Thursday, in case that's relevant. Myself, I quite enjoy a round or two with her."

"What courage you've got. Anyhow, I still have the key you gave me before."

"God knows," she adds, "it would do Seb the world of good if you would teach *him* a wrestling hold or two, if only for laughs. Sometimes lately I get the feeling he's letting go – giving up. And in spite of everything, and days when I really think euthanasia would be the best possible solution, I don't want the old monster to die. It's not that I'm fond of him, any more than he is of me, just that for some reason he's important to me, don't ask me why, a case of shingles would be easier to deal with by far, I suppose it's a question of blood."

His head is hanging off the pillow and in the half-light his skin looks grey, the closed eyelids purplish. For a second – long enough for my own breath to suspend itself – I think he is dead. Then I bend closer and see that a thick artery in his neck is pulsing.

"Sebastian," I say loudly.

He releases a faint snore.

"Wake up, Seb," I tell him. Worried by what Pam has told me, I've left work early to come here. It is not yet five in the afternoon, yet the window blind has been lowered and the bedside lamp switched off. I draw up the blind and pallid winter sunlight bursts into the stuffy room. His wrinkled eyelids twitch.

"Sebastian, wake up."

Blinking, he looks up at me without recognition; then his eyes sink shut again. I go down the hall and bring back a washcloth wrung out in cold water. With this I ruthlessly wash his face, which is thickly bristled with silver beard.

"What the hell do you think you're doing?" he mumbles, weakly trying to push away my hand.

"I am waking you up. This is no time to be sleeping, Seb; you'll lie awake all night this way. Now come on, let's get you sitting up. Then we're going to have some tea."

"Don't want bloody tea."

"Well, I do." Down the hall in her room, Mrs. Blot is occupied with several guests of her own. They are so immersed in loud – even violent – conversation that nobody has noticed my diffident rap at the front door. So letting myself in with Pam's key has been a quiet success, and being here without opposition – in secret, almost – gives me confidence. "Back in a tick," I tell Sebastian, after heaving him into a sitting position and propping him there with pillows. "Don't you go back to sleep now." Down the stairs I go and in the deserted kitchen swiftly brew a strong pot of tea, which I take up to him.

"Now then, have some of this." I hold out a cup from which steam curls comfortably.

"Don't want it," he says thickly. His breath is foul.

I clear room for the cup on his bedside table, which is crowded with various pharmaceuticals, including a plastic cylinder with a child-proof top. It contains a number of yellow capsules.

"What are these for, Seb?" I ask him. "Have you had some of these today? Look at them."

He glances at the container vaguely. "No idea."

"Are you sure? Why is there no label on the bottle?"

"Never touch drugs, stupid things. Nothing wrong with me but a little heart murmur. Silly quack with his whatdyecallit – listener thing. That bastard has grabbed Poland, man, we're at war. I'm perfectly fit, my place is over there, don't wag your silly head at me, it's my duty." He blinks at me and the room around him as if completely disoriented.

"Where's bloody Pam, then?" he demands. "What hospital is this?"

"You're home, Seb. And Pam will be round to see you, probably tomorrow."

"Never said I wanted her here."

"She'll come anyway."

"No doubt."

"Well, tell me how you're feeling. Still a bit sore from that fall, are you?"

"What fall? I don't know what the hell you're talking about. I'm thirsty."

I steady his trembling hands around the cup with both of mine. The dragged-up pyjama sleeve exposes a large green bruise near the elbow. He sups at the tea greedily.

"There. That's better, isn't it?"

He shoots me an irascible glance. "Oh, stuff it, Nurse Bloody Rowena. What the hell is all that din out there?"

"Mrs. Blot seems to have company."

"Ah, yes. Her daughters. They're trying to get the poor bitch to go back to her husband. Lear's offspring, Greek-Canadian variety. Voices like cormorants, they've got, even worse than Lowland Scots. Close the door, will you."

"I thought about you on Christmas Day," I tell him, pulling up a chair.

"Did you?" he says with interest. "I want more tea. Why did you do that?"

"Call it empathy."

"I didn't think about you," he says. "Women are much better at that kind of thing than men. Whatever that proves. Did you not have a jolly yuletide full of merriment, then?"

"No, I did not."

"Join the club. John gave me a tie and Pam a heating pad, no doubt fondly hoping I might electrocute myself with it. The only decent present I got, in fact, was from you, Rowena, and I drank that."

"Good."

There is an easy silence that distances the raucous argument down the hall. Sebastian munches a ginger biscuit, showering his bony chest liberally with crumbs. A sparrow lights on the windowsill and peers in at us with its bright bead of an eye. "Before I go, I'll put out some crumbs there for him," I say. "Birds are nice to look at."

"Better at a distance, like most things. I remember as a small boy seeing a city all lit up at night – must have been Manchester – it looked like something magical out of Revelation; and when we got into the place, all there was to see were grotty streets and fish-and-chip shops. My first lesson in perspective."

"Or maybe anatomy. We had to dissect a frog in high school biology class. I felt a bit sick, but fascinated, because the thing was so much more complicated and interesting inside than it was outside."

"Was it? So are most people, I suppose – at least one hopes so. Let's have a drink, Rowena."

"What has Wittgenstein got to say about outsides and insides?" I ask, to divert him.

"Not a lot. On the other hand he did ask poignantly why philosophy is so complicated, when it should be perfectly simple. He concluded that the problem was not philosophy but our screwed-up thinking. In other words, if we could just think straight, all our confusion would disappear and truth would disclose itself."

"And if it did that, would we all be serene and happy?"

"That he never said. But something of the kind may be implied in *Philosophical Investigations*, the work of his old age." He reaches down a long arm and, wincing, draws up a shabby book from the pile by his bed. "Here, for instance, he says, 'What we are supplying are really remarks on the natural history of human beings.' He was interested, y'see, in abstract ideas only as they relate to our lives – what we do, and in particular what we say."

"Does he ever mention why some people so often say the wrong thing? Seems to me that's not so much because of confused thinking as plain ill will and bad temper. And yet I like Ethel Wilson's muddled sort of philosophy . . . it suits our muddled existence. She says she believes in God, 'and in man, to some extent.' The comma is perfect, isn't it? I'll bring you one of her books next time; I think you'd like them."

"Curious thing, you know, about Wittgenstein – it's always surprised me in anyone so disillusioned – but he's on record as having said he wished his last book could do what Bach tried for – 'to honour the most high God and to benefit my neighbour.'"

"What an aim. Covers everything."

"I want a whisky, Rowena; how about it?"

"I don't think so today, Seb."

"Why not? You turned Moslem or something?"

"No, just that I have to go now. Next time, maybe."

"I'm allowed two drinks, you know, before dinner."

"I'll come Thursday, Seb, and then I promise we'll have a whisky together."

"That's Mrs. B.'s afternoon off."

"I know." Our eyes meet. One of his closes in a wink. Before I go, I heave open the window and scatter some crumbs for the bird. Then, when Sebastian's attention is elsewhere, I slip the container of yellow capsules into my pocket. My quiet departure occurs without any interference or even sign of interest on the part of Mrs. Blot, which is a relief, because I am now not only afraid of her but to some degree afraid of myself.

"Mother."

"Yes, Marion. Something wrong?"

"Have you got any painkiller in the house?"

Painkiller, I think, Sebastian's sleeping face flashing into my mind. There are such things, but are they always a good idea?

"Yes, I think so, dear. Why do you need –?"

"I had a couple of impacted wisdoms out this morning. The dentist gave me something to take, but it's no use at all."

"Well, I think we have some 292s left over from that time your Dad sprained his knee. You just sit tight, dear, and I'll come right over with them. Lucky thing I'm free – the shop's closed because Arlene's mother died."

But Marion is not at all interested in the shop or in Arlene's mother. "Right. Thanks," she says curtly and rings off.

I hurry to ransack the medicine cabinet and pull on my outdoor things. Tom is due to pay his regular weekly call later on, but he (or, come to that, both of us) will just have to do without this time. Marion so seldom asks for help – or for anything – that her call has put me into a fluster. Halfway down the front path I have to hurry back for the tube of pills, and at the bus stop I discover I've snatched up a pair of mismatched gloves.

A ten-minute bus ride brings me to Marion's apartment building, a yellow-brick, art deco structure built around a courtyard that in summer is made hideous by stiff beds of salvia. It looks much better now, heaped knee-deep with fresh snow the wind has moulded to porcelain smoothness. Marion is pacing the floor from front to back of her small space. One of her tight braids has pulled a little loose from its coil. In a controlled sort of way, she looks frantic.

"Here you are, dear. I think one, to begin with. How long ago did you take the other stuff?"

"Oh, I don't know – don't fuss, Ma – just give it to me."

She pauses in her pacing just long enough to gulp down the pill with water I bring her from the bathroom.

"I wish I'd known you were having those teeth out, dear, so I could have arranged to be here when you got home. It's no time to be alone, after a business like that. Would a cup of tea help at all?"

"Oh, don't fuss." She sits down briefly, but a moment later jumps up to pace the floor again.

"Was it one of those clinics they sent you to?" I ask, fidgeting sympathetically after her. She doesn't answer, yet I hover near helplessly. It seems impossible just to sit down and get on with my knitting. "Those places . . . Cuthbert once had a bad time after an extraction . . . It's like an assembly line; they work too fast."

"Oh, it hurts, it hurts," Marion says in a thin voice that seems to belong to someone else. She walks rapidly into and out of the bathroom, holding both hands to her face.

"Poor lamb. Look, let's try an ice pack, it won't take a minute." Clumsy with haste, I crack ice cubes out of their tray and roll them in a clean dish towel. "Now hold this under your jaw, dear. It's sure to help."

Without breaking stride she takes the ice pack from me and continues pacing. For something to do, I go back to the kitchen and put the kettle on. A red geranium on the windowsill makes a little splash of colour in the dull room, but on closer inspection it turns out to be plastic. Everything on the counters and in the cupboards is almost clinically neat and spotless, but when it comes to detail, Marion's taste runs oddly to cuteness. Her pot holders are shaped like pansies, and on the wall hangs a pink linen calendar depicting little Kate Greenaway girls watering flowers, skipping rope and dancing in a ring. When the tea is made I take the pot into the other room where poor Marion is still walking rapidly up and down. She waves away the tea, but I sit down and drink mine gratefully.

"No better at all?" I ask.

"No."

"Well, if you get no relief soon, we'll have to call your dentist."

By the time my cup is empty she is pacing more slowly, but there is still a frightened look in her eyes that touches my heart. I have not seen Marion afraid since she was five and in a high fever cried out, "I'm growing! I'm growing!" It was one of the rare occasions when I felt really close to her; the bizarre size changes of *Alice in Wonderland* had frightened me as a child, too. And yet, the thought of growing shouldn't scare anyone. It doesn't scare Mrs. Wilson.

"Now that pill is starting to help, isn't it, dear? Why don't you sit down."

Mumbling, "Sorry about the fuss," she drops to the sofa where she puts her head back and closes her eyes. I take the ice pack from her gently and renew it in the kitchen.

"There you are. I'm so glad it's a bit easier."

"Bernice said she'd come over, but she hasn't bothered."

"Well, I suppose like me she finds it hard to get away in the afternoon."

"Maybe."

"What's her job again – something in a lab, isn't it?"

"She's a qualified pharmacist now."

"Oh, really? I wonder if – I came across some pills the other day – she could probably tell me what they are."

"Bernice? She can't tell her ass from her elbow these days."

My eyebrows rise high. Marion does not normally use this kind of vocabulary – at least not in my hearing. I glance at her uneasily.

"What's her problem, then?"

Eyes still closed, Marion says incisively, "She's met a man, that's her problem. A divorced man with a Volvo and a pot belly. And she's over the moon because he's taken her out a couple of times to a Thai restaurant, and sent her a fuchsia for Christmas."

"Oh, really. Well, I suppose that's nice for her."

"Is it? Embarrassing, if you ask me, to see a woman make such a jackass of herself. She can't talk about anything else. We were going skiing last weekend, but she wouldn't go in case he called. Silly ass." Here, to the dismay of both of us, her voice shakes. Angrily she roots in a pocket and blows her nose into a tissue.

"Sure you wouldn't like some tea, dear?"

I hang over the sofa, longing to touch her, but not daring to. There are one or two white threads in her dark hair I've not seen before.

"No, don't bother," she says curtly.

"Well, why don't you stretch out here and have a little doze. Maybe that —"

The door buzzer sounds, and when I answer it, Bernice herself stands revealed – a small, sallow, youngish woman in a coat horridly befurred in fluffy blue at neck, wrist and hem. With her receding chin and large, anxious eyes, she looks rather like a goldfish. I have no trouble at all understanding why the attentions of the Volvo man dazzle her.

"How are you, Mrs. Hill?" She has a way of speaking on an indrawn breath, so everything she says has an air of uncertainty and diffidence. "You okay, Marion?" she murmurs. "I brought you over some codeine."

"Thanks. You're a bit late," says Marion, without opening her eyes.

"Well, I'll stick around for a bit, if you like."

"Suit yourself."

"I might as well get along home, then," I say brightly into the ensuing silence. "Before the rush hour starts. You'll be all right now, dear. The rest of those pills are in the bathroom, if you need them."

As I pull on my coat, something rattles in the pocket. It is the bottle of capsules from Sebastian's room. I take it over to Bernice who is flipping through the latest *Maclean's* while Marion appears to doze. "Can you tell me what these are, by any chance? There's no label, as you see."

She breaks open one of the capsules and first sniffs, then tastes the powder inside. Then she says in her half-audible voice, "Nembutal. Sleeping pills. Sometimes pharmacists just slip the label inside. Bad idea; they get lost."

"Yes, I see. Thanks."

That evening as I sit knitting and turning over recent events in my mind, Prince Charles drops in – something he has not done for some time. He lounges in the big chair, legs stretched out, looking (for him) almost relaxed.

"Haven't seen much of Your Highness recently," I remark.

"Well, three's a crowd, isn't it?"

"I suppose so," I admit placidly.

"One way and another, your time is pretty fully occupied these days. True, you only have one gentleman caller these days, but twice a week is going it, rather, with the Rev. Of course, with Cuthbert –"

"Let's change the subject, Sir. I could use some advice, now you're here."

"Whatever about, if not this odd entanglement?"

"About Sebastian."

"Ah. Quite another kettle of fish, then."

"The thing is, I don't know what to do. That is, I do know, but I'm too scared to do it."

"Surely there's no call for you to do anything whatsoever about Sebastian. He's not related to you. You haven't even known him long."

"That doesn't matter. He is related to me, in a way. In that I'm going to be old myself before long, and also in that we like each other a lot."

"Now let's not get too fanciful here," Charles says with some severity. "The man has an attentive daughter, son-in-law and grandson. Come to that, after living in Toronto for fifty-odd years, he must have dozens of friends you've never met. Why on earth do you imagine it's up to you to look after him?"

"I don't know, exactly. I just do imagine it."

"Believe me, you're much better off to keep right out of it."

"You sound just like Edwin."

He frowns. "That's not a friendly remark."

"Well, you could show a bit more sympathy. He's so lonely. And of course that's only one part of what's so sad and grim about his situation now."

"Old age *is* sad and grim, and that's all there is to it."

"But it doesn't have to be humiliating and –"

"Nobody will thank you for interfering, I warn you."

"I don't want to be thanked. I just don't want him victimized by that –"

"Come now, Rowena. Be rational. It's nobody's fault he's laid up, is it? Or that he's a cantankerous old chimp too fond of the bottle?"

"I don't think he'd be either of those things if –"

"Now let me finish. Those capsules you're in such a hoo about. What makes you think Mrs. B. is drugging him? Those pills were probably prescribed by his own doctor. There's no need to drama-tize. A mild sedative to help him sleep, that's all it is."

"Heavily? In the middle of the day?"

"You can't be sure, can you, that wasn't just one of his naps? Of course you can't."

"He was groggy and confused, Charles."

"Is that unusual at his age?"

"It's been worse lately," I say stubbornly.

"And that, too, is unnatural, I suppose."

"God knows I don't want to get involved. And of course it's none of my business. It's just that he's . . . special, somehow."

"Look, if you go over there once in a while to cheer the old boy up, you'll be doing all you can for him. Right? What else can you do, when we get right down to it? Nothing."

"Well —"

"You know I'm right."

"I guess so. Well, I could at least take him over a nip of whisky next time."

"I wouldn't do that, either, if I were you. Alcohol and tranquil-lizers don't mix, you know."

"True."

"That's settled, then."

"I suppose so."

"You know perfectly well I'm giving you good advice."

"Yes, but why did I ask, when I knew beforehand just what you'd say? And also that I'd agree with you?"

"Well, of course people only take advice if it's what they want to hear. If it's right for them, in other words. And that makes per-fectly good sense. For you, in this case, it's right to do nothing."

"I know. That's what depresses me so much."

"Cheer up," he says kindly. "We are what we are. Just have to make the best of it. I ought to know that, if anybody does."

Cuthbert has called to ask, with rather elaborate politeness, if he might come round this evening with more papers for me to sign. I tell him, of course, and firmly resist the impulse to go upstairs

and change or fidget with my hair. Instead I hustle away my
dinner things and sit down to wait for him in the living-room,
after reducing it to a state of severe tidiness. I sit first on the
sofa, then in the armchair. We have not seen each other since
Christmas Day, or spoken about anything personal since our New
Year's conversation. Minutes tick away in the silent house. I get
restlessly to my feet and open the venetian blind to look out at the
empty street. The dark is bejewelled with stars. There is a big
moon with a bite out of it behind the trees. Whatever can be
keeping him? He is never late for anything. Wittgenstein sits in
the window, with the extreme tip of his black tail twitching. With
a start, I move out of sight as Cuthbert's car glides to the curb.
After a pause his small figure emerges, carrying a long florist's
cone and his briefcase.

"Hello, Cuthbert. Come in."

"Hello, Rowena. Here's a bit of spring for you."

Awkwardly he hands over the cone.

"Oh, thanks. How nice."

"They're from Victoria, the man said."

"Really?"

"Yes." He gives me a hopeful, desirous look, and I back away. In
the kitchen I take as much time as possible to fill a vase and
arrange the tulips. In the dining-room I can hear him shuffling his
feet and clearing his throat. Finally with a flop he sets his briefcase
on the table and draws some papers out of it.

"Sorry I'm bothering you this late in the day, Rowena, but I've
been tied up at the office."

"It's no bother, Cuthbert."

"Well, now, if you'll just . . . will you use my pen or would you
rather . . ."

Because I suddenly want one myself, I say, "Can I get you something to drink, Cuthbert? You look a bit tired."

"Actually, I'd appreciate that. Brandy over there, isn't it? Yes, that would be nice."

I pour two smallish drinks and hand him one.

"Thanks. But first if you'll just sign your name here and here, where I've put an X – that's it."

This done, I shepherd him into the sitting-room and we sit down. He looks, I think, not so much tired as deeply preoccupied, or faintly puzzled. We say things about the weather, the news, and our health. Then he gets up and fussily repacks his briefcase. Then he pauses at the front window looking absently out at the moon – or so I think at first. Then I see he is gazing at his own reflection, as if something new about it intrigues him. Eventually he sits down again opposite me.

"Everything all right at work, Cuthbert?" I ask cautiously.

"Yes, fine. Except, of course, for Elaine's misery."

The name sends a light shock through me. I have no wish to hear any more about that girl's problems. Nor do I enjoy this little pang of sexual jealousy, which is not something I expected to feel. It's disconcerting because it's a surprise; and it seems absurdly misplaced, as well, because I never felt like this about Edwin, even after learning about his other life.

"Just look at how fat Witty is getting," I say brightly. "He must be cadging meals next door – getting the best of both worlds."

"How are the Wrights these days?" he asks politely.

"They're gearing up for a couple of weeks in Barbados, lucky things."

"I should have taken you places, Rowena," he says sadly.

"No – no – I never meant –"

"I know, but . . ." Moodily he swirls the dregs of his brandy. "Sometimes I feel I've been very selfish, because you . . . well, you've been so sweet and generous."

"Come on, Cuthbert, if it comes to generosity, you've –"

"After all," he goes on, studying his glass intently, "it's not too late, is it? We could go away for a weekend somewhere nice."

"No, no, no," I say hurriedly. "We agreed about all that, dear. And besides, what on earth would Marion say?"

There is a brief silence. I am afraid he will pursue this topic, but instead he says, "Actually, she called me at the office today." My hand smoothing Wittgenstein's fur gives a little twitch. "She did?"

"Yes. She was – er – asking for an update on things . . . our application and so on. She thinks – I mean I know it seems to be taking a long time in the works, but I explained to her that I've done all I can – once these papers go in, it will be out of my hands till the hearing. People don't realize how long these things take, specially in a case like this where we have an opponent."

"I know you've done your best for me, Cuthbert, and so does she. But her temperament is . . . She likes everything to be cut and dried, over and done with quickly . . . I hope she didn't say anything to –"

"No, of course not," he says too quickly. "It's perfectly natural for her to be concerned. She's a good soul, Marion."

There is another short pause. Then I say with reluctance, "I suppose she means well."

"That's right," he says. His voice sounds tired.

"More brandy?"

"No, thanks, Rowena. I must be getting along." He gets up smothering a great yawn. Winding on his scarf he gives his head a little shake. "You think she's a bit difficult – wow, you should meet Elaine's ex-husband. What a Hindu *he'll* make. He's suing for half of everything they've got, you know – perhaps I told you this before."

With an effort I keep my voice neutral. "Hardly fair, is it, when he's the one opting out."

"Fair is not a word in that guy's vocabulary. The one thing he doesn't want is custody of Sarah. Poor old Elaine will have all the responsibility of that. Poor kid." He yawns again.

"You're worn out, Cuthbert; would you maybe like to –" But fortunately he has pulled down his fur hat snugly over his ears, and fails to hear this.

"Yes, I must get home. Thanks for the drink, dear. Give you a call soon."

He pats my shoulder and takes himself off to the waiting car. The cat and I watch as he pulls away and disappears under the stars. I stand there for a while looking at the empty road. Now you cut this out, I tell myself sternly. This is only the beginning, and it's how things are going to be. At least he didn't mention that ring. We seem to have come out of this without doing any real damage to each other. But it will stay that way only if you're not a fool. And that will be the hard part.

Tom's black umbrella enlarges its own small puddle on the kitchen floor, quietly domesticating nature. Outside a gust of sleet rattles fiercely at the window like a housebreaker. Tom himself sits at the table hunched round-shouldered over his crossed arms. I fill our cups with tea and push his closer. His extended silence has been, in its way, statement enough, but I ask, "Weather got you down, Tom?"

"No," he mutters. "It's not that."

"Well, drink that while it's hot. And try a bran muffin – I made them this morning."

"Bless you," he says a moment later through a well-buttered mouthful. "Delicious." After a loud swig or two of tea he wipes his moustache and leans back with a politely repressed belch.

"It's my day for hospital visits," he says, breaking off another bite of muffin. "And that never does much to lift the spirits. Worst part of my duty, in fact. Today I saw a child with leukaemia – then a parishioner who miscarried in her sixth month. But worst of all was poor Miriam Whittaker. She went in for tests last week – nothing but a stubborn cough, we all thought – but they've diagnosed lung cancer. She's being quite marvellous about it, but –" He pauses here to pull out a handkerchief. With a honk he blows his nose and openly wipes his eyes. "Well, God must be comforting her in this adversity, poor soul, because she was much more cheerful today than I was after hearing the news. I've seen this before in the condemned, of course. The struggle to accept is hard and long."

I touch his hand. It is clear to me now, if it wasn't before, that Miriam has been one of Tom's parochial sheep on particularly friendly terms with her pastor; but this detail seems of no consequence now, if it ever was.

"It won't be long now, Rowena," he tells me heavily, "before I know as many dead people as living ones."

I think of Sebastian's hooded eyes looking bleakly at the future and refill Tom's cup. "Does it help to believe you'll see them all again?" I ask, too curious to keep silent. "I suppose you do really believe that?"

"Our Lord did not tell lies," he says firmly. "Why should the promise of life everlasting be any less true than the other things He said?"

"Well, but that one does ask for such a huge suspension of disbelief."

"That doesn't alter the truth of it." But his shoulders have sagged again, as if he feels both tired and discouraged.

"Why don't you have a little brandy, Tom. You've had a rough day. It will do you good."

He makes no objection, so I bring in the bottle and a glass from the dining-room and pour him a generous tot, not without a rueful sense of *déjà vu.*

"Thanks, my dear. Not joining me? Your health."

Wittgenstein's squawk can be heard faintly at the back door. When I open it he shoots in and shakes himself indignantly, scattering ice-cold drops everywhere. Tom draws his robe to one side to protect it while I towel the cat dry. Under the rubbing a purr like a lion's emerges.

"Doesn't that beast live next door?"

"Not now."

"What a friend to all the world you are, my dear. Myself, I've never seen the point of cats."

"I guess it's a matter of faith, Tom. It's their self-confidence I like so much. And envy."

"This bottle's very low. I'll have to bring along a replacement next time I come." I let this observation pass without comment. "Can we go and sit in the other room?" he says, getting stiffly to his feet. "This chair is hard on my old bones."

Once established in the big chair, feet propped on a hassock and glass in hand, he sighs with contentment. "There, that's better. Tell me, Rowena, how is Marion these days?"

"About as usual, I think. Why do you ask?"

"Well, last Sunday – you know she takes the eight-to-tens at Sunday school (I had to be there because my curate's down with flu), I found her in the vestry telling off one of the youngsters. Now no doubt the child had been very trying; heaven knows these days they can behave like demons. But she said to this one, 'If you can't behave decently, you have no business being alive.' I really did think that was too strong – the child was already in tears. I hate to see anyone cry, you know, so when the youngster was gone, I remonstrated a little with Marion. Very gently, you understand. You know I'm an admirer of hers, and very fond of her, as well. But her reaction quite took me aback. She actually snapped at me. Offered to resign on the spot. Well, of course that was the very last thing – in the end, I found myself the one more or less apologizing . . . At any rate the whole thing made me wonder whether she has . . . Is she unhappy for any reason, do you know?"

"I think," I say with reluctance, "that Marion is far from happy. Worse, I'm beginning to wonder if she ever has been."

"Of course I know she felt her father's death very deeply; but you'd expect a sensible girl like that, after this length of time . . ."

"Somehow, I think that's only part of it. But she's always kept me at arm's length, you know. Perhaps all those years with Edwin, she was afraid I'd cling too much, to compensate for . . . Well, anyhow, that's all over now, but we both appear to be stuck in the old postures. If there's anything I can do about her current frame of mind, I wish you'd tell me."

Tom has laced his hands together and closed his eyes rather in the manner of one hearing confession, but he says nothing. After a silence he murmurs, "If we say that we have no sin, we deceive ourselves and the truth is not in us. I shall put her into my prayers."

"That may be all anybody can do. That is, if you believe we make our own misery, much of the time."

After a pause I glance at him inquiringly. But the conference is over. His head has sunk forward and a faint, sighing snore escapes from under the grey moustache.

An hour or so later a taxi takes Tom off to a synod meeting, leaving Wittgenstein and me alone. Outside the storm is still histrionically hissing and rattling at the windows. We both find the sound of it satisfactory because it doubles the pleasure of being indoors. Over a bite of supper, I say comfortably to Mrs. Wilson, "Pleasant, isn't it, that nothing has happened lately."

"Ah, well," she says, switching her wheelchair closer to the table. "Occurrences can be invisible but still potent."

"Possibly. The thing is, what can I do for my poor girl?"

"Not much one can do for an adult child, is there?"

"No, but if I could just get to the bottom of what . . . It's not just a man she wants, is it? Or a woman, either. I mean, I've met Bernice, and . . . No, I don't really think it's that. Marion's neuter, I've always thought, which may after all be a very disturbing condition. My guess is that a long time ago she might have over-heard something between Edwin and me that put her off the whole thing – traumatized her, if you like those terms. More guilt for me, I suppose. I did the best I could at the time, or tried to, but –"

"Sea gulls," says Ethel. "They pay no bills and have no con-science. They never say 'if only.' What dignity."

"But this worries me, Ethel. I used to admire Marion for making a good life for herself, but it begins to seem I was wrong about that. Do you think it's a child she wants?"

"If that's the case, they're easily available."

"Well, I've been her child, in a way. Till lately, that is. Maybe that's the answer. I'll get her to explain fuses to me or something like that. I'll ask her advice. Come to think of it, I could do a lot worse. She might well suggest some better job for me than those pies. Telling me what to do would probably cheer her up quite a bit."

"In the end she'll find connections of her own," says Ethel. "You can trust things in general to lead somewhere. The whole web is there."

"I want something good to happen to her, Ethel."

"Once you never wanted anything to happen. Now you do. Hopeful sign, that."

"Oh, I don't know. We may be more alike than I think, Marion and I. Nothing will ever really happen to either of us. We're not the type."

"Now you're being pretentious. Everybody's the type. Love, breakfast, death . . . nobody escapes. Besides, by happen, do you mean going over Niagara Falls in a barrel or blackmailing Prince Charles into a divorce? Of course you don't. Making a sauce or laughing in the dark – those are happenings."

"Well, of a trivial kind, yes."

"Have some proper respect for triviality, then."

"I'm going to phone Marion right now and ask her to take me to lunch or something. You once wrote that everything of importance happens indoors, and I guess that's true."

"Everything happens again," says Ethel calmly, "and it's never the same."

CHAPTER NINE

My key in the lock seems to make the loud, aggressive noise of an armed invasion. My heart beats fast as I ease open the door. Cautiously I peer into the dim hallway before admitting myself and the carefully packed basket on my arm. After the bright, gusty sky outside, the old house closes round me darkly, its air confined and unnaturally heavy. I remind myself that this is Thursday and that having arranged for Mrs. Blot's afternoon off and mine to coincide, there is no risk of meeting her here. Nevertheless the sound of my own footsteps makes me nervous. There is not another sound in the place but the ponderous tick of a clock somewhere in the dim cavern of the sitting-room. Also, as I quietly mount the stairs, the regular rise and fall of someone snoring.

In his darkened room, Sebastian lies as before, his mouth fallen a little open. His long face is thickly bearded with white and this, together with his spectral thinness, suggests he is hardly here at all. I draw close to the bed to inspect the clutter on the side table.

There is a new tube of yellow capsules, but this one is labelled with his name and his doctor's. Somewhat noisily I go to the window, raise the blind and pull up the sash a few inches. At once a burst of brilliant light and chill air bursts exuberantly in. His eyelids twitch and he mutters something unintelligible.

"Open your eyes, Sebastian," I tell him loudly. "Wake up this minute."

"Bloody nuisance," he mumbles. With a clumsy smack his lips come together. Then he lifts a thin and tremulous hand to screen his eyes. From behind this barricade a bloodshot eye peers at me suspiciously.

"I've brought you some lunch. Sit up."

"You, is it? I might have known. Get that filthy fresh air out of here – it will kill me."

"Nonsense. This isn't Shangri-La, God knows. Sit up and take notice. I've got something nice here for you."

"Evidence that there is an *a priori* order of the world?"

"No."

"Proof that in diversity there is some unifying essence?"

"Afraid not."

"Whisky?" he says hopefully.

"Wait and see." To make room for my basket I remove an untouched bologna sandwich curling dryly beside a full, luke-warm glass of grapefruit juice. "What do you say to a bit of beef Stroganoff, Seb? And a glass of wine?" I take an aluminum container out and open its lid. The contents are still quite hot. I wave it under his nose to tantalize him with the aroma of beef, garlic and sour cream.

"Whatever that is, it's sure to give me indigestion," he says gloomily. "However, I'll taste a bit. It actually smells like food. Mrs. B. thinks food only comes in vacuum-sealed packets and has to taste of chemicals to be safe to eat."

Having poured the juice down the sink and rinsed the glass, I fill it from the half-bottle of Bordeaux I've brought along. He takes it eagerly in both grossly trembling hands.

"Careful, now." A few drops spill on the sheet, and I mop them up, not very successfully. He tastes the dish without much interest, but the wine immediately brings a little colour into his leaden lips and pale, sunken cheeks. After a moment he struggles to sit more upright, muttering, "Plonk it may be, but the hell with that – I drink for the effect." After that he eats a little more of the beef. I sit down to watch him with satisfaction. The bright air lifts the window curtain a little and throws a delicate pattern of branches onto the carpet.

"I suppose you haven't heard from Pam and John yet," I say. "There hasn't been time."

"Why should I hear from them?"

"They're in Barbados."

"Are they?"

"Yes. Of course you know that."

"I thought you were there."

"Where?"

"Barbados."

"What made you think that?"

He eyes me sharply over the edge of his glass. "You've not been to see me for two months."

"Weeks, Sebastian. Weeks." But I shift a little in my chair. It's disconcerting to find him so much more clearheaded today. And it is difficult to explain, even to myself, why I've postponed this visit so long.

"Why haven't you come?" he asks. "I bore you, is that it?"

"Hush," I tell him. And obeying some impulse probably as mysterious to him as to me, I lean forward and kiss his prickly cheek. We look at each other afterwards with mild astonishment. "You do not bore me," I say.

"Nor you me, Mrs. Nobody."

"Have some more Stroganoff."

"Rowena, don't leave me alone like that again. Tell me you won't."

"It's been like this, Seb; I've been spending a bit more time with my daughter. She's trying to help me –"

But somebody is unlocking the front door below. He gives a start that spills a little more of the wine, and simultaneously a reflex of fear gets me to my feet.

"Bloody Blot," he mumbles. "Home early for once."

"Well, I think I'd better – I'll just –"

"Yes."

Swiftly I repack the basket and put my coat back on. Mrs. B.'s footsteps have retreated to the kitchen. If she has not noticed my boots in the hall cupboard, I might be able to slip away without having to face her.

"Better go," he says. "Scene otherwise. I'm under orders not to annoy. Extend the deadline, girl, just till tomorrow, mind. Pay attention to the footnotes." A vein jerks at the side of his neck. Hastily he gulps down the last of the wine and drops the glass to the floor, where it obligingly hides itself under the bed.

"Yes; take care, Seb. I'll see you next week."

"No use blaming me," he mutters. "Nothing to do with me, is it. Bloody budget."

I pause at the top of the stairs to make sure the hall below is clear; then I descend, trying to tread lightly on the steps that creak most. I am just pulling on my second boot when a hard voice makes me jump.

"Miss Hell."

"Oh, hello, Mrs. –"

Arms folded, she faces me, incongruously bedecked in a fussy purple dress and the once-pink slippers. Doubtless her best shoes hurt. Under its elaborate layer of blusher, eye shadow and mascara, her broad face is red with anger. Involuntarily I step a little back from her.

"You come here is no good for him, Miss Hell. Very sick old man."

"Well, I don't really think he —"

"Sick," she repeats, and stiff-fingers her own temple meaningfully. "You make him upset."

"Mrs. Wright has given me —"

"You don't come here. Get that? No good for him."

"Look, I just —"

She glances scathingly at the basket. "What you give him? I tell the doctor. I tell Miss Wright. I'm the one look after that man. *I* know. You stay home."

My heart is drumming helplessly. My mouth is too dry to form any answer. Without a word I turn away and go.

It takes me a long time to get to sleep the night after this encounter. Then, when at last I do drift off, I wake with a start to hear somebody trying to get in downstairs. There is a fumbling at the door handle; then the door, always a little swollen in wintertime, breaks open with its familiar, stiff creak. I sit up in bed, throat so constricted with fear I can hardly breathe. An eddy of cold air drifts up the stairs toward me. In the dark I grope for and find the big sewing shears. Unhurried, regular steps mount from below. With no relief, but accelerated panic, I recognize the tread as Edwin's. He stands in the bedroom doorway, his insignificant height extended with anger. "I am the resurrection," says Tom's voice from somewhere near the altar.

"Well?" Edwin says. "What explanation have you got for this?" He is holding out a collection plate, which immediately turns into a small jeweller's box.

"You were buried," I say through stiff lips.

He comes closer to the bed. As always when in a rage, his eyes protrude and his skin has a yellow tinge. His sex grows enormously, threateningly huge. Then the heavy, arms-akimbo bulk of Mrs. Blot superimposes itself on the darkness at the door. I try to run down the hall to escape them, but my legs are made of stone, I can barely drag one after the other. Cornered in the bathroom, I grip the ice-cold shears and in desperation lift them high. The thin street light gleams on the double blade as I drive it into the side of his neck where, like a phantom weapon, it makes no wound and leaves no mark. What jerks me awake is someone shouting, "You go home. I tell the doctor."

I grope for the bedside lamp and all but overturn it before my trembling hand can find the switch. Bewildered, I look around at the familiar, empty room. On the dressmaking table, the shears rest calmly in their accustomed place. My windpipe feels sore as if I have been running for a long time. And instead of fading out of focus, the dream's bizarre details only seem to intensify as I recall them.

Well, I think, clumsily thrusting my arms into a dressing gown, that's natural enough. It wasn't a dream at all, really; more a play-back of a memory tape. Switching on every light along the way, I creep downstairs and put on the kettle. Black night stands at the window. From time to time a chill roughens my skin, and my heart is still pounding. The dream is over, but it has demonstrated, as dreams do, that the past is the present, a fact basic enough to frighten anyone.

"I don't remember being consulted about this," Edwin remarked with unpleasant politeness. "No doubt that's because you knew very well what I'd say. But you obviously felt a bit uncomfortable about spending my money on something I disapprove of, or you wouldn't have hidden it, would you?"

"*She has to have a birthday present, Edwin. And all her friends have a quartz watch.*"

"*I don't believe it does a child any good at all to have the gimmicks everybody else has. But apparently you have no respect at all for my opinion.*"

"*Well, I don't see how it will make Marion a better human being to be deprived of everything other kids have. We have no TV, for instance, which itself – In any case, the watch was on sale; it only cost –*"

"*It's the principle, Rowena; can you not get that into your head? I get no co-operation from you. You've spent money I can't afford – but that's not the point. What I can't accept is your brand of passive resistance – worse, your deceit; your disloyalty.*"

I had no answer to that; the raw truth of it silenced me. Next day I took the little watch back to the shop where, after some unpleasantness with the manager, Edwin's money was refunded. Marion got a new winter coat for her birthday instead. But that was not the end of it. For days afterwards his silence constricted the very air in the house to an unbreathable substance. Because I had nothing else, still less anything better, the withdrawal of whatever he felt for me, even if it was only approval, could not be endured. In the end I wept.

"*I'm sorry, Edwin. I was wrong. It won't happen again.*"

"*So you say. It's easy to promise, isn't it, just for the sake of peace?*" *He was sitting on the side of the bed taking off his socks, and this domestic intimacy added its own ingredient of ugliness to the scene, as did the fact we had to keep our voices low to avoid waking Marion.*

"*Why do we go on with this?*" *I asked desperately.* "*Why do we keep on together when –*"

"*I made a certain commitment. And so did you. That's all.*"

"*But what if that's not enough?*" *The tears had dried up and I was proud of that, but when he stared at me I could not meet the challenge and my swollen eyes filled again.* "*Whatever else can be said about me," he said, "I do look after you. Don't forget that."*

"I'm not – I don't. But I still say why go on when there's so much bitterness ..." It was raining heavily outside, a dark nighttime downpour that made me ever afterwards associate rain with misery.

"You don't want to end it," he said flatly.

There was a silence. Then I said, "No."

He looked at me again. There was a sly, dry pleasure in his glance; it was the satisfied look of the winner, which I saw again this afternoon on the face of Calliope Blovantasakis.

Shivering, I fold my hands around my teacup in an effort to warm them. In the eastern corner of the sky an immaculate pink streak is opening, delicate and luminous as the pearly inside of a shell. It slowly expands, shining its impersonal, impartial beauty over this dirty world and all its inhabitants. It makes its own wordless comment on that long-ago scene between me and Edwin. I sit there pondering the immortality of such defeats. The hot drink has calmed me, but I am still not brave enough to go back to bed, where that and other surrenders have so often been consummated. I sit at the kitchen table watching the radiance outside gradually thin and brighten to mundane daylight.

The dream plays and replays its tape in my mind. Its details, down to the murderous lift of the shears, need no interpretation. What poor, battered Mrs. Blot was doing in my subconscious as a threat puzzles me at first. Then, when I understand it, something like relief steals over me.

Finally I can think calmly, almost with regret, "Well, there it is. I can't do it. I'm a casualty and that can't be altered now. Nothing's left over to help anybody else with. Never mind whose fault it all is . . . that's beside the point now. What it means is I can't risk – I can't face – sorry, Sebastian, but there it is. I can't afford to see you if it's going to rake up all this . . . Not with my limitations. Sorry, but that's it."

Once this decision is made, I feel released. A wave of drowsiness makes my head swim. Yawning, I go to the sofa and, pulling the afghan over me, fall into a deep sleep.

Midway through February, my birthday rolls around. Almost nothing distinguishes it from any other day. Marion sends me a card with kittens on it, wishing me many happy returns. Cuthbert calls me up to convey the same message.

"Thanks, Cuthbert."

"I'm up to my eyeballs here or I'd suggest dinner or something. But everything at the office is jumping and tonight I've got to take Basil to the vet; I think he has pip. And on top of it all, Elaine's car blew its brakes today and I had to drive her to the day-care place to pick up Sarah. Actually it wasn't the drag I thought it would be, though, because she's really a cute kid. Great big blue eyes, and she chats away – a really big vocabulary for a two-year-old. She waved to me when I dropped them off and said, 'See you around, Cupboard.' Cute, eh?"

"Yes."

"There's no more news except that one of my partners has taken on an interesting case . . . a lady politician under investigation for conflict of interest. That could turn out to be a real can of worms, but Jack will get her off, I'm pretty sure. And how are things with you, Rowena? Marion well?"

"Yes, though I think she could use a holiday . . . or something. There's no news here, really. I'm still chopping chickens for a living and with some help from Marion I'm managing all right."

"That's good," he says comfortably. A clicking noise now breaks out on the line, and he says rather hurriedly, "Someone's trying to get this number, I think, Rowena, so I'd better ring off. Talk to you again soon."

"Yes. Goodbye, Cuthbert."

So much for any hope I may have had, then, that this birthday might actually see the emergence of anything new, much less a new me.

Next evening, the familiar stamp of snow boots outside the door makes an official announcement of Marion's arrival. With some reluctance I put down my book and get up to greet her. She disposes tidily of her outdoor things and then stands a moment smoothing her already smooth hair. There is something in the lift of her arms and the set of her back that suggests tension, even a state of heightened emotion, and this disquiets me.

"Hello, dear. Thanks for the birthday card."

"Everything all right here, Mother?"

"Everything's fine," I tell her, wishing it were true.

"Actually I meant to drop in yesterday, but things piled up and I couldn't make it."

"Have you eaten? I've got some –"

"No, don't bother. I mean, I haven't, but I don't want anything."

Marion has always regarded food as an uninteresting interruption to more important matters; hence she has always been thin; but tonight I notice egg-shaped hollows under her collarbone that seem new. Her colour is high, and she moves around the room as if charged with more nervous energy than she knows what to do with. On her way past the sofa she picks up my book – Mrs. Wilson's *The Innocent Traveller*.

"But you've read this before," she says, tossing it down.

"Yes, I have."

"Why on earth read it again, then? You know what happens – what's the point?"

"With her books, it's not what happens, because not much does, generally. It's how and why and to whom that –"

"Makes no sense to me."

I let this go. She fidgets the venetian blind straight, tidies several library books into a neat pile, then brusquely turns the cat out of the big chair and drops into it herself. A second later she jumps up and heads for the kitchen. "Stay where you are," she tells me. "I'll make us a pot of tea."

In her absence, Wittgenstein repossesses the chair. Once back with the tea, she turns him out again. He stalks out of the room in dignified offence.

"I've just come from the East General," she says.

"Oh?" I look at her anxiously. "What took you there?"

"Bernice. The stupid fool swallowed a hundred aspirins last night." What perplexes me is not this news, but the note of something almost like elation in Marion's voice.

"No, really. The poor creature."

"You'd think a pharmacist would make a better job than that of knocking herself off, wouldn't you. Aspirin, of all things."

"Yes, but Marion –"

"All it did was make her vomit."

"But isn't that a dangerous dose?"

"Not unless you choke to death."

"But poor Bernice. I suppose that man with the Volvo lost interest?"

Her shoulders lift in a contemptuous shrug.

"Is she going to be all right then?"

"Of course. The idea wasn't to die, just to get everybody in a flap. And it was a terrific success as far as that went. Her room-mate Gertie Payne called me at three this morning, she's a nervous Nellie at the best of times, and much worse since she got engaged . . . Anyhow she was in such a panic I had to call the ambulance for her. Right now, Gert is the one who needs the hospital bed, if you ask me. They'll keep Bernice in the psychiatric ward for a week to assess her, and she'll enjoy the drama of that."

"You don't seem very sympathetic," I venture.

"Why should I be? Imagine getting into a state like that about a potbellied little man with dentures."

"Well, these things are all in the eye of the beholder."

She gives a snort. "Then she needs glasses. Imagine at the age of thirty-five not realizing he was just putting in time between divorces. Anyone could have told her. Come to that, I did tell her."

"Which didn't help much, I imagine."

"There's no cure for stupidity, if that's what you mean."

"Had you been in touch with her recently? I mean, you couldn't have seen this coming, or you'd have –"

"Haven't laid eyes on her for weeks. I just couldn't stick it any more. Whining away about why didn't he call and so forth – enough to drive you dippy. So I just left her alone."

After an uncomfortable pause I say, "Well, I'm glad you went to see her today. I'm sure she was glad to see you."

"Oh, yes. In her fashion," Marion says carelessly. For a moment she looks uncannily like Edwin. I pull my sweater more closely around me. "Anyhow," she goes on, "we had a long talk. With Gertie moving out this spring, we thought the two of us might share a two-bedroom, if one comes up in my building. Wouldn't live in hers, it's got cockroaches. Anyhow, we'll see. It won't make any difference to you, if it turns out you need a place; we'll still have the sofa bed. As a matter of fact, Mother, what I really dropped in for was to ask you over for a meal some time soon. You need to get out more, and I doubt if you're eating properly. That extra weight on you obviously means too much carbohydrate. Say Friday night."

"Oh, that's nice of you, dear, but . . ." My voice trails away as I wonder what would happen if I were to say, Friday, dear, is Tom's regular time to call here for various kinds of intercourse.

"Yes, that would be lovely." I look at her, perplexed. She is adjusting her braids at the back of the neat Guides hat.

"Friday at six," she says briskly. "I'll do you a wok dinner."

"That sounds good. Thanks, dear."

"Haven't seen enough of you lately. Been busy, but that's no excuse. It's not that I don't care, you know." Then, to my surprise, she leans forward and drops a peck of a kiss on my cheek. The next moment she is gone.

"Good heavens, she's happy. Will wonders never cease," I say to the empty hall.

"Luckily, no," Mrs. Wilson answers.

"So it was Bernice after all. Well, I'm glad for her. I just hope it will be a good thing for both of them."

"It probably will."

"It's a bit of a shock just the same. I feel I'm just beginning to know Marion."

"Maybe till now you haven't been equipped for it."

"That could be."

"Always rather disturbing," she says calmly, "to recognize the truth. Strains our very limited capacities. No offence meant."

"None taken."

A hard, bright winter morning. I'm on my way to work. Blinking in the glare of sun on snow, a few people like walking bundles scurry along our street trying to achieve minimal exposure to the cold. For once I am no more anonymous than anyone else, though only a small segment of my face can be seen between my woolly hat and big muffler. John Wright is a stride past before he recognizes me. Then his red face – what is visible of it between coat collar and fur hat – breaks into a smile.

"Morning, Rowena. Bloody cold, eh?"

"Awful. How was your holiday?"

"Great. Shock getting back to this."

"It must be. Pam well?"

"Fine, thanks."

"And how did you find Sebastian?" I had no intention of mentioning Seb, and wonder with annoyance what has made me do it. On his new (or old) footing as a friend, Cuthbert is coming to dinner, I've been pleasantly planning the menu, and have no desire to hear anything whatsoever that might prove disturbing. I eye John sidelong, hoping he has not heard the question. But the bit of his face I can see is folded into a frown.

"Not well. Fact is, we're worried."

"Oh, dear. That's too bad. Well, I must be –"

"Nothing specific wrong. Just deteriorating. Hardly bothers getting up now. Stopped grumbling. Bad sign, that." His breath smokes in the frigid air. I tap my feet together to keep them warm. But he seems to have more to say, little as I want to hear it.

"Problem, really. Nursing home next stop. Pam looking into it. Depressing business."

"Yes, of course. Well –"

"One of those things. My old ma, too, making life hell for all. What can you do?"

"Nothing. That's just it."

"Not much, that's it. Well, *ciao*."

He strides off and I go my way. With a little effort of will, I find it's not too difficult to put this conversation out of my mind. It's sad, but it doesn't concern me. That fact has been firmly

established for some time now, and I have no intention of thinking any more about it.

With a contented sigh, Cuthbert pats the little tummy he has
recently developed. "That was a lovely meal, Rowena," he says.
"And I thought I was too tired to eat."

"Basil all right now, is he?"

"Oh, yes, thanks. He's fine." Here, for no apparent reason, he
sighs.

"Something on your mind, Cuthbert?"

"No, no. Just . . . rather a lot happening all at once, this last little
while." He sighs again. Somewhere in the distance a dog barks for-
lornly at the night.

It's more or less safe for you to tell me about her now, I think.
He has settled back in the big chair and put up his short legs on
the hassock, but he does not look really at ease or at home; in fact,
I feel his separateness, as perhaps he feels mine.

"I daresay that politician they're investigating is a bit of a
problem, is she?" I suggest.

"Oh. No, not really. She's been very careful. Jack won't have
much trouble getting her off. The ideal client, in a way. She tells a
consistent story, it can be corroborated, and he doesn't need to
know any more than that."

"You mean she's guilty, but –"

"We don't look at it that way, you see. She has a case that can be
won. That's our job. The rest is beside the point."

"Seems pretty cynical, doesn't it?"

"Not really. It's just common sense. We don't arbitrate morals."

"But surely the law is all about guilt or innocence."

"The law is about what can be proved, my dear."

"And that doesn't bother you?"

"Not a bit. It reassures me. I'm not here to pass judgement. That *would* bother me."

"Yes. You have a very sensitive conscience."

"That's right."

It occurs to me as curious that intimacy with two lovers – each representing, you might say, a code, whether ethical or moral – has only succeeded in puzzling rather than improving me. Perhaps women by their nature are more or less impervious to codes.

Sharp blades of moonlight shine at the edges of the venetian blind. He draws another brief sigh. Then he says, "What's the hardest decision you ever made, Rowena?"

I think about that for a minute. "Well, the way things used to be here for me, I very seldom got to make any decisions. Any major ones, that is. And not many minor ones. Once, years and years ago, I did get angry enough with Edwin to decide to leave him. There was enough in the housekeeping for three nights in a hotel; after that, I thought I could be somebody's cleaning woman or something. But the only cheap hotel I knew anything about was way across town. I had no idea what bus to take to get there, and there wasn't enough cash for a taxi ride that long; so of course I never left. Ludicrous, isn't it?"

"By the way, Rowena, speaking of money, have you really looked absolutely everywhere for that will? I still can't believe a careful man like Edwin . . ."

"I've searched everywhere, Cuthbert."

"Well, don't give up, will you?" He crosses his legs; then recrosses them. Far away somewhere out in the dark a siren wails its reminder that disaster randomly occurs.

"About decisions," he says, and I know he would not say even this much if it were not so late at night. "It's so hard sometimes to know what's best. Not just for myself, you understand. That part is more or less easy."

"Someone else is involved," I say carefully.

"More than one."

I try not to smile. "That's complicated, all right."

"People you care about . . . you want to protect them, and yet it can be so . . ."

Yes, I think. And has one of them by any chance got a big vocabulary for a two-year-old?

He sighs once more. "And emotions – I mean, how can you tell whether your judgement's functioning, or just your glands? It's all so complicated. And meanwhile, how much, if anything, can you tell anybody?"

There is a longish silence. A diesel train defines distance with a long, flat hoot. Then I say, "Well, it's been my experience that hardly anything can actually be said, not without the most disastrous consequences. How could I ever tell Marion, for instance, that I didn't let Edwin know I was pregnant till I was in the fourth month, because I was so afraid he'd insist on an abortion? It would devastate her to know that, about both of us. Come to that, it's unfair even to tell you this, because in fact Edwin turned out to be a very loving father to her. But the whole experience turned me into that old joke, a silent woman. Otherwise there's a lot I could say to you about . . . what's on your mind. But maybe between you and me, dear, silence can say a lot, right?"

"That's true. Anyhow, there are moments – and places – where it's absolutely impossible to say – to say anything." He rubs his hands over his face and adds, "Well, it's time I was off. Actually I think I'm starting a cold. You know that sort of burning you get in the back of your throat before it begins to be sore?"

"Mm. Try a salt-water gargle."

"Everybody in town's got something. What a winter it's been. Zero again tonight, and flurries coming tomorrow. Well, thanks again for dinner – I must be on my way. Lord, I meant to be home hours ago – I'm expecting a call –"

At the door he pauses to polish first one lens then the other of his thick glasses. Without them, his round face with its dimpled chin is that of a sorely perplexed baby. While he is pulling on his galoshes, I go swiftly upstairs and bring down the small velvet ring box. Without a word I push it into his coat pocket, and without a word he accepts it. Neither of us says anything more about silence and the many things it can communicate.

Late next afternoon, the doorbell rings – a long, loud peal suggestive of urgency, even desperation. I start up to answer it; then hesitate. How typical of me, I think, to be torn between fear of action and fear of inaction. Householders have recently been warned not to open the door to strangers. On the other hand this is not a time of day when armed robbers are normally active. It's possible that Tom or Cuthbert might have chosen to make an unscheduled call, and seeing all the lights on, will surely be offended if I fail to answer the door. Still, something tells me that at best, whatever is out there will prove disturbing in one way or another, and I have planned another search through shelves and drawers for that will. However, in the end I recklessly draw back the chain and open the door.

"Rowena, come next door and have a drink with me at once," Pam says loudly. "It's urgent. I'm depressed." She does not look depressed, with her scarlet jersey and silver hoop earrings big enough for a parrot to swing in; but there is a strained note in her voice that suggests she is, for once, not exaggerating as wildly as usual.

"Oh. Well – er – I was – but all right. Hold on while I get my coat."

In silence we pick our way down my snowy steps and up hers. Once inside she sweeps up the wildly barking Arthur in her arms to silence him, then switches off the TV and picks up some snarled knitting from the floor, where it seems to have been thrown.

"John's in Montreal on business," she says, "and Colin's sleeping over with a friend, so there's nobody around but LaVerne, who is not a chatty animal; as for Arthur, he's beautiful but dumb. So frustrating to have nobody to bitch to, so I thought of you." She gives a sudden giggle. "Scotch and water?"

"Mostly water," I say, smiling in spite of myself. I do not ask why she is depressed, because that might lead to a subject I hope to avoid. In fact I intend to steer her erratic conversation in some other direction entirely, and this, given her temperament, shouldn't be difficult, I think cheerfully.

"You know, Pam, I nearly didn't answer the door. Did you read in the paper about that pair of women going from door to door in this neighbourhood?"

"No, how odd, I thought they cruised the streets downtown." She hands me a drink and sits down opposite me with a tall glass for herself, murmuring, "Ah. Lovely gin."

"They ring the bell arm in arm, and one of them says her friend feels faint, could she have a glass of water. While you're off getting it, they snatch up anything small and valuable you happen to have sitting around. In my case, that would be nothing, but still."

"But I would *love* that," she says, glancing around as if her own sitting-room presents new and interesting possibilities. "Anybody who wants those silly brass bellows is welcome to them, since we have no fireplace anyway; and as for those Doulton figurines on the mantel, they bore me horribly, people give them to you as presents when they don't really like you and can't think of anything else, an aunt of John's gave us that woman selling balloons when we got married and never spoke to us again."

"I ran into John the day after you got back from your holiday. How did you enjoy it?"

"Oh, my dear, all that sun, it was bliss, but you know day after day lolling on the beach and drinking out of pineapples, it's heaven at first, but in the end it just seems a bit futile somehow, and furthermore, every time I looked at all those good-looking black people who spend their lives making up our beds and washing our dishes, I felt horribly guilty, it just isn't fair, in their place instead of smiling all the time and exuding charm the way they do, I'd be whacking off white heads in the most revolutionary way, wouldn't you?"

"Actually, I daresay I'd be as repressed black as I am white, if not more so."

"Besides," she goes on, having abruptly lost interest in the black race, "the whole point of the islands used to be to get a tan so everybody would eat their hearts out with envy, but one doesn't dare any more because of skin cancer, and John actually got bitten by some kind of very tropical spider and his whole leg got infected, it just shows. One might really be better off to stay home, or just shack up in a local hotel and stay drunk for a couple of weeks, it would cost a lot less."

"I'm glad I'm not your travel agent."

"Anyhow," she continues, lifting her trousered legs straight out in front of her as if to admire them, "it's not all that bad being home. What do people in the tropics do for something to grumble about weatherwise? Fancy having to rely on hurricanes, because they don't come round all that often, do they?"

"Yes, that must be rough." I sip my drink contentedly. So far at least, her conversation has made easy listening.

"Of course we got back just in time for that awful cold snap, you'd think God would have some decency right at the end of February, but no. And to think we rushed back to be here for reading week when Max came home (though the last thing in the world they do is read, of course), and there he was simply brimming over with appalling news."

"Oh, really?"

"My dear, full of great plans to drop out of university and form a rock group. It sounded at first like one of those vague projects they get in their heads and then forget, but he's actually going to do it, Rowena. All those music lessons, think of it, just so he can play the trumpet in some awful club smelling of toilet deodorizer. John is so miserable he can't even get into a rage about it. As for me, while I'm generally in favour of people doing their thing, I do feel this particular thing is pure lunacy. I mean other people's sons go in for engineering or law, or at worst push off to Kathmandu to find themselves, why does ours want to dye his hair pink and make videos of people who look epileptic, it's too depressing. He tells us he'll be rehearsing in a friend's basement, which is some relief, and Jim's father is stone deaf, which is a bit of luck for him, but Max will live at home and there's no use pretending this will not be a severe bind. How's your drink? Mine's gone, and no wonder."

I shake my head, but she replenishes her own glass with generosity. "Yes, one of the least attractive details of this plan is that he'll have to live here, there being no prospect of making any money at this rock thing, not for a long time anyway, if ever, and that means daily warfare with Colin, they get on each other's nerves quite horribly and in this little house you can imagine . . . And that in turn brings me to the problem of Sebastian –"

"Pam, is it really six? – I must go –"

"Well, if I thought things here were fraught with doom, it just shows how wrong you can be, nothing is apparently so bad it can't get worse, and that certainly goes for Pa. As soon as we got back we found he was rapidly falling to bits one way and another, occasional incontinence now, for instance, and Mrs. Blot can hardly be expected to deal with that, even if she were a lot nicer than she is. So I'm trying to find him accommodation in some kind of nursing home. And Rowena, before John's mother had to go into one, I never really believed those horror stories, who possibly could until they've seen some of these places with their own eyes, not to mention smelled them, and believe me –"

Something like acute indigestion or malaise is gripping me inwardly. I begin to move rapidly towards the door. "Sorry, Pam, but I really have to –"

"I went to one in Scarborough yesterday run by a very kind, sweet woman – a nice big house with a verandah where they can sit in the summertime – the place was very clean inside and the old bods looked well cared for, but Rowena, they were lined up in a row in chairs and wheelchairs, all of them white as chalk, and all of them absolutely silent. Not a sound. Just sitting there waiting to die. It was perfectly horrible." She pauses here to blow her nose fiercely. "And the worst of it is that that place was much the best of all I've seen."

Murmuring something sympathetic, I pull on my coat.

"John's been so sweet, he says why don't we have him here, but now that Max will be home, it isn't physically possible. And we agree the boy has a right to come home, after all . . . But even if we had room, it would be a question of how could I cope with the old blight on a day-to-day basis without falling to pieces myself, a process I can feel setting in already . . . Well, I mean Florence Nightingale herself couldn't hack it, could she, actually spent all the rest of her life in bed, and as for me, I would immediately become a falling-down drunk, which is fun in its way once in a while, but not as a full-time future, don't you agree?"

The doorknob in my hand, I pause just long enough to say, "Couldn't you all move in with Seb? There's plenty of room at his place."

"My dear, that's been considered, but even if I could bear the thought of it – which I can't – the thing is, the mere mention made him fly into a major tantrum. He said if we really wanted to finish him off that would be the quickest way to do it. You see how totally impossible he –"

"I really must get home now, Pam. Sorry to hear about all this, but I'm sure you'll work something out. Give my best to Max and John. And thanks for the drink."

I am quite proud of this masterful exit, the first of its kind I have ever made. It surely indicates the development of qualities I've all my life seemed to possess only in the most stunted form. Better yet, with a little concentrated willpower, I am able to put all of Pam's family problems right out of my mind for the rest of the evening. On the other hand, a thorough ransack of the house unearths no will.

Early next morning, out of the confused landscape of a dream, a spectrally thin figure in pyjamas moves swiftly away, though I urgently want to see his face. A mournful voice says, "No proposition has only one complete analysis." Sebastian then lays a wreath on a new grave – Edwin's – and looks squarely at me from watery blue eyes. Resentfully I jerk awake. It really is not fair to be invaded like this when asleep. And how irritating to be plagued by a dream that seems to mean something, but is manifestly nonsense. When the phone rings I hurry down to answer it, glad to be called away to the real world.

"Rowena? Cuthbert here. Look, things have moved a bit faster with your case than I expected. The hearing's been fixed for tomorrow at nine, in the district court. We'll be before Madame Justice Hart."

"Tomorrow!" My heart has given a great leap of fear. The tops of my knees begin to tremble. Somehow – though Cuthbert has mentioned it several times before – I've never actually believed I would have to stand up in court before a judge. After all, what have I done? And what excuse can I offer for it? The prospect is so appalling I can hardly take in what Cuthbert is saying.

"I didn't tell you the date before, dear, because I didn't want you worrying way ahead of time. There's nothing to it, really, you know. We'll just go along there quietly together, and the whole thing may be over by noon. These hearings are open to the public, but I'm sure nobody will be there but Hill and his lawyer. And Corinne Hart is a good sort. Not like some of the old grouches on the bench. I'm reasonably sure she'll decide you're entitled to some support. So I'll pick you up at the house a little after eight, all right?"

I try to swallow. "All right."

"Now cheer up, dear. You probably won't have to say a word. Hill's lawyer and I will do all the talking. Just try to relax now. Oh, and no need to dress up or anything."

"Will Marion have to be there, too?"

"Not unless you want her to be."

"No. Please, no."

"Then we won't mention it till later."

"She's so likely to –"

"Yes, I know. Well, see you tomorrow, then."

"All right."

"And don't worry, now."

We both know I cannot possibly accept this good advice, but I am grateful for the gentleness in Cuthbert's voice. As soon as he hangs up, a dozen questions buzz into my mind – will the judge want to see my housekeeping accounts, for example, and what will she say when I admit I haven't kept any since Edwin's death? But the most urgent question of all is one I can hardly ask him, or anyone: namely, what can I say in my own defence at this hearing, when the very thought of it makes my head swim with guilt, stress and fear.

By the time I get up next morning, after a white night, I feel peculiarly unreal, almost disembodied. Even my strongest brew of tea cannot dispel the sense of living in a dream. It persists all the way downtown as Cuthbert's Buick floats us through rush-hour traffic, and only intensifies when I find myself on a hard seat in Courtroom Six. Two strange men are already in conference there, and when one of them remarks, "Hem – good morning," with vague surprise I recognize John Hill. His strong resemblance to Edwin further disorients me. There is an institutional smell of floor polish in the room strong enough to make my eyes water. A nervous tickle at the back of my throat makes me cough persistently.

A clerk in a grey jacket entering by a side door says in a loud voice, "Oyez, Oyez, Oyez. Anyone having business before the Queen's Justice of the Ontario Court of Justice, attend now and you shall be heard. Long live the Queen." By all means, I think confusedly, though what Her Majesty can have to do with my case is obscure to me. A bent old gentleman now shuffles in, followed by a small woman. He is formally dressed in grey flannels and a crested blazer. The woman with him wears shabby black.

"That's the sheriff's deputy," whispers Cuthbert. "He's here to protect the judge."

After obeying the bawled order, "All rise," we now sit down again. The small lady in black takes a seat on the dais facing us, and I realize she is not a petitioner like me, but the judge. That surreal sense that none of this can actually be happening closes over me again, bringing a sort of comfort with it.

Cuthbert is now on his feet talking in a rather high, nervous voice. Then Hill's man gets up and takes his turn. Very little of what they say seems to be in English. Try as I will, I have great difficulty following their arguments. So, it would seem, has the elderly official scribbling shorthand notes, who holds up a hand to rebuke Cuthbert for talking too fast. Somewhere out in the street a pneumatic drill chatters.

I gaze curiously at Madame Justice Hart. She has very thin brown hair; indeed she is nearly bald on the crown. I daresay she wishes Canadian legal people wore wigs. I fumble in my purse for a throat lozenge and remind myself to buy milk on the way home for the cat. Bits and pieces of phraseology float around me, released like a shower of confetti by the Hill lawyer, an almost supernaturally beautiful young man with thick gold hair and pink cheeks. "Exemplary wife and mother," he is saying. "Resumption of full marital relations. In very frail health. Financially straitened circumstances over a long period of time . . . The other establishment. Stress of recent events. In need of medical treatment . . . Change of climate advised." Trying to separate which of these statements applies to me and which to the other Mrs. Hill only further muddles me. The one clear impression I have is a Kafka-like one: I am the accused in this room, on trial for some serious but unnamed crime.

Eventually there is silence. The old gentleman appointed to protect the judge is asleep. The worried-looking little lady on the bench puts on bifocals to peer again at some papers handed up to her. Cuthbert bobs up and says something indignant. The shorthand man scrawls it down and then sits back to steal a glance at the *Globe and Mail* under his documents. Then the judge unhooks her glasses and rubs her nose rather fretfully. When she speaks it is in a voice so soft I have some trouble hearing her.

"The deciding factors in this case appear to me to be the poor health and advanced age of the legitimate spouse." Here she looks directly at me in a friendly, even kindly manner. "The deceased having made no provision for Mrs. Rowena Hill, a relatively young woman," she goes on, "it must be assumed he thought her quite capable of self-support, as I do myself. I therefore cannot find in favour of her application for relief. The claim of John Hill to the estate, on behalf of his mother, is valid."

Here, after gently nudging her bodyguard awake, she rises. So, to my surprise, do I. In an almost audible voice I say to her, "Thank you." Once more the clerk bawls, "Oyez, Oyez, Oyez. The sittings of this court are now concluded. Long live the Queen."

Once the judge and her escort have gone, the rest of us stand about for a moment uncertainly. Hill and his lawyer are shaking hands with effusive good will. Then, approaching me with a tight little smile, Hill offers me his hand. I stare at him frigidly and turn away. Cuthbert, looking pale and rather distraught, takes me by the elbow and hurries us out of the room. As we speed along the polished corridor his lips are set in such a grim line over the dimpled chin that he looks quite unfamiliar.

"Moonshine," he says with a vehemence better suited to a much stronger word. "All that medical testimony – pure moonshine. Sorry, Rowena, it's turned out this way. I'm honestly not just surprised but shocked – and truly sorry. If I'd maybe had more courtroom know-how – well, who knows. I did my best, but –"

"Of course you did, Cuthbert. It's all right. Truly, I almost feel as if in a way we've won, not lost."

"You do?" he says, pausing to stare at me curiously. "Is that why you *thanked* Corinne?"

"Well, you heard what she said. 'Capable of self-support . . . as I do myself.' That's a lot. I mean a judge actually thinks I can cope. She assumes Edwin thought so, too. Never mind the estate

– such as it is – that's a lot for her to give me, you must see that."

A gorgeously braided commissionaire whisks open the door for us and we are abruptly out in the bright street. Cuthbert hugs my arm to him. We both blink in the sunlight that is winking gaily off melting icicles and car chrome and the courthouse windows.

"Well, I want you to know, Rowena," he says, looking earnestly at me through his thick glasses, "that ring can still be yours, if you want it. You're not alone, you know. You can still have me. I mean it."

I stop to look at him while lunch-hungry lawyers and litigants jostle their way past us. "No, dear," I tell him. "Thanks, but all that's quite settled and final." And though he mumbles something, I can see relief in his face. Not that this or anything else seems to matter much. All I know is that Edwin's dead hand can never reach out to me again; not after today. This itself is such a discovery, and such a release, that nothing else really counts.

"My dear," says Tom, looking shocked, "I'm terribly sorry. I always understood Cuthbert was a first-rate . . . Well, it certainly leaves you in a most unfortunate position. I wish to heaven I could help, but as you know the Anglican Church of Canada doesn't pay its clergy very much or I'd –"

"Thanks anyway, Tom. Don't worry about it. I'll manage somehow. Have some more tea."

He has the resigned look of a priest experienced enough to know that human problems tend to be much more often financial than spiritual. "Yes, well, you're a brave girl, but you must let me help with the practical side of things. A dear little woman like you who's always been protected, after all . . . Now obviously it's domestic work you have the skills for – the question is, exactly what kind. You don't drive, do you? – that rules out some possible –"

"One way and another, you can rule out pretty well everything, I'm afraid. Marion and I have been over it and over it. Nannying is out, we've decided. I couldn't even be a good cleaning woman – haven't got the knees for it any more. Also forget news anchorwoman and cover girl."

This levity draws a reproachful glance from Tom. After all, earning money is serious business, second only, perhaps, to godliness. It pains him to find me taking my plight so lightly; indeed, the mood of almost reckless detachment I am in seems odd even to me.

"I'm trying to think who in the parish needs . . . Don't you agree that some kind of housekeeper-companion job would be most suitable . . ."

"Live-in," I contribute helpfully. "Since the legitimate spouse will now legally inherit this place. Otherwise, I'll be of no fixed address. All my worldly goods in a paper bag. Drinking vanilla in doorways. Can't say the prospect appeals. So it will have to be live-in. If you can call that really living."

Tom waits patiently for these remarks to end. I refill his cup and discourage Wittgenstein from advancing his nose towards the milk jug. "Now let me see," he mutters, smoothing his moustache with his thumb. "There's old Mrs. McNair . . . her daughters have done their best to dry her out at the Donwood, but she keeps relapsing . . . No, that would be quite impossible. I don't think . . . No, now wait a minute – there's Miss Waterman on Birch Street. She's getting on and needs someone – her last housekeeper walked out recently without notice, and her nephew –"

"Why?"

"Why did the housekeeper –?"

"Yes."

"Oh, I think we can assume she was just one of these irresponsible people. Anyhow, the nephew is our People's Warden – a first-rate chap, but he has a busy dental practice, and – anyhow, this seems to me like a real possibility. Shall I give Brian a call when I get home?"

"What's Miss Waterman like?"

"Oh, an excellent lady. Elderly, you know. Touch of arthritis. No doubt that's why her disposition is a bit . . . After the active life she's had, it can't be easy. She was a missionary in China for more than twenty years – ran a girls' school there. A little fixed in her views, perhaps – very high moral standards . . . yes. Splendid woman."

I murmur something polite.

"Devoted to her three little Pekinese," he goes on, "and her game of bridge. Unfortunately a chain-smoker, but poor soul, I suppose she finds some consolation in it. I really think you'd find . . . She lives in a bungalow, so the housekeeping part wouldn't be too burdensome, and she spends a lot of time with her ham radio, so that occupies . . ."

"Can you give me a few days, Tom," I say rather desperately. "I'm still – I don't think I can make any decisions about this right away."

"Of course, my dear. Most understandable. There must be many things to consider. And naturally you'll want to consult Marion. I would have thought – I mean you could always move in with her, couldn't you, on a temporary basis, at any rate?"

"No, I couldn't. She and her friend are going to share an apartment this spring, that's all settled. To everyone's satisfaction, Tom."

"I see. Well, no harm, is there, in my sounding Brian out – he'll be at the vestry meeting tomorrow."

"Wittgenstein." The cat, crouched nearby over his own folded paws, blinks at me inquiringly.

"Eh?" says Tom.

"I've been dipping into his book. He believed the daily dialogue mitigates dogmatic assertion because it reminds us of the different ways we apply words."

It is now Tom's turn to blink. He steals a rather baffled look at me. Then, with a sigh, he levers himself to his feet. "Well, I must move on."

For a moment I think I hear Sebastian's voice saying, "Give me proof, woman, that in diversity there is some unifying essence." His face, with its long, flat cheeks a little flushed with whisky, and his young blue eyes, hangs a moment in the air like a mirage, and to exorcise it I follow Tom out to the hall.

"Tell me how Miriam is. Have you seen her lately?"

"Ah, it's going more quickly than they expected. She's very weak now. Needs oxygen nearly all the time. Poor soul, it's sad to see her brought to this." He clears his throat noisily. I push cold hands deeper into my cardigan pockets.

"How on earth do you manage to comfort the dying, Tom? Come to that, how can you forgive God for inflicting things like that on helpless people?" Even as I say this, though, I know I am doing it chiefly to blot out that other matter in my mind, or at the back of it, which I have been so resolutely not thinking about.

Tom pauses in the act of putting on his hat. He sighs, but is too professional to let my question pass. "It's not easy," he says. "You just have to hold onto the central truth – that in the end God will defend us from all danger, ghostly and bodily." He looks tired, this having been one of his hospital-visiting days, but speaking these words seems to give him a kind of refreshment. He chafes my cheek affectionately with the back of his square hand.

"That's all very well, if you can believe it. Go home, Tom; you look exhausted."

"The giver of all goodness also gives us grace to believe, you know."

"Does he? Well, grace is a pretty word. And when you say 'in the end,' that doesn't help much here and now, does it?"

"You've become a bit of a radical lately, haven't you, my dear? Quite a rebellious questioner. A splendid start."

"Start! I have no intention of starting anything." I go on despite the fact it is clear we are talking at cross-purposes. "All I hope for is the sense to keep my head down and escape as many threats as possible. It's only in Victorian novels, thank God, that people had to face a moral crisis. I'm just an obscure citizen of the twentieth century, so I'm quite safe from all that."

Tom resettles his hat, at the same time allowing a large yawn to escape him. He embraces me, says "Bless you," and goes out into the frosty, star-bright evening. When I return to the kitchen to tidy away the tea things, I find Mrs. Wilson at the table looking into an empty cup.

"Reading the leaves," she says. "I do like emblems."

"Fortune telling? Well, Nana and I once had our teacups read. I was going to rise to a great challenge in the middle of my life, the woman said, and she was annoyed when we both immediately got the giggles. When I was a toddler, I was afraid to step off the pavement onto the grass, that's what a bold adventurer I was. And still am. No, I'd much rather not know what's coming, if it can be known. It's almost sure to be nasty or frightening, or both." Here I am referring, of course, as Ethel and I both know, not to the search for employment I must soon come to grips with, but to that other matter at the back of my mind.

"But have you no curiosity?" she wants to know.

"Not about myself. I know me too well. Which means I can pretty well predict my own future. Besides, it's safer not to know."

"Nothing is safe. Surely you know that."

"Oh, you're wrong there. Some things are. Minding your own business and keeping out of other people's, for example. All that. It's the only safety there is."

"Certainly most things are risky; even dangerous. Is that a good reason to refrain from doing them?"

"The best reason in the world, if you ask me."

"You poor creature," says Ethel with sincerity. Her voice is gentle, but there is a faint note of contempt in it none the less. I frown. And after an uncomfortable moment – it is our first disagreement – she vanishes.

I lie in bed next morning before daybreak, arms folded behind my head, and think hard. I think about standing for hours peeling skin off chickens and whacking a cleaver through their pinkish bones at six dollars an hour. I think about emptying ashtrays and walking three Pekes for Miss Waterman. Light slowly filters into the room. I wonder quite seriously whether praying might help; or perhaps a confession of sin. "We have followed too much the devices and desires of our own hearts . . ." and here I sit up. I go to the cupboard and fumble in the pocket of my old beige cardigan. There is the curled-up label reading "Handmade for Devices and Desires, Queen Street West."

Some hours later I am walking along Queen Street past shops selling used comic books, wicker furniture, pets, shoes, furs and hamburgers. This is a part of the city so unknown to me it might almost be a foreign capital in some exotic corner of the globe. The illusion is heightened by the astonishing number of African and Oriental faces I encounter. Amid all the urban grind and clutter of traffic, a sudden thaw has created glittering sidewalk puddles and a chitter of birds. Glad of the excuse to loiter, I slow down, searching shopfronts for the right number. At a red light, I wait beside a toddler in a winter space-suit, holding the hand of its mother, a melancholy Pakistani in boots and leather coat, under which the gilt hem of a sari trails wistfully. A truck cutting the corner short sends a spray of filthy water over her, at which the toddler laughs with delight. The mother and I exchange a rueful smile.

Before I am really ready for it, Devices and Desires presents itself. It is a double-fronted shop with one window full of implements and materials for sewing and knitting; the other stocked with finished articles – samplers, table linen, shawls and the like. Allowing myself no time to pause, I step inside. A pleasant smell of coffee and new fabric inhabits the place. So does a large number of people examining things in the boutique or standing around waiting to be served. The only staff on hand, though, seems to be a small, stout woman in a smock who darts among the customers in a distracted sort of way, talking all the time as if to keep the forces of chaos at bay.

"Yes, we have the fifty-four inch – you'll need six metres to cover – now where's that tape measure? – Yes, madam, I'll be with you in just a – oh, bother that phone – I'll just have to let it ring – now where are my scissors?" Reaching out, I lift a corner of the fabric for her and reveal the handles of a pair of scissors.

"They seem terribly short-handed here today," remarks a woman at my elbow, unbuttoning her fur coat patiently. She extracts from a plastic bag a large piece of Fair Isle knitting which is in a state of extreme confusion. "This thing is driving me crazy, Mrs. Barnes," she adds, raising it and her voice to catch the attention of the stout woman.

"Ah – yes – get to you in a minute – now my pen's gone – my daughter's usually here to help out on Tuesdays, but she's – and my assistant's got flu and can't keep anything down – I don't know –" She lifts both hands to her bushy grey hair and extracts from it with an air of pleased surprise a red ball-point pen. "Now your bill –" she says. "So sorry to keep you waiting," she adds, looking at me in a hunted manner.

"Maybe I could help this lady for you," I suggest, indicating the Fair Isle customer. "I know that pattern well."

"Oh, would you – how very kind – yes, just coming," and she darts off into the boutique.

I see at once what is wrong with the Fair Isle project. Swiftly ripping back I find and pick up two dropped stitches. "Aren't you clever," says a gaunt girl in a blue ski cap. She edges closer, opening a carrier-bag of her own. "Could you just have a quick look at my armhole? Something awful's happened, only a midget could get into it, and I don't know why."

I take the sweater from her. "Ah, well. You've been decreasing one stitch every row instead of one every other row. That's why. Pull it out and start again back here."

Satisfied, both knitters depart. Quite a few of the customers have by now given up and gone home, and Mrs. Barnes in her desperate way trots to and fro dealing with those who remain. Eventually the two of us find ourselves alone in the empty shop. We look at each other amiably.

"Nice of you to help out like that," she says. Now that things have calmed down, she is capable of finishing her sentences. Sighing, she lowers her broad bottom onto a stool. "Now what can I do for you?"

"You could use some of my work, I hope." I grope in my bag for the small teddy bear bought weeks ago at the Yankee Doodle shop. As a sample of my handiwork I've knitted him a miniature duffle coat, using some leftover navy wool and a couple of toggles off an old jacket. Mrs. Barnes touches the small hood and patch pockets with an amused grin.

"Damn nice," she says. "Sure. We take a fifteen per cent commission, of course, but if that's all right – we sell a lot of gifts for brides and newborns – can you do that kind of thing? Shouldn't be hard to agree on a price. People will pay very well for work like that. Otherwise, as you can probably see, I'd have gone out of business a long time ago."

Without bothering with any polite denials, I tell her, "I crochet and embroider too."

"Great. Bring your stuff along. And I often get orders for initialling and so on, if you're interested."

"I'm interested in surviving."

She darts me a quick, interested glance. "Me, too. What's your name, anyway?"

"Rowena Hill."

"I'm Kate Barnes. Not in a rush, are you? Hang on a minute, then."

A minute or two later she reappears with two steaming mugs of coffee. "My daughter's getting married and she just can't help me as much now; as for Judy, the kid's always got something wrong with her, and I really need somebody –" I am much intrigued to discover that she is nervous, even slightly apprehensive of me. "I wonder if by any chance you'd be interested in working here three or four mornings a week?" she goes on, cramming both fists into her smock pockets. "For instance we get so many people coming in with knitting problems. I can't turn them away, for the sake of good will, but the buggers take up so much time – and you obviously have the know-how and the patience. Pay twelve dollars an hour, if you're –"

"Done," I say promptly. To reassure myself that all this is actually happening, I sip my coffee. It is quite dreadful.

"Oh, that's great. I've really needed somebody for weeks and it's frazzled me half to death. Like to start Monday?"

"The sooner the better."

"Right. Monday, then." The door opens and three customers straggle in. "We'll get everything organized then. I'll need your social insurance number and your OHIP and all that – Yes, can I help you?"

I step out onto Queen Street in a state of euphoria. I am an employee with fringe benefits. I don't know exactly what a social insurance number is, but I intend to find out, and get myself one. Cuthbert will know what to do. Down the wet pavement I stride, walking on air.

"So you've got a job," says Charles. "I wish I could say the same." He perches on the end of my sewing table with his usual well-meant but futile effort to seem at home anywhere.

"I haven't seen you for ages!" I say cheerfully. "Where have you been?"

"Ah," he says, looking thoughtful. "I only come along when needed, you know. What with this new interest in your life, maybe . . ."

"Are you surprised? I am, I can tell you. Imagine me in a shop, waiting on customers – talk about radical changes –"

"Radical?" he asks, raising his eyebrows quizzically. "You and I are not people who can change our essential nature, you know. That may be regrettable, of course; but there it is."

"I guess to me even small changes are radical."

"Which illustrates my point."

"Yes, it does."

"What are you making there?"

"Hemstitching some pillowcases for Mrs. Barnes."

"Making things. Inaugural stuff. I like that. It's vaguely encouraging. Well, I must be off to cut a ribbon or two myself. Nice chatting to you, Rowena."

"Always a pleasure, Sir. My regards to your mother, by the way. Her name was mentioned in the courtroom the other day."

He makes me a ceremonial bow. Then, with dignity, but swiftly, he fades and retreats towards the bedroom window. As I watch, hand lifted in farewell, he gracefully melts into the bright air, his ears lingering a second after the rest of him has vanished.

Sunday is a very slow and empty day, because I'm so eager to begin my new career. The house is quiet, the phone mute. I sit about, fidgeting from one room to another, unable to settle to my sewing. I gaze curiously at the faded upholstery of Edwin's chair and the end of the kitchen table where he always laid his carefully folded newspaper, marvelling that these things remain while he is so totally and finally gone. I ponder this for some time. Until now I haven't found it possible to think of him with any kind of detachment. But today for the first time I can consider him almost – though perhaps not quite – kindly.

I wander into the sitting-room again and look at the shabby books in their case. He always resented them ("Why have you always got your nose in a book?"), but perhaps that was an admission of loneliness. They were my defense and refuge, and they shut him out. The one item on those shelves that was his own was the prayer book. After a moment I take it out, and sitting on the edge of his chair, riffle idly through its pages.

It's not the hypocrisy of his churchgoing now that strikes me, but the possibility that he sincerely needed his religion. The communion service, after all, is all about guilt. "We do earnestly repent, and are heartily sorry for these our misdoings," and all that. Yes, it would have been in church, if anywhere, that Edwin might have felt like making me an act of atonement.

But this prayer book is the new one Marion gave him for his birthday just five or six years ago. What happened to that little scuffed red one he used before that? He would never have thrown it away. It must be somewhere in the house . . . Yes, I remember now seeing it when I searched that old trunk in the basement in the days when Cuthbert was nagging me to look everywhere for a will.

Something gets me to my feet. More for something to do than for any clear purpose, I go down the cellar stairs and once more lift the domed lid of the trunk Edwin brought from his Ottawa home all those years ago. It's rather sad that after that it travelled nowhere, but instead served as a sort of burial ground for transient domestic interests of his like home upholstery or do-it-yourself barbering. Here is a packet of yellowed letters to him in my untidy schoolgirl writing, together with some loose snapshots of my old, rounder-faced self in that long-ago park. I saw these on my earlier visit to the trunk, and tossed them aside. Now it seems to me rather touching that he should have kept them. I have no wish to look more closely at them – the whiff of orris-root I used to romanticize the notepaper embarrasses me now; yet somehow they humanize Edwin. They remind me how private his emotions always were, and how much more of him I might have known if –

But there is the little red prayer book, under Marion's badge-covered Brownie uniform. Now those thirty married years are over, I can admit they included moments of satisfaction, even happiness – not many, perhaps, but some. Suddenly I see again Marion's thin little six-year-old legs running eagerly up the path to the camp lodge. She was so impatient to begin the adventure of camp that she forgot to turn and wave goodbye to us, and Edwin silently reached for and took my hand. My eyes ache in the poor light. Out of somewhere there drifts across my mind Wittgenstein's dictum: "Whereof one cannot speak, thereof one must be silent." No doubt I have not been entirely fair to Edwin. Perhaps it would do me no harm, in fact, to ask somebody's forgiveness for sins of my own.

I take the little red book upstairs and sit at the kitchen table to examine it. The binding is broken with long handling, and loose sheets of sallow India paper protrude on three sides. The flyleaf, foxed and creased with age, drifts free, and I catch it before it reaches the floor. Something is written there in blurred pencil. My breath snags in my throat and the words swim under my eyes: "I mean Rowena to have the Don Mills house." It is signed Edwin John Hill and dated eight years ago. And it is a valid will. I know this because months ago Cuthbert lectured me on the subject. A signed holograph will, even one as rudimentary as this, is quite legal.

For minutes I stare at the pencilled words for clues to Edwin's motives and feelings, but cannot find them there. The facing page in the book lists the moveable feasts of the church year. Bemused, I wonder what impulse made Edwin, perhaps at some pause in morning prayer, scrawl this statement of intention. It seems bizarre to be elated over such an enigma. Nonetheless, I go swiftly to the phone and call Cuthbert.

"My dear, how marvellous!" he all but shouts. "Yes, it's perfectly valid . . . we can easily prove it's his handwriting. Oh, glory, to think all along I had this gut feeling he left a will, and here it is!

"So now you can count on a roof over your head at least. First thing tomorrow I'll apply for probate of the first will to be set aside. Then we apply for grant of probate to yours –" Here he gives a tremendous sneeze and adds, "I've got a filthy cold, but I'll get this in the works first thing in the morning. The whole business will take a few months, of course, but what the heck – oh, I'm so pleased for you."

But the joy in his voice tells me he is pleased for himself, too. And I don't resent that in the least. This liberates him at last, and we both know it.

CHAPTER TEN

❧

I've been behind the counter at Devices and Desires for a week now. It's still rather a nervous business confronting customers, getting used to the stock, travelling in rush hour . . . It all seems not just to fill my time but cram it to overflowing. I find it a scramble to fit in my own household routine. It's sometimes even difficult to find time for a peaceful bowel movement. And some of Kate Barnes's scattiness may be rubbing off on me. I left my wallet on the supermarket counter the other day and had to run back to retrieve it. And now I come across a key in my kitchen that I don't recognize at all. My own house key is on a ring. Where on earth have I acquired this one? Then I remember, and drop it into my handbag. Don't forget, I tell myself, to return this to the Wrights some time. Then I set out for the shopping plaza, this being my morning off.

Melting snow soaks the yellow grass and makes a blue glaze of wetness on the pavement. Not a leaf or blade of green shows itself yet, but the air feels faintly warm and smells of earth. Winter-pale people, still padded in their heavy coats, wait at the bus stop, turning their faces wistfully up to the sun. With cautious half-smiles they say things to each other like, "Nice change, eh?" and, "Thought it would never come." Among them, with a slight jolt of recognition, I spot Mrs. Blot in the armour of a raspberry-coloured down coat that doubles her bulk and clashes with her blusher. The bus sweeps to the curb and gathers them all in, and I walk on.

At the corner of McKenzie Street, without any instructions from me, my feet pause. Well, after all, I think; why not? Just a brief look-in for old times' sake, since the coast appears to be clear. After all, I haven't seen him for a couple of months. I'll just stay long enough to say hello. At his age, you never know – it might be the last chance. And perhaps that will get the old brute out of my conscience and my dreams.

The key turns with such reluctance in its slot that I think for a moment the lock has been changed. But Mrs. Blot has not carried the war that far. I step inside to find everything unchanged . . . the brooding silence, the smell of dust, the stuffy darkness that makes its own glum statement in the midst of the radiance outdoors. As always the place both intimidates and depresses me, because it seems to prove that time and circumstances can crush even a strong personality like Sebastian's. I climb the creaking stairs calling his name into the stagnant gloom.

There is no answer, but I find him slumped in a bedroom chair, head back, exposing a ropy neck, eyes half closed. He is not asleep or even dozing, but his thoughts, whatever they are, appear to oppress him. A sour smell hangs about the room. The fingernails of his slack hands are yellow and broken. His beard, now raggedly thick and stained with food, gives him a helpless air that suggests suffering. When the hooded blue eyes open briefly they are quite blank. No recognition brings them to life; no intelligence moves there; no interest keeps them open. My heart begins to beat hard and fast, as if I have been accused.

"Sebastian," I say loudly.

He mumbles something inaudible and rolls his head away from my voice. I touch his shoulder where the sharpness of his bones startles me.

"Open your eyes," I tell him. "Do you hear me, Seb? It's me – Rowena."

"No," he mutters. "No point in that."

"*Sit up*, Sebastian." I give him a none-too-gentle shake. "Wake up."

"Wha' for?" he mumbles. His head sinks forward again.

There seems no appropriate answer to his question, so I go to the window and draw back the curtains to let in more light. Dust released from the faded fabric spins aimlessly in the bright sunlight. It's too late, I think; but instead of accepting defeat and simply turning away to go, I stand there with my heart banging faster and louder than ever. Then I go back to his chair and bend over him.

"Sebastian," I say, quietly this time. Oddly enough, this rouses him. He looks at me vaguely, lips fumbling for words. I take his bony hand in both of mine. It is icy cold.

"Mrs. Blot has gone downtown," I tell him. "Now sit up. Wake up. I want to talk to you."

He blinks at me, frowning.

"Listen to me. Are you listening?"

"You look awful. Why have you let yourself get in this state? It's disgraceful. Have you no pride? Seb, do you hear me? You've deliberately let go, haven't you? It's true, isn't it? Just to get attention. Admit it. You don't have to be in this mess."

"No." He closes his eyes again.

"Then why stay in it?"

"Good question. Nobody pays attention. And why should they? I'll soon be nothing but a bit of atomic garbage in the winds that howl around the universe."

"Now, Seb, answer me: do you want to go on, or are you really giving up? Come on. *I* am paying attention."

"Extendicare," he says, for the first time looking at me directly. "Bastard term. Bastard concept. I'm on a waiting list – can you think of anything worse than that? What's to do but give up? That's where pride comes in. Go with some kind of dignity."

I take the skeletal hand between mine, trying to warm it. Instead of calming, my heart is drumming more insistently than ever, with something unfamiliar that feels like rage, or resolution. The glass of water by his bed containing dentures is cloudy and bubbled. His breath is bad. The tumbled bedclothes, the stale disorder of the room, the unbuttoned, crumpled pyjamas he wears all fuel this anger.

"Tell me the truth, now, Seb. Do you want to get out of here?"

"Where to – the knacker's yard?" he mutters.

"What about coming to my place?"

"Your place?"

"Yes. As it happens, I own a house. Come on home with me. We'll explain to the Wrights later. I'll look after you – that is if you behave decently. Are you game for it?"

He stares at me. "You're mad."

"Yes, I am. Come on then, if you're coming."

There is a pause while he deals with his pride. "Get some clothes on," I urge impatiently. "You can't go anywhere like this. I'll call a taxi."

A flush jumps into his hollow cheeks. After a moment he takes my proffered arm and with its help hauls himself up on unsteady legs. "Got to pee first," he says breathlessly.

"That's right. Here we go, then." We shuffle along to the bathroom. Once he is safely inside I hurry back to the fusty bedroom and snatch up the array of medications there, stuffing them into a couple of carrier bags together with some clothes from the bureau drawers.

"Put these on," I tell him, handing shirt and trousers through the bathroom door. "And don't you dare fall in there, or they'll send me to jail." Hastily I add slippers and his teeth to the bags, and then call a taxi. My fingers are shaking so much I have to dial three times before getting the right number. When Sebastian creeps back down the hall, bracing himself along the way with one hand on the wall, he is more or less dressed, but he has flushed a rather alarming, mottled colour and is breathing heavily. Prince Charles's voice inside my head remarks, "This could kill him," but I tell him fiercely, "So what?"

"Wait," says Seb. "Can't do this, you know. The stairs. Can't manage them."

I look at him desperately. We have to get out of here somehow, and soon. Mrs Blot might come in at any moment, and that will be the end of it all for him.

"Look – you could get down those stairs on your seat."

"Eh? My what?"

"Yes – just sit down on the top step and grab the banister. Come on – it's perfectly simple. You must have done it when you were two. Try, anyhow. Hurry, now, before –"

Wheezing and shaky, he manages to lower himself by degrees until he is sitting perilously on the top step. His skinny legs gawkily rest on the next step down. From that height he peers down at the dim hall below as a mountaineer might look giddily down at a remote valley. "That's right," I tell him. "Now just lower your bottom onto the next step. Come on, man, think of England; we've got to make it." The doorbell then rings, making us both start horribly.

"Oh, God, there's the taxi."

I scramble past him to answer the door, dragging with me the bags of his clothes. With maddening slowness Sebastian lowers himself down one more step. The cab driver, a swarthy East Indian who takes the bags from me kindly, tries not to look astonished by the sight of an elderly gentleman coming downstairs on his bottom. "Could you please give us a hand out to the car," I ask him breathlessly. "Just two more to go now, Seb. Take it easy. You're doing fine."

By the time he reaches floor level and in stiff instalments gets himself upright, Sebastian's face is crimson and he is wheezing in long spasms that frighten me. Then I realize that for the first time since the Korean War, the old man is laughing.

"What the hell are you doing here, Rowena? Where are we?"

"I live here, Seb. We came here together this morning – don't pretend you've forgotten that. I certainly never will."

"Ah, yes. We eloped, didn't we? So this is your house, is it?"

His eyes travel around the banal little sitting-room, and Wittgenstein, sitting primly on the rug with tail curled around his paws, examines him with the same blend of curiosity and surprise. As soon as we arrived, Sebastian sank into the easy chair, trembling, and minutes later, worn out by exertion and stress, dropped then and there into a deep sleep. My own first act was to phone the Wrights, but though I've called repeatedly since then, there is no answer next door. Between calls I sat on the sofa watching my guest sleep, and trying not to think about all the probable consequences of my crazy act of kidnap. Curiously enough, though, now the deed has been done, nearly all my qualms of fear seem to have vanished. I feel, in fact, serene, even amused.

I smile at Seb, who also seems at ease, almost happy, snapping his fingers and trilling at the cat. His long legs are crossed one over the other, revealing the fact that he has put his trousers on over his pyjama bottoms.

"I remember when these semis went up in the late fifties," he says. "Architecture like this amounts to a criminal offence, wouldn't you say? Or perhaps you wouldn't. I'm not famous for tact. After that tomb I've been living in, I guess you could call this cosy. Where's your bathroom? Nature calls. In fact, her voice is getting a tad shrill."

"It's upstairs, I'm afraid."

He frowns. "This is grave news, you realize."

Instantly my calm vanishes and agitation sets in once more. Here is only the first of what will doubtless be a long chain of unforeseen, small but insurmountable problems.

"Well, Seb, we'll just have to get you up there somehow."

"Frankly I don't see how."

"Come on, you didn't think you could get downstairs, either, and you managed it. Let's go. I'll help you."

In a Mutt and Jeff fashion we tackle the stairs. I prop and push fervently while he hauls himself up, one step at a time, with the help of the banister and occasional profanity. There is a perilous moment near the top when he totters, but that crisis passes, and he shuffles at last into the bathroom, wheezing, "Excelsior!"

While I wait for him to reappear, I put clean linen on the bed for him in my room, and move my own things across the hall into Marion's old room. With the padded rocker and some of my books about, the big bedroom will make a pleasant enough bed-sitter for him. I open the window a crack to let in the clean-smelling, moist air and the sunlight that lavishly irradiates the deep blue sky. This clear light lies like a blessing on the rough trunk and bare boughs of the back-yard maple tree.

"Now this is going to be your room," I tell Seb when he shuffles into view. "Try out the rocker. I'm going down to get us a bite of lunch. If you feel like coming down for it, do – on your seat, please. We don't want any broken bones. Later on, when you get some muscle back in those legs –"

A loud rapping at the front door cuts me off. We exchange a hunted glance. "I'm not here!" he says hoarsely, gripping my wrist in a bony hand.

"Take it easy," I tell him, and hurry downstairs, my heart rattling noisily inside my rib cage. When I open the door the sight of two large policemen, one fat and one thin, makes me gasp.

"You the lady of the house?" the fat one asks, squinting at the pocket notebook in his meaty hand.

"Yes."

"Your name, ma'am?"

"I'm Mrs. – Mrs. Edwin – I'm a widow."

"Mrs. Edwin?"

"Yes."

"This four-seven-six Maple?"

It occurs to me wildly that they are not here to retrieve Sebastian but to claim the house for John Hill. Either way, I don't mean to give up without a struggle. "This is four-seven-two," I tell them, doing my best to sound calm. "I've lived here for thirty years. What are you – are you looking for someone?"

The fat one eases his leather holster with a menacing creak. "Witness to an accident is who we're looking for."

The thin one says, "Not the right address, Joe. We want four-seven-six." The fat one sighs and puts away the notebook. "Sorry to trouble you, ma'am. Good day." And they thump off down the wet steps.

I close the door and lean against it for a moment. Sebastian's long face appears over the stair banister.

"Gone?" he asks cautiously.

"Yes."

"Splendid. Weren't looking for stolen goods, were they?" His wheezing laugh floats down to me like a pat on the back. "Now how about that bite of lunch, Rowena? For some reason, I feel hungry."

"Coming right up." But before getting out the omelette pan, I try the Wrights' number again. There is still no answer. In a way, this is a relief. As I break eggs into a bowl, I wonder what name the law might have for what I've done. Is stealing an old man grand larceny? Rape? Pillage? It must come under the general heading of felony, and I am not looking forward to what Cuthbert will say when he hears the story. Or Marion. Or the Wrights; or, come to that, Prince Charles. What I've done is surely going to be far beyond even my ability to excuse or explain. And yet I can't help feeling proud of myself for committing a misdemeanour on such a grand scale.

In the middle of the night, a muffled crash wakes me. Judgement, I think, still entangled in light sleep, and seizing a bedside torch I scurry across the hall. As I grope towards Sebastian's bed, my bare feet encounter his overturned bedside lamp with its long, cold snake of cord. Then the narrow ray of my torch reveals Seb himself, standing, a preternaturally tall figure in pyjamas, on the other side of the bed.

"Seb, what happened? Are you all right?"

He turns aside to snatch up his dressing gown and wrap it round himself apron-fashion. "Do you realize it's three o'clock in the morning?" he asks austerely.

"Yes, I realize that. What got you up?" Fumbling, I set up his lamp on the night table, discovering at the same time he has upset his water glass, which now lies half under the bed, spreading a wet patch shaped like a swan.

"Bad dream," he mutters. "Bloody pills. Go back to bed." He avoids my eye; then, after a pause, adds only half audibly, "Thought I was in the loo, actually."

"Oh, is that all? Can happen to anyone, of course." I pick up the glass, adding untruthfully, "Happens to me sometimes. Here's a set of clean p.j.s."

"Bloody cousins of mine used to beat me every day for wetting the bed." His voice trails away as he turns the corner into the bathroom. I rapidly check that the bed is dry and straighten the tumbled blankets.

"Sorry to be such a bore," he says, reappearing at the door.

"I'll just get some paper towels to mop this water up. Would you like a hot drink while I'm down there?"

"Make it a double," he says cheerfully.

Ten minutes later I am back with two steaming mugs of cocoa and sit down beside him to share it.

"This is better for you than a pill," I tell him.

He sniffs his drink pessimistically. "That's not claiming a hell of a lot for it. But cheers anyway."

"Next time the doctor pays you a call, let's ask him to review all your medication. After a point I'm sure all these pills clash with each other, and after that with you. Or maybe we should just review the doctor. Does he really pay attention?"

"Oh, he's not a bad chap for an existentialist."

"Anyhow, we'll see what he says."

"Before I dozed off, Rowena, I was thinking."

"Were you, now. What about?"

"About money, among other things. You haven't got much, have you?"

"Very little – only a small salary from . . . This house is really my only asset. Why?"

"Whereas, you know, I have my various pensions, plus that mausoleum on McKenzie Street. Satisfactory, isn't it? King Cophetua. Of course that house of mine is falling to pieces, but given its size, it would probably fetch quite a preposterous sum. Now I was thinking, with the cash from that, we could buy some-place, maybe out of town, if you'd prefer that – or we could enlarge this potty little house, what d'ye think of that idea? Put an exten-sion on at the back – have another bathroom put in downstairs, and a sitting-room with a fireplace. And up here a big sun-room for your sewing things." He makes an extensive gesture with his long arms. "Well, what do you say to that, eh?"

There is something about his use of pronouns that pleases me so deeply I can make no answer. Over my shoulder I glance at the table with my machine, shears and sewing basket, which have so long occupied a crowded corner of the room. It is strange how unfamiliar everything suddenly appears, now that his long red dressing gown hangs on the door and his leather slippers lie on the rug beside the wet patch, which now looks more like a ship on its way somewhere. Because he is looking at it the room has quite a new presence. Cramped, shabby, nondescript, it nevertheless sud-denly seems to have possibilities not before perceived. And when his hooded eyes, alert and astute now, rest with speculation on me, his gaze has a further, curious effect: it makes me feel significant. This sensation is so novel it puts me into something of a fluster and turns my cheeks hot.

"You see, I've put insomnia to some practical use for a change," he says. "Unless," he goes on, putting down his cup with a tremu-lous hand, "those red cheeks mean you're furious with me. I meant no impertinence, you understand. It's not that I'm ungrateful for your hospitality. But you must agree this place will need some improvements if we stay here. And as for money – you realize what I was paying that slut, the Muse of Don Mills – just to warm up junk food and never dust the furniture? If you look after me, Rowena, I shall insist you accept the same. That way we'll both have what we need, except that I'm the one who will get the best of the bargain by far. It's been amusing to lie here planning the house extension. Did you know, by the way, that Wittgenstein designed and built a house for his sister in Vienna? He also designed a jet-engine propeller, but I know my own limitations." Here he yawns widely and slides farther down on his pillows.

"You can pay me room and board," I tell him, not without pride, "but I have a part-time job downtown, you know. Anyhow, you go to sleep now. We'll talk some more in the morning. I mean later. And if the Wrights ever get home – I can't think where they've got to – we'll have to discuss all this with them, as well."

"None of their affair," he says drowsily.

"Oh, I'm afraid, one way and another, they're going to think it is."

But to avoid further discussion, he is officially asleep.

As I creep into my own bed, I think with a kind of defiant satisfaction, "Yes, Seb. You'll die before long and become an atom in the wind that howls around the universe. But in the meantime you're here, with me."

Next afternoon, in an aisle of the supermarket perhaps appropriately labelled Cleansers, I encounter Tom, whose pouched and tired face lights up at the sight of me.

"Ah, my dear Rowena, this is a nice surprise."

"Hello, Tom. Good to see you – I've been trying to get you on the phone but you're never in lately."

"It's high season for funerals, my dear. Actually, I was planning to drop in to see you – so why not now – I could carry your groceries home into the bargain. We haven't had a get-together for some time, have we?" He beams down at me genially as various impatient shoppers push past us to get at the boxes of detergent.

"Er – no – we haven't; but you see, Tom –"

With a quick glance round to make sure none of his parishioners are within earshot, he goes on, "Been wanting to discuss that matter with you we talked about last week."

"Oh, yes, that – Well, you see, Tom, since then –"

"Because I've had a word with the nephew, and he seems very –"

"Tom, let's get out of the traffic a bit here." I draw him around the corner to an unfrequented alcove displaying dog collars and dishcloths. In a crowd his slight deafness is more apparent than usual; furthermore, accustomed as he is to having no competition in church, he tends in public to pitch his voice louder than is welcome at the moment.

"There; that's better. You see, Tom, a lot has happened since I saw you last. I've tried several times to phone you, but – The thing is, I've found myself a job in a handicraft shop. And a will of Edwin's has actually turned up, leaving me the house. So I'm not in such a needy position as we –"

"No! Really? A will leaving you – well, my dear, I do congratulate you! That's excellent news. Excellent!" Smiling broadly he frees one hand from the wire grip of his basket to pat my shoulder. His shopping, I see, consists of several TV dinners, a large chocolate bar and a bottle of club soda. My basket, on the other hand, is loaded with eggs, flour, sugar, vegetables and a large chicken, and I now set it down on the floor to ease my arms.

"And that's not all," I continue, edging us aside while an old lady in a fur coat pauses to examine the dog leashes. "I've got a lodger now."

"A lodger!" he echoes, staring at me.

The old lady, having chosen a blue leash, exchanges it for a red one. Then she changes her mind again, and in attempting to replace the red one on the rack, knocks the whole display to the floor. Tom gallantly stoops to retrieve and replace them while she drifts pensively away, perhaps having suddenly remembered she hasn't got a dog. Tom rises, flushed with exertion. Rather testily he says, "Whatever do you mean – somebody's actually rooming with you?"

"Yes. You see, my neighbours the Wrights – you don't know them; they're not churchgoers – anyhow her old father needs a bit of looking after, and so I – well, the whole thing was done on the spur of the moment, and . . ."

"Purely a temporary arrangement, then," he says more pacifically.

"Well, I'm not sure about that."

But he brushes this aside. "I still think, my dear, you should really consider Miss Waterman. Her nephew is very anxious to meet you. He's greatly concerned about her and he seemed delighted to know you might consider . . . Of course I haven't committed you to anything, and they might agree to a live-out arrangement if you prefer that." He fixes me with a commanding gaze that makes me fidget nervously with the clasp on my handbag. Patiently he waits for me to answer.

At last I find my voice, surprised to hear it emerge quite clear and steady.

"Tom, as I told you, I have a job now downtown. But even if I didn't – I'm afraid the very sound of Miss Waterman appalls me. Please don't be annoyed – you've been so good and kind, and I do appreciate it, but now I have this job and a home of my own, I have to tell you that wild horses couldn't get me into that bungalow with the ham radio and the three Pekes." This declaration, firm as it is, leaves me rather breathless. With dismay, I see that Tom is becoming not only justifiably irritated, but quite unfriendly. The timid little woman he thought he knew has metamorphosed into someone he does not really like much, if at all. My first impulse, of course, is to apologize, and the second to retract. That was what Nana taught me a good girl did when faced with male opposition. It's the reflex of a lifetime that makes me say, "I'm really sorry, Tom. I know you've gone to a lot of trouble for me, and I'm grateful for it. Only you see for the time being I'm committed –"

"It's up to you, of course," he says stiffly.

There is an uncomfortable pause. This is obviously the moment to go on to phase two and recant; but somehow, stubbornly, the words refuse to come. And really, I tell myself, there seems no good reason why they should. Surely I needn't become the hireling of Tom's missionary friend simply out of politeness or fear of giving offence – specially when there are other things I much prefer to do. Just the same, Tom's displeasure makes me so uncomfortable it's all I can do not to hang my head like a child in disgrace. I make a last, lame effort to placate him and my own conscience.

"You see, Tom, I'll be paid for looking after . . . Mr. Long is going to be a paying guest, so –"

"I quite understand," he says, in the huffy manner of one who does nothing of the kind. "Of course if I'd known this before, I wouldn't have wasted anybody's time. Regrettable all round. However, I'll tell Waterman at once that your circumstances have changed and you're not available. Now I must really get along. Good day, Rowena."

He makes off with his basket so crisply I have no chance even to say goodbye. It's clear I have lost more than the chance to have my groceries carried home. For a few minutes I stay there among the dog leashes feeling downcast and guilty. Then I begin to remember with some complacence my speech about the wild horses, and my spirits lift a little. Once outside in the sunshine, I suddenly break into a broad smile, which manifestly puzzles passersby.

It's unfortunate that Marion should have chosen to drop in on Sunday just when I am on my knees in the kitchen trimming Sebastian's toenails. They are in a sorry state – horny and over-grown, curling over his toe pads like claws, and I've been working on them for half an hour. While he soaks one foot in a basin, I clip and file away at the other, and we are so busy arguing about deter-minism that neither of us hears her key in the lock. When she appears at the kitchen door and says, "Hello, Mother," we both start as if caught in some clandestine act.

"Oh – there you are, dear," I say, trying to dispose in haste of Sebastian's large, naked foot so that I can stand up. "This is Mr. Long. Seb – my daughter, Marion."

She took the news of my employment on Queen Street with something almost like approval; but when I phoned her soon afterwards to explain I now have a boarder, she was quite openly dubious and disapproving. At that, I avoided burdening her with any details. Without actually lying, I described him lightly as elderly, and implied he was quite active. Now her clear eyes rest judgementally on his white head, the cane hooked over his chair back, and his gnarled, blueish feet. The floor around us is liberally splashed, and bits of yellow toenail lie scattered about.

"Well, I was just – we were just finishing up here – would you like some tea, dear?"

"It's all right, Mother, don't get in a flap."

"Well, perhaps you could fill the kettle while I –"

"Yes, of course."

Sebastian contemplates her trim, uniformed figure with ironic curiosity. "In the police force, are you, Miss Hill?" he asks.

"Division Commissioner with the Girl Guides," she tells him crisply.

"I've always admired the Guides," he says. "They combine moral uplift and practicality in the most ingenious way. Christianity and knots. It's a combination I'd have thought only a man could take seriously. It's a fact, isn't it, that Baden-Powell from the start turned over the Girl Scout movement to his sister? I think he suspected the female branch would never stay the course for giggling."

"If so, he was wrong, wasn't he?" Marion returns coolly. "We'll celebrate our eightieth anniversary next year."

"I celebrated mine some time ago," he says, grinning. "But it's nothing to brag about. *Au contraire*, in fact."

This is not a good beginning. Seb's mocking conversational style, which I enjoy so much, seems to her, I can tell, merely silly. With little ceremony I dry his feet and thrust them into his broken old slippers. "Will you have tea down here with us?" I ask him, trying to telegraph wordlessly the hint that a sense of humour is not one of Marion's chief assets. With a twitch of his heavy eyelids he gets this message, but interprets it to mean he'd better disappear.

"No, thanks, Rowena, you ladies enjoy your visit alone. I'll go on upstairs. Charmed to have met you, Miss Hill." Creakily rising, he takes possession of the cane and begins to shuffle off. I start to offer my arm, but he impatiently waves me back. "I can manage perfectly well," he says, and I let him go without protest. Through the kettle's shriek I strain to hear him reach the landing safely. With relief a few moments later I hear the creak of the bedroom floor, which means he has made it to his room. It irritates but does not surprise me that Marion's presence has so put us on the defensive. I might have known in advance that she would take a dim view of Sebastian's personality. The nakedness of his feet no doubt created a bad first impression, too, and this seems to me unfair. To conceal these thoughts and quell certain anxieties about the future, I fold the towels and empty the basin, creating small talk as I do so.

"Well, dear, how are things with you? When do you and Bernice move into the new place?"

"Not till April first. I told you that the other day."

"Yes, I remember now. And she's quite . . . recovered now, would you say?"

"Of course. From the start it was all mostly a performance."

If that's true, and you know it, how can you possibly be so matter-of-fact about it? I wonder privately. She claps the lid on the brown teapot and drops the knitted cosy over the brew. "And this lodger of yours," she asks, turning to look squarely at me. "How's that working out?" With reluctance I meet the challenge.

"Why, just fine, dear. He's no trouble really. In fact –"

"Oh, come on, Mother. Of course he's trouble. Looking after anyone that age is a big responsibility. The thing is, does it make sense to take it on? It might be a good idea to rent out your spare room, but it would make a lot more sense to have a single woman here, with a job – someone who'd be out all day. As it happens Moira Baxter in our office is looking for a room – bed-and-breakfast sort of thing. Her diabetes is no real problem as long as someone keeps an eye on her. Decent type, Moira. You'd like her."

There is a brief silence.

"I like Mr. Long."

"That's fairly obvious," she says tartly, "or he'd hardly be getting a pedicure in your kitchen. It doesn't alter the fact that it's crazy to take on an old man in bad shape, on top of this new job of yours. For one thing, he's bound to deteriorate as time goes on. You know that's true, Mother."

"Marion, I –"

"The whole thing was decided on impulse, you told me so yourself. Tom, I know, thinks the whole arrangement is quite deplorable. And when the Wrights get back from wherever it is they've gone, they're sure to agree with me. That old man is too much altogether for someone like you with no training or –"

She pours tea with brusque efficiency into our cups and gestures me towards a chair, which I do not take.

"Tom has reasons of his own for disapproving that I'd rather not go into right now. As for the Wrights, let's let them speak for themselves, shall we?"

"By all means. But you'd better be ready for it, Mother, because –"

"And if it comes to speaking, Sebastian and I are both entitled to a voice as well, surely."

"Nobody said you weren't. I'm simply trying to point out that you're proposing to take on a real burden – a thankless kind of custodial job with no future. With somebody like Moira, you'd at least have your privacy and no problems. I'm thinking of you, Mother, that's all."

"Are you, Marion?" I say sadly. "Well, I suppose you believe you are."

"That's a peculiar thing to say. Honestly, since Dad went, there are times when I wonder whether you – whether you aren't – well, in some ways maybe you're still in shock. But it's obvious that ever since that will turned up you've been –"

"Been what? A little less easy to manipulate?"

Two angry spots of colour have begun to burn in her cheeks. "I really am beginning to think your common sense is gone," she says tartly. "If you honestly can't see the foolishness of having a senile patient in the house instead of –"

"Marion." I take a moment here to muster my forces, inadvertently creating an impressive pause. "Your intentions are good, I suppose, though there's plenty of room for doubt about that. The point is this: I have never since your teens burdened you with unwanted advice. I have nothing to say about your own living arrangements, for instance. Now it's high time you returned the compliment. For better or worse, I'm an adult capable of making my own decisions. What's more, you owe me, whether you like it or not, some tact and consideration. No matter how much your nature and judgement differ from mine, they don't entitle you to dismiss me as if I were nobody."

With something like astonishment I find myself able to reach the end of this pronouncement without once faltering or melting into tears. It is clear that Marion, too, in her fashion, is astounded. Her face could not express more consternation if the cat had suddenly risen to his hind legs and begun to quote Shelley. With frigid dignity she pushes aside her cup of tea and gets to her feet.

"I'm sorry my concern offends you," she says. Pulling on her coat she makes off down the hall in long strides. But when she turns at the door with a stiff farewell nod, I see, just for the fraction of a second, that she is afraid to say anything more. For the first time in our joint lives, in fact, she is afraid of me. And this brings me a dry, grim kind of satisfaction I'm half ashamed of – but only half.

"**I** was in this neighbourhood to see a client," Cuthbert says, blinking at me through his thick glasses, "so I thought I'd drop in for a minute . . . just for a bit of a chat." He leans forward to place a decorous kiss on my cheek.

"Of course; come on in, my dear. Always nice to see you."

I whisk his coat into the cupboard while he tugs down his waistcoat and adjusts his tie as if preparing for some obscure kind of confrontation. "How's your job going?" he asks.

"I'm enjoying it. The owner is a nice woman. She makes me feel efficient – strong – capable."

"That's nice," he says vaguely. "Well, I have nothing new to report on the legal front. Of course Hill's lawyer's been put in the picture – literally – I faxed him a copy of the new will – so we should have no problem at all. What I actually dropped in to tell you was –"

"Come on in here, Cuthbert. We were just about to have a drink while dinner's cooking."

I usher him into the kitchen where Sebastian is ensconced doing the *Times* crossword instead of shelling peas as requested. He rises slowly to greet the guest, his old cardigan drooping from his bony shoulders.

"This is Cuthbert Wesley, Seb, my, er, lawyer. Sebastian Long." They shake hands, exchanging a glance of mutual assessment and curiosity. "Rowena's spoken of you," Seb remarks rather grudgingly, as if this fact to some extent validates Cuthbert's existence.

"Yes. How d'ye do," says Cuthbert without enthusiasm, pushing up his glasses with a short forefinger. I hastily measure out malt whiskies and bestow one on each of them, hoping to create a more cordial atmosphere. "Do sit down, both of you. Better still, go into the sitting-room; I'll join you in a minute as soon as I deal with these peas."

"I like it here," says Seb, repossessing his straight chair. "So do I," says Cuthbert, and sits down opposite him. I add potatoes to the roasting pan, shove it back into the oven, and then get to work on the peas. As soon as all of us are seated, one of those deadly social vacuums develops, in the form of a silence more assertive than any noise. Seb swirls his drink moodily and squints through the bottoms of his glasses at his puzzle. Cuthbert fidgets with his silk tie. I rack my brains for something to say. "Hasn't the weather been lovely," I finally bring out in a tentative voice. And the setting sun, as if to snub this platitude, breaks out of a dark cloud bank to flood the window with radiance.

"Oh, it promises to be a lovely spring, all right," agrees Cuthbert politely. "Rowena tells me you're from the Old Country," he says to Seb. "You must miss the early daffodils and things."

"I don't miss the early rheumatics, I can tell you that."

Cuthbert looks down at his polished shoes. Wittgenstein, who has taken a violent fancy to Seb, now leaps into his lap and begins to knead vigorously. Seb dumps him off without ceremony. "Get off, you old sex maniac," he says. Cuthbert clears his throat.

"I understand you were a philosophy professor, Mr. Long. That must have been an interesting career."

"In the end," remarks Seb, looking severely across the table, "the concept that every proposition has more than one complete analysis brought on a sort of intellectual hernia, from which I suffer to this day."

"Er – you don't say. I never took Philosophy at Queen's."

"Well, it's hardly something one takes like a pill."

"Too abstract and theoretical for me. I've got a very literal sort of mind."

"Then you probably saved yourself a lot of heartburn."

"Well, I'm afraid I have to drink and run, Rowena. Thanks for the whisky, but I must get along now. Nice to have met you, sir." And he offers his hand to Seb. "A pleasure," murmurs Sebastian without much conviction. I follow Cuthbert into the hall.

"Pity you can't stay, dear. Perhaps you could come for dinner some time soon."

"Sorry to rush like this, but you see, I really just dropped in to – I forgot you had a lodger, to tell the truth – but I wanted to tell you . . . something personal." Here he lowers his voice till it becomes almost inaudible. In the not very clear light of the hallway, his face looks dark, and peering closely I see that he is blushing.

"Something personal?" We retreat towards the front door and I, too, cautiously lower my voice. Sebastian's hearing can be acute at all the wrong moments. "What is it, then?"

"Well, I just wanted you to know right away that . . . I mean, it's right you should be the first to . . ."

"Yes?"

"Rowena, dear, you've been so sweet to me."

"That's not what you want to tell me, is it?"

"Well, not exactly, but it's part of it." He takes both my hands in a rather feverish grip and looks at me helplessly.

"It's about you and Elaine, isn't it?" I ask, since there seems no other way out of this verbal impasse.

"How on earth did you guess?"

"Ah, well. It was not really difficult, dear."

Relief makes his round face shine like a happy child's. "Yes, Elaine and I are engaged. Isn't it wonderful? I'll be husband and father in one fell swoop. It happened last night, and I'm just in some kind of daze. I can hardly believe my luck – a beautiful girl like that accepting me . . . it's like a dream or something."

I smile, repressing at the same time a faint reminiscent pang as I picture the engagement ceremony.

"Wonderful. I told you something like this would happen, didn't I?"

"Actually you did. And you were right. About that and lots of other things. You've been wise and wonderful about everything, Rowena dear, and I'll never forget it."

"Yes, you will, and that's just as it should be, Cuthbert. I wish you both all the happiness in the world."

We embrace and he trots off down the path, his short legs twinkling so exuberantly he might almost be dancing. When I turn back to the kitchen, a rich smell of roast chicken drifts out to meet me. The cat is curled on Seb's bony knees and he is reading *The Innocent Traveller*, glasses perched on the end of his long nose. Without glancing up he says, "How come I never heard of Ethel Wilson before? Listen to this for a nutshell description of progress: 'Down came the forests. Chop. Chop. Chop.' Marvellous."

"Yes, isn't she?"

The second week of Seb's residency has begun, and we are playing Scrabble over a nightcap. The game is new to me, but I liked it immediately after discovering it is not at all like chess, Edwin's game, whose strategies and aggressions I always found so disconcerting. As for bridge, its intricacies are such that Tom and Marion long ago gave up trying to teach them to me. Scrabble seems to me, in fact, too verbal, amusing and civilized to be a game in that sense at all, which is perhaps why I enjoy it so much. Now I wait impatiently for my turn to add *ed* to the word *exist*.

Breathing loudly down his long nose, Seb studies the board, then fumbles his squares into a vertical line to form *existence*.

"Darn you, Seb."

While I brood over my collection of letters, the phone rings. "Ignore it," he advises me. "It's sure to be someone far keener to speak to us than we are to hear them." But the old moral compulsion to answer every call makes me put down my drink and go to the phone.

"John Wright here."

"Oh, John, I'm so glad you're back! I've tried and tried to –"

"Seb there, is he?"

"Yes, he's –"

"Right. Worried. Naturally. All right, is he?"

"Oh, yes, perfectly –"

"Pop in then, if we may."

I find his telegraphic style contagious. "Do."

He rings off without further ceremony. An uneasy feeling in the pit of my stomach warns me that the coming encounter is not going to be a pleasant social call. When I go back to the sitting-room it is clear that Sebastian shares this feeling. Throwing an apprehensive glance at me, he dumps the Scrabble back into its box with so unsteady a hand that half the letters spill to the floor, where the cat jovially rolls on them. We are both glad that Seb is shaved and fully dressed, even to an ascot. He smooths both hands over his white hair while I brush a few crumbs of after-dinner cheese off his front. The bell then rings in a peremptory way.

I open the door to find Pam there, her tumbled hair pearled with rain and a sweater slung haphazardly round her shoulders. She looks very pale. John stands behind her, his expression austere. He is wearing a dark suit and a black tie which gives him such an air of official solemnity that he looks quite unfamiliar.

"Come on in," I urge them. They do this in silence. Seb has laboriously risen to greet them and now stands leaning on his cane, holding himself as upright as he can. John shakes his hand. Pam offers him her cheek. Her unnaturally wordless state is ominous.

"Do sit down," I urge them, trying to sound natural. "Can I offer you a drink?"

They both look without enthusiasm from our nearly empty glasses to the Scrabble tiles on the floor, and murmur, "No thanks." Together they sit with stiff decorum on the sofa, but Seb remains standing.

"Well, from the doom-laden look of you, I imagine Mrs. Blot has been in touch," he begins.

"In touch!" Pam bursts out. "If you mean mid-Europe hysterics, missing-person reports, police, et cetera, you couldn't be more accurate, and coming on the heels of a funeral, then driving home with one's mother-in-law in a vase in the glove compartment, the whole thing's enough to put one in the psychiatric ward. What on earth possessed you, Dad, to rush off like that without a word to a soul, not even a note?"

"There *was* a note," puts in Sebastian. "I wrote, 'Visiting a friend,' and propped it on the bureau in the best tradition. There was no pincushion, but I did my best."

"Anyway, nothing Mrs. B. could make head or tail of. I do call it totally inconsiderate and heartless of you just to nip off like that, after all we've done for you, do you realize the police have your name, I mean how shaming, and as for Mrs. Blot, she is under a doctor's care and threatening to sue absolutely everybody, and how can anyone blame her, left in charge like that, she's been screeching at us innocent victims for the past hour on the phone, with her daughters taking turns in the background, I honestly think your arteries must have hardened to absolute *wires* to do a thing like this the minute our backs are turned, and I really think you owe us some kind of explanation for this whole business, Rowena."

This abrupt switch to me as target makes my heart jerk in alarm. With as much calm as I can muster, I say, "Sebastian wasn't doing well in that woman's care. I invited him here, and he accepted. You weren't here to be consulted and we –"

"If you'd let me know you were going to be out of town, it would have been considerate," Sebastian puts in. "Then you could have avoided this unpleasant surprise."

"Yes, well, there simply wasn't time, we had to leave in such a rush and poor Ma hung on longer than anyone – then there was the funeral to organize, the point is this whole thing appears to have been done to give Blot, and consequently us, the maximum aggro, and when I think of all the bother and exhaustion I went through to find a decent nursing home it really does seem like total ingratitude."

John here clears his throat in a corroborative sort of way, though he says nothing.

"Have you quite finished?" Seb asks her politely.

"Not at all, I'm just getting warmed up, but by all means go ahead, I wonder what earthly excuse you can make for doing this to us."

"But I make no excuse at all, my dear. Nor do I apologize to anyone, including your mother-in-law, simply for exercising freedom of choice. Mrs. Blot was your idea, not mine. I did my best to get rid of her, but you insisted. The nursing home was your idea, too; not mine. I do not need a nursing home."

"That's a matter of opinion. It's not what your doctor thinks. Or what we think, who know you better than anybody." Here she casts me an unfriendly glance.

"The point is," says Seb, "that my opinion hasn't been taken into account by anybody except Rowena, not for a long time. Why should it be assumed that a man of eighty is no longer a man but a sort of deformed or deficient child? Why should I submit to be hustled into an institution – not for my comfort or convenience, but for yours?"

"There you are, you see." And Pam makes an ample gesture as if appealing to some invisible jury. "You are utterly unreasonable. Paranoid, even. If I haven't got your best interests at heart, who has?"

A pause follows: the kind that follows formalized questions like those asked in church – for example, Wilt thou have this man. Then, to my considerable surprise, I hear my own voice say, "I do."

She stares at me. "How can you possibly say a thing like that, Rowena? I thought you were a friend, and yet here you are –"

"Pam, he was neglected over there. Bored. Regressing, if you like. But not mentally incompetent, or even physically ... There's a difference between senility and plain misery. What the two of us did was get him out of there, and it seems to me we had a perfect right, both of us. It's unfortunate it all happened while you were away, that's all."

"Unfortunate my foot!" she says angrily. "You never would have dared influence him to do such a thing if –"

"Steady, girl," murmurs John.

"Me influence anybody?" I say, charmed by the idea. "Influence Sebastian? It's the other way round, if anything."

Seb smiles with a certain complacence, which is not lost on Pam. She takes a deep, outraged breath to continue; but John now intervenes. He stands up, taking her arm and pulling her up firmly with him.

"Well, all I've got to say is it's a damn pity I didn't get that power of attorney arranged before we were called away," says Pam, becoming tearful, "because it's obvious, Seb, you no longer have a full set of marbles, otherwise you never would have tumbled into this infatuation or whatever it is."

"Take her home, John," says Sebastian grimly. "She can apologize to Rowena and me some other time."

"Upset," mutters John, looking uncomfortable. "Home, Pam. Be in touch later."

He puts his arm around her and leads her away. We are left to eye each other ruefully over the Scrabble pieces.

"I suppose they'll get over it – all of them – in time," I say, hoping this will turn out to be true. Pam might; but in Marion's case, I doubt it.

"They don't, in fact, have a lot of choice, you know." He lowers himself with caution and a faint groan into the easy chair. "Why don't you get us another drink, Rowena?" he adds. "I think we've earned it."

I pick up our glasses in silent agreement. The now quiet room has the disorderly, depleted look common to domestic battlefields. But insofar as there can be any victory in such wars, we both feel, with all due modesty, it rests with us.

The sun swings in and out, blown by a spring wind that dances with the clothes on the line, and glazes the red twigs of the old maple tree. In the narrow strip of our back garden a few intrepid crocus plants lift yellow and purple faces to the sun. High in a nearby tree a cardinal plays over his rocking sequence of notes. Our patch of grass is half obliterated by builders' lumber and a pile of cement blocks on which Wittgenstein crouches, warming his black coat.

"Marion's coming for tea, and I must say I dread it," I confide to Mrs. Wilson. "Seb is sure to be rude to her, for one thing."

"That might do her a power of good."

"And she's sure to object to these renovations. Don't ask me why or how, but she'll find a way."

"Relatives," she says, "are no exception to the general rule. Some are agreeable and some are not. Marion is your daughter, but she is not agreeable. I never had a daughter, except for dream children like Lilly and Topaz, but if I had, quite possibly she would have been difficult, or even actively unpleasant. There are a lot worse fates than being childless."

"True. But it's only lately – I think – that her attitude, which I used to accept quite easily, now just seems unacceptable."

"Then don't try," she suggests, half-closing her eyes in the sun rather as Wittgenstein does when he feels particularly comfortable. "Absurd to try. And few people, I think I can truly say, know more about absurdity than I do. The fact is, you haven't realized yet that you're not obliged to love Marion. Not at all."

"But I do love her," I say feebly. "That's what's so painful about it."

"Attempting to love anybody a hundred per cent of the time is never advisable." She pulls the end of her nose thoughtfully. "Ten per cent, in this case, I would call generous."

Across the yard young Colin Wright scrambles from a fence post to the sloping roof of his parents' garage. On this elevated perch he often sits, chin on knees, contemplating his world in solitude and peace. Turning his curly head towards me now, he says briefly, "Hi, Rowena," before biting into a banana.

"Well, she really shouldn't treat me like something substandard that ought to be sent back to the factory. I've always found it discouraging, but now it annoys me intensely."

"Only carrying on the good work begun by her father, isn't she? Loyal to him, as ever."

"Oh, yes. Completely loyal."

"And it's one way of keeping him alive, isn't it?"

"But actually, you know, he's dead at last. She hasn't realized that yet, though. Maybe she never will."

"Well, as I say you're under no obligation to love that, or even like it. Do look at that cloud, it's shaped exactly like a bird."

Pulling in the line I briskly begin to unpeg Sebastian's shirts and drop them into the basket at my feet. Through the kitchen window I can see him at the table having a beer with the contractor, who studied Kant at McGill. Given the time they spend discussing pure reason, I wonder whether this extension will ever get off the ground.

"Isn't it curious," says Ethel dreamily, "how much of life is international? I mean, here we are, two natives, sitting in the middle of Canada, talking about Marion and Edwin – and yet their humanness has no boundary, any more than a horse or a blade of grass is particular to any special place or time. I find this extraordinary and very reassuring somehow."

"Oh, Lord, there's the doorbell. It must be Marion. Why on earth doesn't she use her key?"

"Think about it," advises Ethel with a smile.

"Don't ever leave me, will you, Ethel."

"Oh," she says serenely, "I'll be around."